SEEKER

The Seeker Series: Book One

By Amy Reece

Seeker

Limitless Publishing, LLC
Kailua, HI 96734
www.limitlesspublishing.com

Formatting: Limitless Publishing

ISBN-13: 978-1-68058-114-0
ISBN-10: 1-68058-114-7

DEDICATION

To all the girls who seek to be extraordinary. Never stop seeking. And to the boys who are strong enough to love them.

CHAPTER ONE

"Belief is the burden of seeing...To see into the heart of something is to believe in it."
–N. Scott Momaday, *"The Man Made of Words"*

I can't really tell you the best place to have your first psychic vision. I can, however, tell you the worst. That would be in 7th period English 11. Veronica Albluth was droning on about *The Scarlet Letter* at the front of the room and I was minding my own business, doodling in my notebook and mostly tuning her out when my core body heat suddenly skyrocketed. My hands began trembling so violently I couldn't hold my pen. Some of the other students began fanning themselves with notebooks and papers while our teacher, Ms. Gonzalez, leapt up from her desk and started to mess with the thermostat, punching buttons randomly and muttering under her breath. Veronica kept right on babbling through it all, even though no one was listening to her anymore. I dropped my forehead to the cool surface of my desk to avoid passing out and hoped no one could hear me groaning. Through the buzzing in my ears I'm nearly certain I heard someone say they thought I was going to hurl.

"Hey, are you okay?" came a male voice from behind me.

I think I nodded, but I'm not sure because he suddenly called out to the teacher, interrupting the presentation. "Hey, Ms. Gonzalez! I think Ally needs to go to the nurse." Then he was prying me out of my desk and moving me toward the front of the class. I have a fuzzy memory of a pink hall pass being shoved into the guy's hand and then I was being propelled out of the room and down the hall toward the nurse's office.

At this point I finally gathered my scattered wits/senses/whatever, stopped in my tracks, swayed a bit, and shrugged out of his hold. "I'm fine. I don't need to go to the nurse. I just need a bathroom." I steadied myself with a hand against the brick wall, trying to refocus my vision.

"All right," the guy said as he scrutinized me a bit too closely for comfort. It was Jack Ruiz, who sits behind me in English and is also in my physics class. He was new this year and seemed to keep pretty much to himself, but when I walked into this class the first day of school I had noticed him in the back row with an empty seat in front of him. I didn't stop to analyze, but immediately eschewed sitting in the front of the room like a good little nerd and instead opted to sit in front of the new guy everyone else seemed to be avoiding. Perhaps it was due to his classic bad boy look, complete with leather jacket, tattoo, and scowl. Plopping bravely down in front of him was, however, the only move I had made. This, so far, was the extent of our relationship: me sitting in front of him, occasionally turning around to pass papers back, him occasionally muttering "thanks." That's it.

"There's a bathroom at the end of C Hall. I'll wait for you and make sure you're okay. You could pass out in there and hit your head on a sink or something. We don't want you turning the girl's bathroom into a scene from *Dexter*. Come on." This time he simply ushered me to the bathroom.

As I stared at myself in the grease-smudged mirror above the girl's bathroom sink, I thought back to what had happened in class. Snotty Veronica Albluth had been presenting her essay in front of the class, prosing on about how *The Scarlet Letter* was really a re-telling of Adam and Eve and the consequences of sin, while I was thinking that she was repeating what she had skimmed from *Wikipedia*. Suddenly, my vision had blurred around the edges and Veronica's voice faded as a buzzing in my ears grew louder. I glanced up and zoomed in on the shiny red belt Veronica was wearing around her rich-girl thin waist and the classroom disappeared.

Veronica was leaning against a bathroom vanity, staring at her cellphone, which was running a timer app. The clock hit 0:00 and she took a deep breath, turned around, and picked up the white plastic stick lying on the counter. After staring at it for a few seconds, she turned and flung it in the trashcan. It landed on about 4 or 5 identical white sticks, each one sporting a little pink plus sign in its window. She crumpled to the ground and started sobbing.

I wish I could tell you that nothing like this has ever happened, but that would be a bold-faced lie. Although I have had these really weird, strong feelings off and on for most of my life—it actually runs in the family—this was the clearest, strongest episode I have ever experienced. I felt like I was actually *there* in the bathroom with Veronica. I heard her cry and I felt her sink down to the bathmat, almost as if it were happening to me. I didn't like the feeling at all. For one thing, it made snotty Veronica seem almost human. I don't want to feel sorry for her—it's so much easier to dislike her for everything she stands for: rich, privileged teenagers who have nothing more to worry about than what color BMW their daddy will buy them and OMG it better have seat-warmers! And now she was pregnant, which didn't come as a huge shock to me, given that she was constantly wrapped around some guy in the hallways. Her current boyfriend, Danny Burkhart, was on the football team—the quarterback, I think—which completed the stereotype perfectly since she was a cheerleader.

The funny thing was, Veronica and I had been friends once. Back in elementary school we had lived next door to each other and spent hours at each other's houses, mostly playing Barbies. My Barbies were always setting off on great adventures and solving mysteries, while hers were hooking up with Ken and having babies. She moved away when her mom divorced her dad and got remarried to a lawyer.

It was time to pull myself together and slink out of this bathroom to face Jack; if he was even waiting for me. He most likely lost interest and retreated back to class. I splashed water on my face and tried vainly to tame my obnoxious, curly red hair and exited the bathroom. To my surprise, Jack was leaning against the wall with his hands in his pockets, staring at the ground. He looked up and smiled slightly at me, one corner of his attractive mouth inching higher than the other. His big, nearly black eyes were full of concern as he asked, "You feeling better? I thought maybe you were gonna puke all over the place back there."

Perfect. Exactly what I wanted him to think of in connection with me: the girl who looked like she was going to puke. "No, I'm fine. I needed to get away from the Wikipedia re-hash, that's all. Thanks for the escape." I tried to scoot by him.

He laughed a bit under his breath and reached out, gently grabbing my arm as I passed. "Hey, don't run off. You looked really upset. I want to make sure you're all right. Besides, Ms. Gonzalez thinks we're at the nurse. No need to rush back for more coma-inducing book reports. I'm Jack, by the way. Jack Ruiz." He pulled me directly in front of him and again examined my face. An intoxicating aroma wafted to me from his warm skin; a sort of warm, spicy scent that instantly became my new favorite. I might have swayed toward him a bit.

"Yeah, I know, Jack. I've been handing your papers back all semester." I struggled to sound unaffected.

He nodded. "You still look really pale, Ally. And you seem a bit unsteady. Sure you're not gonna puke?"

Really? Why me, God? I stood up straight and gently shrugged off his hand. "Yes. I had a, uh...a moment. I'm okay. Thanks for getting me out of there." His dark eyes looked like melted dark chocolate. Life is so not fair. On the bright side, he actually knows my name. I wouldn't have bet on that. I'm not the kind of girl who stands out—well, except for the crazy red hair—or attracts much attention. I'm short and small, wear really plain clothes, and I don't say very much at school. I have a few good friends and we pretty much fly below the radar and try to stay out of the limelight. I like it that way. High school seriously sucks and I just want to get through it quietly and without a lot of drama. Please, God, life will be better in college.

"So, this is gonna sound pretty weird," Jack started hesitantly, "but, uh, when it got really hot in the classroom, it, well it kinda felt like it was, uh, emanating from you." He laughed once, quietly. "That's crazy, huh?"

Wow. Did he just use the word "emanating" in a sentence? Who does that? I mean, in high school? I wonder what he got on his ACT? I had always had the sense there was more to him than meets the eye, and this cemented that feeling.

"Yeah, that sounds kinda weird. I mean, I felt really hot and dizzy for a minute. Maybe flu or something. But I'm not going to throw up, I promise." I couldn't quite meet his gaze. I'm terrible at lying and I felt like he knew it. When I looked up I saw he was staring at me with raised eyebrows and patent disbelief. Just then the bell rang—saved by the…well, you know—ending the day. I started to head back to the classroom, fighting upstream against the deluge of students eager to escape another day of American compulsory education.

He caught up with me easily. "How 'bout we grab our stuff and I walk you to your car? Unless you have practice or something? I want to make sure you're really all right."

I appreciated the sweetness of the offer and any other time would have jumped at the chance to spend more time with the gorgeous Jack Ruiz. But today I needed to get away by myself to process what had happened. "No, I don't have practice or anything, and if by car you mean bus stop, that's okay. I really am fine." We were at our classroom door and Veronica breezed out, stopping very briefly to give me a haughty stare before turning abruptly away.

"Jeez," said Jack, watching her march away. He turned back to me, and with a rather stubborn look on his face said, "I'm not entirely convinced you're feeling well enough to be alone, and you wouldn't let me take you to the nurse, so the least you can do is let me drive you home. I don't want you passing out on the bus." He steered me into the classroom, grabbed his notebook and backpack, and stood by while I packed up my stuff. Then he held out his hand, motioning to my backpack.

"I can at least carry my own backpack," I argued,

recognizing I had lost the battle of the bus.

He shook his head, so I surrendered it to him with a sigh and he hefted it over his shoulder. He didn't appear the least bit phased to be toting a bright pink bag as he guided me out of the classroom, stopping briefly to explain to Ms. Gonzalez that I was feeling much better. I felt quite overwhelmed by this take-charge attitude—it was pretty sexy, not gonna lie—so I meekly followed.

***

I was surprised to find myself chatting amiably with him on the way to the student parking lot. We shared our complete lack of school spirit or interest in extracurricular activities and arrived at his car in a few minutes. We may never have conversed before, but once we got the ball rolling, it turned out we had lots to talk about. His car was a grey primered-looking thing, probably something classic—I don't know—that was surprisingly nice on the inside.

He unlocked and held open the passenger door for me saying, "I'm gonna be painting it pretty soon. I thought the inside was more important to restore first." He looked adorably unsure of himself for a moment.

"It's really nice," I hastened to reassure him as I breathed in new leather, Jack's spicy cologne, and old car funk. "What is it? It's classic, right?"

His pained look plainly said I was the worst sort of neophyte. "Yeah, it's a '65 Mustang." As if that should clarify all. He stared at me like he couldn't believe I wouldn't know something like that.

"Oh, that's, um, old," I fumbled.

"Yeah." He laughed briefly, shaking his head. "So, we've established you know nothing about classic cars." I gave him an indignant look. "My uncle gave me this car. It was a complete wreck, but I've been restoring it a little at a time, when I'm not busy working."

"Oh, where do you work?" I asked, suddenly curious to know everything about him.

"I work for my uncle at his auto body shop. He's been teaching me the craft, and I get to use all his equipment in my off time. There's not much off time so it's slow going." He shrugged. His cell phone alarm suddenly beeped a reminder. He grabbed it and cursed softly. "Sorry. I forgot I have to pick up my sister from school today." He put the car in gear and began to back out, his arm slung across the seat back. "It's really close and won't take but a minute. Then I can drop you off."

"I can take the bus," I began.

"No, it's no problem. Where do you live, by the way?"

I gave him the directions. "Oh, great. That's pretty close to my sister's school." He reached to turn the volume down on the stereo, which was booming out the latest Arctic Monkeys CD. "Sorry. I crank it when I'm by myself."

"That's fine." I smiled. "I like Arctic Monkeys. What else do you listen to?"

We discussed music the rest of the short drive to pick up his sister. We turned out to have fairly similar tastes, except for his unexpected love of country music, which I abhor. He also confessed to liking a lot of Tejano music, which I guessed was part of his upbringing. He was able to scoff at my liking for Broadway soundtracks, so we were even. I could listen to his voice all day, a deep cadence with a hint of an accent, like maybe his first language was Spanish instead of English.

I was a bit surprised when Jack pulled the car into the roundabout at Sombra del Monte Elementary School, a half mile up Candelaria Boulevard from Oso Grande High School where we attended. I had supposed his sister would be more in the middle school age range. He pulled forward as directed by the security guard and parked.

"I'll be right back." He gave me a half-smile then strode up the front walk of the school as a swarm of small children poured out the front doors, diverting around him as he waited. One of the last to emerge was a very small black-haired girl holding a teacher's hand, which she dropped when she saw Jack and skipped excitedly to him. He scooped her up, Hello Kitty backpack, lunchbox, and all. She plastered a sloppy-looking kiss on his cheek and began what looked like a very one-sided chatter to him as they walked back to the car. He loaded her into the back seat, buckling her into a booster car seat I hadn't noticed before.

"And then Joshua called Tonia a poop-head and Teacher heard him and he got sent to the time-out chair and who's that?" she quizzed, finally stopping for a breath.

"That's Ally. She's a friend of mine," he said as he finished fastening her seat belt across the booster seat. I really liked the thought of being a friend of his. "We're gonna drop her off real quick, okay?"

"Okay. Hi, Ally. I'm Megan. I'm six. I'm in first grade. I like dogs. Do you like dogs? I have a dog named Sodapop. Your hair is pretty. Do you think her hair is pretty, Jack?"

Jack concentrated on pulling safely onto the street, but spared me an apologetic smile and said, "How much sugar did they give you today, Megan? Yes, I think her hair is very pretty."

Darn my red-haired complexion that blushed so easily! I turned in my seat to address Megan. "Nice to meet you, Megan. Yes, I like dogs, but I have a cat. His name is Mr. Wickham but we call him Wicky. Why did you name your dog Sodapop?"

She giggled a cute little-girl giggle. "Wicky! That's a funny name! My brother named Sodapop. It's from a book."

I turned and raised my eyebrows expectantly at him.

Another self-deprecating half-smile. "It's from *The Outsiders*. You know, Sodapop Curtis?" He turned onto my street.

"Yeah, I read it in middle school. Sodapop, huh? There, on the left." I directed him to my house and he pulled to the curb.

"Wait there." He jumped out and ran around to open my door, holding out his hand to help me out. Who does that anymore? His hand was rough with calluses, probably from the manual labor he did at his uncle's shop. I liked the warmth and the feel of it a lot. He again grabbed my backpack and walked me up to my door.

I don't think I've mentioned yet that my mom and I live with my grandmother. I mention it now because my grandmother opened the door as we approached and stepped out on the front porch to greet us. How to describe my grandmother? How do you describe a truly indescribable person? Well, today she appeared every inch the southern lady of the manor, with a silk beige dress, pearls, and ivory cardigan. With her slim form and a smooth blonde bob, the image was one of genteel class. Looks can be deceiving. More on that later.

"Why, Ally. I've been waiting for you. And who is this charming young man?" she purred in a slightly southern accent that is totally fake. She was born and raised here in Albuquerque and we don't have southern accents.

"Hey, Grams. This is Jack. He gave me a ride home." I tried to take my backpack from him quickly so he could leave—preferably before she got her devious hooks into him.

"Hello, ma'am. I'm Jack Ruiz. Ally and I go to school together." He had apparently saved up all the charm he had been keeping in and decided to let it loose today, judging by the disarming smile he gave her as he took the limp hand she proffered. "She wasn't feeling very—" he stopped as he saw the hopefully very slight shake of my head. "Um…very much like taking the bus. And I was going this way…so it was no problem," he finished rather lamely.

Too late. She hadn't missed the gist of his first statement. "You're not feeling well, Ally? Oh dear. Well, I'm sure you what you need is a nice cup of tea. Won't you join us, Jack?" She was already pulling him toward the door.

"No, Jack doesn't want tea, Grams. His sister is in the car. He has to go." I tried to spare him, but his little sister had sneakily slipped out of her car seat and the car and now insinuated herself into our conversation.

"I like tea," she implored my grandmother, with huge, brown puppy-dog eyes. "I'm Megan. Jack's my big brother." She was so cute, and obviously a gifted manipulator.

"Well, hello," my grandmother purred victoriously. "Of course you do. Let's go inside and have tea and cookies and get to know each other." She took Megan by the hand and led her inside.

"I am so incredibly sorry about this," I apologized.

"Don't worry about it," he said. "Your grandmother seems really sweet." He held the door open for me and we followed the other two inside.

"She's anything but sweet," I cautioned him as we entered. He flashed me a strange look, but really, he had no idea what he was getting into. Grams and Megan were already seated in the living room, with Megan on the floor beside the coffee table, which was set with all the accoutrements for tea for four, including a plate of dainty-looking cookies. I really hope you're asking yourself how she knew to prepare for this supposedly impromptu tea party. I absolutely guarantee that she doesn't make a habit of greeting me and my friends with afternoon tea.

She poured a cup of tea for Jack and asked, "Do

you take sugar? Cream or lemon?" Oh my God, it was like a twisted scene from *Downton Abbey*.

Jack shot me a slightly panicked look and addressed my grandmother, saying, "Uh, just some sugar. Uh, please." Megan was happily slurping away at her tea and munching messily on a cookie, blissfully unaware of the awkwardness Jack and I were experiencing.

Grams directed an indulgent smile her way before her eagle eye zeroed in on Jack. "So, tell me about yourself, Jack. Where does your family come from?"

Seriously, Grams? This is Albuquerque in 2013, not Atlanta in 1912.

"Well, um," he stammered. "I, uh, moved here this summer from Taos. My sister and I live with my aunt and uncle." There was a world of questions left unanswered, but I silently begged her not to probe. It was absolutely not our business why he lived with an aunt and uncle instead of parents.

"That sounds nice." She let it alone, thank goodness. At least she was showing some hint of sensitivity, rather unusual in someone usually so forthright. "So what do you like to do in your spare time?"

"Uh, well, I guess I like to work on cars. I work at my uncle's body shop. And I go to CNM for dual credit classes. I hope to have an associate's degree when I graduate high school." CNM is our local community college. I was impressed that he was already taking classes there, something I hadn't thought to do.

"That's very admirable," she said smugly. "I do

admire your 1965 Mustang. You'll be painting it soon, I expect? What color have you chosen?"

Well, that won him over completely, as I'm sure she meant it to. "It has to be cherry red. Is there really any other color for a '65 Mustang? I'm hoping to have time to paint it this weekend or next."

"Be sure to bring it by so I can see it. I used to go with a young man who drove a Mustang, although it was blue." She was really getting her hooks into him. I wondered why? He was certainly not the kind of guy most normal grandmothers would want their granddaughters bringing home. Then again, she was not most grandmothers. She would be one to approve of a guy with tattoos, a leather jacket, and a muscle car. "It must be nice to have such a lovely car to take the young ladies out. Do you date often, Jack? Do you have a special young lady?"

"Grams!" I squeaked. "That's none of your business!" All right, so I really wanted to know too, but I like to think I would have been subtler about finding out. "Leave him alone, please." I gave her The Look over the rim of my teacup. I noticed Jack looking back and forth between the two of us, but I couldn't quite tell if he was amused or horrified.

"Oh, I'm sure he doesn't mind, dear. Do you, Jack?" Nobody can really resist her when she turns on her full quota of charm.

"Um, no, I, uh, guess not," Jack stuttered.

"Well? It wasn't a difficult question, Jack. Do you have a girlfriend or not?" Grams was like a pit bull with a rabbit in its teeth.

"No, ma'am. I don't have a girlfriend." It looked like he might be blushing under his dark complexion. I shook my head. Megan giggled.

Grams was momentarily diverted, giving Jack a much-needed reprieve. "Now, Miss Megan, tell me all about yourself. What grade are you in and what is your favorite subject?"

As Megan began to chatter with some crumb spewage involved, when my cat deigned to make an appearance, winding himself around Jack's legs and purring. Jack reached down to scratch his ears and Wicky actually jumped up into his lap. This surprised me since he's usually not quite so friendly with strangers. What can I say? My cat and I apparently share an interest.

"Hey, Kitty." Jack continued to rub Wicky's ears. "So, Wickham, huh? You don't get to be Mr. Darcy? That's a raw deal, kitty." Wow. How many guys his age would get a Jane Austen reference? I was totally impressed.

Grams continued to chat both Jack and Megan up until the teapot was empty and nothing remained of the cookies but a few scattered crumbs.

"Thanks for the tea, ma'am. We need to get going, though. I gotta get Megan home and I need to get to work."

"Of course, come anytime. I so enjoyed the company. Thank you for taking such good care of my granddaughter when she wasn't, um, *feeling* very well. I do enjoy a chance to use my mother's beautiful tea set. She brought it all the way from County Mayo in Ireland when she emigrated." She looked like butter wouldn't melt in her mouth.

"Wow," Megan breathed.

"Yeah, well, it's been great." I vaulted out of my seat, desperately trying to end this ridiculous encounter. "Thanks again for the ride, Jack. I really appreciate it." I practically shooed him and his sister out the door and then followed them out to his car.

"Hey, tell your grandmother thanks again for us. She didn't have to go to so much trouble. Jeez, I'm glad Megan didn't break her cup. I had no idea it was so old." He looked somewhat worried.

"She got it on eBay a few months ago. My grandmother is, uh, interesting. You can't take her at face value. I'm so sorry you had to do that." I gestured back at the house.

"It was no problem." He looked carefully at me. "I liked meeting her. You don't have to apologize. Hey, you sure you're feeling better? You had me kind of worried at school."

"Yeah, really. I'm fine. Don't worry." I was simply embarrassed at this point, but his concern was flattering.

Megan pulled at his arm. "Let's go!" she whined.

"Uh oh. The princess is starting to get cranky," he said but he didn't sound bothered. He scooped her up and put her on his shoulders. "See you tomorrow." He bent to buckle Megan in the car seat, affording me a peek at his boxers escaping the top of his jeans. Sigh.

I marched back inside to beard the lion in her lair.

CHAPTER TWO

"The truth is rarely pure and never simple."
–Oscar Wilde, *The Importance of Being Earnest*

"Grams! Grams!" As I expected, she was nowhere to be found. I finally tracked her down in her bedroom closet, beige dress and blonde bob wig gone, replaced by a short silk robe and her natural—with a little help from Ms. Clairol—short, spiky blonde hair. "Grams! Really? What was that all about?"

"What was what all about, sweetie?" She bustled by me with her arms full of dresses. "You're gonna need to scootch 'cuz I've gotta get ready for a date."

"Oh, you've got nothing I haven't seen before." I flopped down on her bed, determined to wait her out. "So, you've been going through my stuff, huh?"

"What do you think of this one? I want to look good for Roger." She held up a red spandex sheath and waggled her eyebrows up and down. She had been systematically working her way through all the eligible men at her senior citizen center. She was only 58, but she started going to the center on her 55th birthday, saying she intended to make the most of this new chapter in her life.

I waited, my arms folded and jaw thrust forward.

She cast aside the red dress and picked up a blue floral one for my inspection, but I would not be moved. I glared. She finally threw the dress aside in frustration, sighing. "Oh Ally. I go through your things all the time. Who else is going to save you from yourself? Don't be so fussy." She plopped down on the bed next to me. "He's so cute! Why haven't you told me about him?"

"There's nothing to tell, as you well know. Do I have any secrets from you? Ugh! I feel so violated, Grams."

"Oh, seriously, Ally! I worry for you. And a good thing, too. You would have let that handsome boy slip through your fingers if I hadn't had a lovely tea party set up!" She had the audacity to look hurt.

"Grams! He's just a friend! Actually more of an acquaintance. I don't even know him."

"Well, you should get to know him." More eyebrow waggling from her. "And what is this about you not feeling well? Why don't you tell me about what happened at school? I was putting some of your laundry away when I got a strong feeling that you were upset somehow. Then I felt that you weren't coming home alone." She put her arm around me. I leaned into her, inhaling the faint, yet comforting scent of Chanel No. 5. Under all the craziness, she's still my grandma.

"Oh, Grams. I think I might be going insane! I had a vision in the middle of class today that was so realistic and I almost blacked out! This wasn't like the other things I know." I'm ashamed to say that I started to cry a little bit.

"Sweetie, tell me everything. This is really important." She hugged me briefly and set me away from her enough to look into my eyes. "I need to hear exactly what happened."

"Well, I was listening to this really snotty girl plagiarize Wikipedia, and I was looking at her red belt around her super-skinny waist…"

"You do have a way with words, dear," she interjected.

"*Anyway*, as I was saying…I got really hot and heard a buzzing in my ears. All of a sudden I *saw*, I can't really describe how, but I saw her in her bathroom doing a bunch of pregnancy tests. They all came back positive. It's like I was in the bathroom with her, seeing everything she saw, almost like I *was* her." I clutched her arm, looking up into her face. "What does it mean? Am I going nuts?"

"Oh, that poor girl! No, sweetie, you're not going crazy. You know the women in our family are a bit, well, different, right?" She brushed my hair back from my face.

"Well, yeah, but you and Mom don't have weird episodes like this! You touch stuff and you know what's going on with the people who own it. And Mom is pretty awesome at finding stuff that's lost, but nothing like this!" The tears were back.

"Shh. Don't cry. No, we haven't been through

20

anything like you described, but we each had to deal with our 'gifts' around the time we turned 17. That's how it happens. It sounds like your gifts may be a bit more extreme than any that have shown up in a while, that's all. We'll figure it out, don't worry."

"That's not all. Jack totally noticed! He said he felt the heat 'emanating' from me—his word, not mine—and he dragged me out of class because he thought I was going to puke! Nice, huh?"

"Hmm," she sounded thoughtful. "It's usually a good idea to keep these gifts in the family, but I sense that he's very trustworthy. He's trying to impress you," she said with an arch look.

"Really? I didn't think he'd ever noticed me. Oh, Grams, I've gotta tell you: I don't really want this kind of gift."

"Ally, you can't choose these things—the gift chooses you. You have to learn to use it to the best of your abilities. You have to be willing to be used." She was rubbing my hands between hers.

"What does it mean, Grams? Why would I get a 'vision' or whatever about some slutty girl who has gotten herself knocked up?"

"Ally, don't be mean. There is sure to be a good reason for this message to come to you. There always is. You have to be ready to listen and act."

"Sorry, but if I have to have visions, why can't they be about something important? It's not going to be any kind of big revelation that Veronica Albluth is pregnant. Sorry to be so blunt, but—"

"Veronica Albluth? Didn't she used to live next door? You were playmates, weren't you?" At my nod she continued, "I don't know why you had that vision, sweetheart, but I have a feeling you're going to find out. You need to be patient and wait for more. I'm going to do some research into our family and see if I can find a record of anyone else having this kind of gift. I have to admit that I've never heard of visions so vivid and clear," she mused.

"Grams! I don't want this! I'm already a freak! I don't need any more attention at school."

"Well, whining won't help any." And she was back. "Now scoot so I can get ready for my date! Your mom has a date too, so I'm afraid you're on your own tonight. Don't wait up." She waggled those dang eyebrows yet again. Gross. I didn't even want to think about it.

"That's okay. Tara's coming over later when she gets done with orchestra practice." I referred to my best friend who was a fantastic oboe player, which unfortunately meant that she had a lot of late afternoon band and orchestra practices.

***

Tara showed up late, at about 7:30, but bearing a peace offering of my favorite Thai Curry Noodle Bowl with tofu so I readily forgave her. Sitting on my bed, shoveling noodles in my mouth, I related the events of the afternoon.

"Ugh! Stupid oboe! I miss all the good stuff. You really got a ride home with Jack Ruiz? And your grandmother invited him in for tea? That is so awesome! He's kinda hot, don't you think? What was he like?" She flipped her long, blonde hair behind her shoulder and plucked a tofu chunk out of my bowl, making a face as she chewed. "How can you eat this crap?"

"Did you miss the part about the freaky vision I had in the middle of class?" I was incredulous.

"I heard that part—but the part about the hot guy is more interesting. I've known you were a complete freak for some time now, so the weird vision really comes as no huge surprise." She dodged my half-hearted attempt to throw my stuffed dog at her, and then got intense for a brief moment, grabbing my foot. "Seriously, are you okay?"

"Yeah. I'm fine. It was pretty freaky, but Jack was really nice about getting me out of the classroom." I looked at her from under my eyelashes. "He *is* pretty hot, huh?" We both dissolved into a fit of girlish giggles. "Oh, Tara! He was sooo nice! He insisted on giving me a ride home and we stopped to pick up his little sister and she's so cute!" I finally ran out of breath and shoved more noodles in my mouth to forestall any more gushing.

"So, what was he like? What did you guys talk about? How old is he?" she prodded.

"Well, we didn't talk about anything important; just small talk. My grandmother got more info out of him than I did. He moved here this summer from Taos and lives with his aunt and uncle. He doesn't have a girlfriend. I don't know how old he is, but doesn't he seem older than the rest of us juniors?"

"Yeah, he does," she agreed. "You've heard the rumors about him, haven't you? Word on the street is that he has a mysterious criminal past."

"*Word on the street?* Seriously, Ice-T? But yeah, I've heard the rumors. I'm having a hard time reconciling the really nice, polite guy that took me home and had tea with Grams with a hardened criminal."

"So, did he ask you out or anything?"

"No, it wasn't really like that. I don't think he *like* likes me. Ick—that sounded so middle school boy-crazy, huh?"

"A little bit, but I think you can be forgiven this once, since you've never been boy-crazy. You've always left that to me." She patted my foot in comfort.

We continued to dissect my afternoon experience until she had to go home without coming to any sort of conclusion. I needed Tara's perspective on what I was going through. I know Grams said to keep it in the family, but Tara *is* family. I can't keep anything from her. We've been best friends since 6th grade, when we joined band together. We both played the flute, but she was clearly talented and was switched to oboe and given private lessons whereas I was so clearly not talented and made my way steadily farther down the flute section until I opted out of band in high school and shoved my flute to the back of my closet. She knows all about our family "curse" and has patiently listened to me complain through the years about Grams constantly going through my stuff when I'm not home—sometimes even when I am home! I've kept her apprised of my previous episodes of—what should I call them— ESP? Yikes, I don't know what to consider them—I just sometimes can tell when what a person is saying or showing is not the whole truth. Yep, I'm a real Deanna Troi. That's a *Star Trek Next Generation* reference for the non-nerdy. Up until earlier today, though, I've never *seen* what the truth actually is. Knowing, seeing that Veronica is pregnant is really creepy. Why should it be any of my business? I don't know her at all anymore, except by reputation—which is not great. She has constantly had a boyfriend since middle school; she doesn't seem to be able to function without a guy hanging on her, and I've witnessed her and her flavor-of-the-month playing tonsil hockey in front of her locker more times than I care to. Gross. So not classy.

Later that evening I was lounging in bed, reading my assigned chapters from *The Scarlet Letter* when my mom poked her head in. Is it sick and twisted that I actually like this book? I mean, nobody *likes* the books they make us read in school.

"Still awake?" She was still dressed up from her date, wearing dressy black slacks and a blue satin top that suited her petite figure. Her glossy auburn hair flowed around her shoulders in a way that my crazy red hair never would. She sat beside me on my bed, saying, "How are you doing, Ally-Bear?" The childhood endearment brought tears to my eyes a bit. "Grams said we need to talk." She brushed my wild hair behind my ears.

I cleared the emotion out of my throat and tried to lessen the tension. "Cool, Mom. Are you finally going to tell me about the birds and the bees? Speaking of birds and bees, how was your date with new guy?" My mom had me in college, the result of too much fun her freshman year. She said she barely knew the guy and certainly never contemplated marrying him. I had always lived here with her and Grams.

She chortled slightly. "My date was fine and not the subject of this discussion. You're almost 17 years old. If you don't know about the birds and the bees, you've got big problems. Seriously, what happened today?"

I filled her in on the details, majorly downplaying the part with Jack. I ended with, "And I'm really worried that I'm going to turn into the biggest freak this family has ever seen! I mean, you and Grams don't nearly pass out when your ESP goes off or whatever," I wailed.

"Well, that's certainly not how I think of it," she said. "Your grandmother and I both have fairly mild, mellow versions of our family 'gift.' But there are stories of some of our ancestors who had very powerful gifts."

"Ugh. I really don't need this in my life right now." I flopped back on my pillows. "I mean, yeah, I would love to be really, really good at something—you know, better than anyone else, but I was thinking of something a little more normal. Something I might actually be able to brag about someday!"

"Well, you've told Tara about this already," she countered.

"And you say your gift's not very powerful," I admonished.

"I don't need any special gift to know that you tell her everything. Did you tell that boy what was going on?" I wondered when she would finally get around to bringing him up. She was examining her nails, oh-so-innocently.

"Mom! I barely know him. Of course I didn't tell him anything. Grams is making way too much of it. He thought I was going to throw up. Do you realize that Grams had a whole tea party waiting for us when we got home? She had four places set! How would a regular person know to have four places set—including one for his little sister? He's not stupid! He may have some very awkward questions for me tomorrow."

She gave me a sly look. "Well, at least you'll get to talk to him again. Grams said he was pretty cute." She got up and smoothed my quilt around me like she used to do when I was little. "And try not to worry too much about what's happening to you. Grams is going to do some research into the family tree and see if she can find out about any other women in our family that went through what you described. Goodnight, Ally-Bear." She turned off my overhead light and shut my door as she left.

I had a hard time getting to sleep; I kept replaying the afternoon in my mind: Veronica's stupid face, Jack's sweet, concerned one. Grams and the tea party. Megan eating cookies, Tara and I eating noodles. I tossed and turned for hours until I finally dozed off around 3 a.m. Ugh! This lack of sleep would make tomorrow/today ugly.

CHAPTER THREE

"If you are out to describe the truth, leave elegance to the tailor."
–Albert Einstein

We had a lab the next day in physics and were allowed to choose our own lab partners. I really dreaded not being assigned a partner because I had no friends in this class. I was mentally preparing myself to be the one Mr. Chiszowski had to stick with an unlucky pair to make a group of three when Jack Ruiz slid onto the lab stool next to me saying, "Is it all right if we're partners? I promise I'll do my share."

"Sure." I tried to sound nonchalant. I'm pretty sure that was a total fail because I had a hard time not staring longingly at his handsome face. Wow, he smelled really good too: that same spicy, warm scent I had noticed yesterday. "You should know I'm fairly hopeless at physics, however."

"Oh, well, in that case," he said, pretending to get up and leave. "I'm kidding. I'm sure it'll be fine. We're just doing some simple vectors." I was barely able to stop myself from asking what the heck a vector was as he sat back down on the stool next to me.

Mr. Chiszowski explained that we would be finding the distance between two points that he would give us. Well, that did sound pretty easy. You just measure it, right? I should have known better. He gave each pair of students a protractor, a meter stick, a metric tape measure, and a roll of string. He then handed us a Xerox copy of a school map with points A & B highlighted and told us to go outside and figure out the solution. It still sounded fairly simple, until we all realized that the two points were on opposite sides of the school building. Yikes. Whatever happened to good old worksheets? What is it with all this newfangled 'critical thinking' stuff they're trying to foist on us? What, do they want to turn us into a thinking citizenry?

I followed Jack outside and we spent the next few minutes tromping around the school building finding the two vector points. He seemed to have a plan or at least some idea of how to tackle the problem, so I happily took on the role of lab assistant. Can I just say that if we had to write a paper of any sort I would be a more active participant? Science is so not my thing.

As we began measuring the distance between our first point and the building, Jack having said something or other about establishing an x-axis baseline, he asked, "Are you feeling better today? I wasn't sure if you'd be at school or not... You know, if you had the flu or something."

"Oh, no." I brushed off the suggestion. "I'm fine. It was a momentary thing. I'm sure it won't happen again." I sincerely hoped it wouldn't.

"Well, good. Here, hold the end of this string." As he back-stepped away toward a trashcan, he said, "I was really worried about you, you know." He looked up at me as he kneeled to take a measurement.

"No, I'm really fine. Don't worry, please." As we gathered up our supplies, ready to go to the other side of the building, a nearby group of boys who seemed to be doing a lot of pushing each other rather than measuring anything, glanced our way and started murmuring. I caught the words "red" and "criminal." I saw Jack's jaw clench and a vein started to pound in his temple. "Hey," I set my hand on his arm. "Don't. They're just stupid, rude jocks." Oh, I made sure they could hear me. Nobody calls me "red" and gets away with it. They moved away, one of them giving me the finger. Jack made as if to start after them. I touched his arm again and shook my head. He visibly deflated, running his hands through his inky, black hair.

"Sorry. Old habits die hard. I used to get in a lot of fights," he admitted quietly.

I thought about the "criminal" comment. According to the rumor mill that Tara mentioned last night, he had been in trouble where he lived before and had even served time in jail. As I told Tara, after starting to get to know him, I didn't really believe any of it. He was way too nice to his sister and my grandmother to be a hardened criminal. Besides, I pride myself on making up my own mind about people. I am not a sheep. No, sir.

I held out the meter stick to him. "Come on. Let's finish this up." He gave me a half-hearted smile and took the stick. I tried to cheer him up, regaling him with stories of some of my grandmother's more mild antics. It felt nice to be the one looking after him today. I really don't want you to get the idea that I'm some sappy, helpless female. I'm a take-charge kind of gal. Really. Again, I marveled at how easy it was to talk to him. I could really like this guy. What would it take to get him to like me back?

We finished our measurements and trekked back inside to work on the math to get our solution. It was gratifying to be one of the few pairs that got very close to the true measurement. The stupid jocks were nowhere near correct. I couldn't help giving them a superior look as I left the classroom.

We both had lunch right after physics and it somehow seemed natural for us to drop stuff in our lockers and walk to the cafeteria together. I thought Tara's eyebrows were going to slide over the top of her head and down her back when Jack and I walked up to her table together.

It turns out Jack and I are both part of the un-cool minority that brown bags it. I personally am a vegetarian who wouldn't dream of eating the disgusting slop they try to pass off as food in the cafeteria. When I asked Jack if he always brings his lunch he replied, "Most of the time. It's way more economical than buying the cafeteria crap every day." He unloaded a packet of what looked like three sandwiches, chips, cookies, and an apple. I unpacked my hummus, carrots, pita, and edamame somewhat self-consciously, aware of his eyes on my lunch. "Jeez, that looks disgustingly healthy," he said with a shudder.

I introduced him to Tara and our other friend, Travis. I have to admit something here. I had a wild crush—that I now heartily regret—on Travis freshman year. We actually had a brief "thing." Really brief because he soon decided he was gay and I had helped him clarify his feelings and he finally felt ready to come out. Great. Really boosted my self-esteem. I mean, I was happy for him, but I'd had a bit of a dry spell guy-wise since then. Dry as the Sahara Desert, actually, if you must know. As in nothing. Nada. Since freshman year. I know, right?

"So, Jack," Tara wasted no time. "Rumor has it that you're actually a criminal on the lam. Is it true that you murdered two of your teachers?"

I thought Jack was going to choke on his sandwich. "Wow, way to get right to the heart of things," he said. "You should consider a career in journalism."

"Tara!" I hissed, appalled.

"No, it's okay," said Jack. "I can respect the direct approach." He set down his sandwich, took a sip of soda, and then said, "No, I did not murder any of my teachers. I'm not on the lam, either." He looked at me hesitantly. "But I am on probation. Sorry. I should have told you yesterday, Ally, before you got in my car."

I melted a little at the worried look on his face.

"Hey, there's no reason you should have told me. I like to think I'm not a judgmental person. So, why are you on probation…if it's okay to ask?"

"Yeah, it's fine." He sighed. "I'm trying to make a fresh start here, so I really don't want it spread around." We all made noisy assurances that we wouldn't tell anyone. "I'm on probation for various delinquent offenses, including distribution of a controlled substance. I got caught trying to sell drugs. I was a mess my first couple years in high school. But I don't do any of that stuff anymore," he assured us.

His honest admission seemed to win Tara's approval. I was proud of her non-judgmental attitude. And being a truly critical thinker—Mr. Chiszowski would be so proud—I wondered why he was such a mess, but I thought this probably wasn't the time to probe. So, clearly, no journalism career for me.

"So, welcome to the Island of Misfit Toys." Tara gestured around the lunch table. "You're in good company. Not of the criminal kind, but none of us fit into the 'high school norm' very well."

"You seem rather proud of that fact," Jack challenged.

"Damn right," she countered.

He raised his soda can in salute. "What is the 'high school norm'?" he continued. "Does such a fearsome thing truly exist?" I met Tara's eyes, both of us with raised eyebrows. He didn't talk like a typical 17-year-old, and I was sure he must be older.

Travis piped in, "Someone who fits into one of

the cliques? You know, jocks, popular girls, brainiacs, druggies, etcetera?" He gestured around the cafeteria, which were fairly homogenous within each table.

"I'm not sure I buy that. It's so cliché," Tara began. "Aren't people, even of the high-school variety, more complex than that? Can we truly be reduced to our lowest common denominator?"

"And what clique would we be?" I asked Travis. "I mean look at us: Tara's a band geek…"

"Hey, that's uncalled for!" she inserted.

"But where do the rest of us fit?" I felt like I had been asking that question my whole life.

"Well, I'm starting my own clique: the fabulously well-dressed, urban metrosexual clique," Travis pronounced.

"But you're not metrosexual. According to the Urban Dictionary, a metrosexual is actually heterosexual," Tara pointed out.

"Well, yeah, but I like the word," Travis countered.

"Hey, I don't like labels," Jack began, "but if I had to pick one for you guys, I would have to say semi-hipster group. I'm not sure you have totally committed to the hipster lifestyle, but you are definitely leaning that way." We all began to object noisily. Jack broke in, "Travis, where did you buy your pants?"

"Well, I got these at Salvation Army. They have really great stuff there."

"And do you own a Blu-Ray copy of *(500) Days of Summer?*" Jack questioned.

"Of course, but that doesn't mean—" Travis

sputtered.

"And you deny being a hipster?"

"Of course, even though I—"

"I rest my case." Jack sat back with a satisfied smile. We all laughed, even Travis, after a minute. "But like I said, I don't like labels. I think people should be what they want to be and not worry about fitting into a category."

"So what category would you put yourself into, if you had to pick a category?" I inquired pointedly.

He pretended to think deeply for a moment. "Well, I would have to say the category that is sick and tired of eating lunch by myself every day. Since juniors aren't allowed to leave campus for lunch, I've been relegated to either sitting by myself or just wandering around. Thanks for letting me crash your party." His admission of loneliness was both sad and sweet.

We spent the rest of lunch dissecting high school subculture and went our various ways when the bell rang.

**

I had pre-calculus after lunch and then met up with Jack again in 7th period as we were filing into our English 11 class. Today was more of the same from yesterday: presentations about "the true meaning of *The Scarlet Letter*." Yawn. I mean, I like the book, but listening to my classmates butcher it kinda kills my buzz, know what I mean? I had given my presentation on the first day, so I was off the hook, but it turned out to be Jack's turn today.

He grabbed his notebook, muttered, "Here goes nothing," and shuffled to the front of the room. Wow, he actually seemed nervous about presenting to the class. He seemed so confident about everything else that I was somewhat surprised.

"In preparation for my presentation," he began quietly, "I read several critical essays on Nathaniel Hawthorne."

"I'm sorry, Jack," interrupted Ms. Gonzalez. "Could you speak up, please?"

"Oh, sorry. Yeah," he apologized, looking even more embarrassed. "The one I found that most resonated with my thinking talked about how Hawthorne took the symbols, such as the scaffold, which typically represented sin and penitence, and turned them completely around. Hawthorne manages to turn the tables and point out the evil lurking beneath the prim and pious outer shell of the Puritans. Hester is portrayed as a sensitive human being with a real heart and true emotions who has unfortunately been trapped by circumstances that don't affect her unknown lover in the same way."

I was amazed at the way he was able to convey his thoughts and synthesis of stuff he had read about the book, even though he was clearly not comfortable with public speaking. He didn't come off sounding like he was trying to take credit for someone else's ideas, unlike some people I know who copy Wikipedia, but instead made it clear that he read and thought about what experts had to say and put his own spin on it. I was momentarily distracted from my overall and over-the-top admiration of Jack Ruiz by a movement in my peripheral vision. Veronica was seated immediately to my left in the next row. She was gripping the edge of her desk really tightly—true white knuckles. I thought that was only an expression, but she had them. She noticed me looking and let go. I watched the blood flow back into her hand as she brought it back to her lap. I couldn't help noticing that her nails were really ragged and chewed. Didn't I remember them being perfect and fake? I know I shouldn't care—it's not like I'm jealous or anything—but they looked really bad now. She saw me looking and gave me a mean look. I was again reminded that I really, really don't like her. But it was odd, on top of that ridiculous vision I had of her yesterday. I guess the stress of her pregnancy was getting to her. Oh, well. I tuned back into what Jack was saying.

"So, overall, the theme that was most significant to me throughout the entire novel was the idea of 'the secret sinner.' The Puritan community assumed it was Hester, but in truth it was the other characters like Dimmesdale and Chillingworth that had committed the true sin." He returned to his seat, giving me a rather self-deprecating smile as he passed. "Whew, glad that's over."

I was again momentarily distracted as Veronica surreptitiously wiped her eyes. I remembered my grandmother referring to her as "that poor girl" when I told her about the pregnancy and felt a little bit sorry for her. I mean, yes, I think girls shouldn't be stupid enough to get pregnant in this day and age of easily accessible and economical birth control, but it's still so much easier for the guy involved.

A few more people presented and I thought I was going to get through a day without any drama or episodes. I was wrong. When the bell rang, I stood up to start packing up my stuff and turned back to tell Jack what a great job he had done on his presentation. Veronica got up at the same time and stepped into the same aisle as me. You know how some desks are designed for right-handed kids and some are for left-handed kids? They open in different directions and they're usually placed in the classroom randomly. She's not one to wait until somebody moves out of the way before pushing past and she bumped into me rather rudely. I was about to turn around and let her know that was not okay when it started: my ears began buzzing, my vision clouded up, and I got really warm. I felt myself begin to pass out; it was such an intense sensation. I barely noticed Jack pushing me back into my seat and shoving my head down to my lap.

Veronica was with someone, a man, but not one I recognized and I couldn't see his face clearly. I saw Veronica, but the man was fuzzy, out of focus somehow. He had his hands on her upper arms, shaking her roughly. His arms were bulging with muscles; he looked like he could be a bodybuilder. "Who have you told? You better not tell anyone it's mine! You have told, haven't you, bitch? Tell me!" He shook her again and called her some very foul names. This obviously wasn't her boyfriend, Danny. This was someone older, judging by his deep voice and huge muscles.

"No, Nick! I swear I haven't told anyone! You're hurting me!"

He abruptly let her go, stepped away, and turned around. Both Veronica and I breathed a sigh of relief. It was short-lived, however, as the man suddenly turned back around and hit her, open-handed, on the side of her head. She fell to the ground, sobbing.

He looked shocked at what he had done. "I'm sorry. I'm sorry, baby. Please forgive me." He was kneeling down by her side, pulling her into his arms.

I came back to my senses with Jack squatting down next to my desk, rubbing my back lightly. "Hey, Ally," he whispered. "What's wrong? You look like you're gonna pass out."

"Jack, Ally, is everything all right here?" Ms. Gonzalez was standing at the front of our row.

Jack looked at me questioningly. I shook my head very slightly and gave him an imploring look.

"Yeah, Ms. Gonzalez," he said, without looking away from me. "I had a minor misunderstanding with my girlfriend. Sorry to bother you. Let's go, Ally. We can talk about this later." He started to gather up our belongings.

"Oh, well," Ms. Gonzalez said "I'll let you..." She retreated back to her desk, apparently unwilling to get involved in any of our teenage drama.

We made our way out of the classroom as quickly as possible. Jack put his hand on the small of my back and guided me into a fairly deserted side hallway. Although I was still fuzzy from the vision,

I couldn't help thinking how much I liked being described as Jack's girlfriend.

"Listen, Ally. What's going on with you?" He backed me against the wall as he confronted me. "This isn't normal. It doesn't seem like you're sick, but something's wrong. I really wish you'd tell me. Maybe I can help. Did that girl do something to you? I mean, yesterday you got all weird when she was presenting and today she practically knocks you down and you get all hot and look like you're gonna pass out."

I looked up into his sweet, caring eyes and thought it was amazing that before yesterday I had never spoken to him. Today I felt like we had been friends for a while, yet I still didn't know very much about him. I shook my head slowly. "No, I'm fine, Jack. Thanks for that, back there," I motioned vaguely toward the classroom.

He looked at me, staring, really. It was unnerving. "Come on, Ally. What's up with you? Something's going on. I've never seen you like this. Let me help." He reached out and pushed my hair behind my ear.

Well, when he did that, I was putty in his hands. "Listen. I'll tell you what's going on. I don't know if you'll believe me or if you'll think I'm insane and never want to speak to me again, but I'll tell you. It's just…is there somewhere we could go? A bit more private? I don't mean to be creepy or anything." I didn't know what I planned to tell him, but I figured he deserved some sort of explanation.

He looked deeply into my eyes, searching. "Sure. How about if we go grab a Coke or something and then I can drive you home. I have a class at CNM in a couple hours, but I've got some time." I nodded and he shouldered my backpack and his and led the way out to the parking lot.

Wow. This guy is super sweet and polite and everything wonderful. Too bad I'm about to completely scare him off with my freakishness.

A surprisingly short time later—how time flies when you're dreading something—he pulled into the parking lot at Flying Star, a local gourmet coffee chain restaurant. Our high school is conveniently located in the Northeast Heights area of Albuquerque, which means we're really close to several malls and lots of restaurants. I love living in this area of town because, as a girl without a car, I appreciate being within handy walking or bus distance of a lot of choices for shopping, and so on. It's not exactly like we live in a major metropolitan area like Chicago or New York—this is New Mexico, after all—but for Albuquerque this is a great part of town. As we approached the glass case full of baked goods and the counter, Jack turned and asked if I was hungry. I shook my head. "Just coffee, thanks."

He ordered two coffees and a piece of Rio Grande Mud Pie with two forks. "You like chocolate, don't you?" he checked. I assented with a slight shrug. Sweet, but I doubted I would be able to keep down any kind of food right now. I was so nervous about the forthcoming conversation I thought I might actually throw up. He picked up our tray and carried it to a booth beside the windows. He placed a cup of strong, steaming coffee in front of each of us and placed the pie in the middle of the table, equidistant between us. He held a fork out to me, saying, "Ally, I know you think that whatever it is you have to tell me is horrible, terrible, and in all other ways a deal-breaker, but I have to tell you that it will be so much better if you have a bite of this amazing pie first." He dangled the fork in front of me, raising his eyebrows hopefully. How could I resist?

I laughed and took a small bite of the pie, a layered concoction with a chocolate crust, a fudgy, dark chocolate layer, and a creamy caramel layer, all topped with whipped cream and chocolate sprinkles around the edge. It was pretty much the trifecta of delightfulness. I moaned as I chewed. It was nearly a *When Harry Met Sally* moment. "Wow. This is wonderful! I've never tried this before." And then I started to tear up—the thought of losing this, this *camaraderie* we were building, for lack of a better term, was heart breaking. Add to that the stress I was under with these crazy visions popping up and you've got the makings of a real drama scene. Now, let me let you in on a little secret: redheads are not pretty criers. We get all blotchy and red with a tendency towards swelling—not attractive. I so needed to get myself under control.

I've got to give Jack a huge amount of credit; when confronted with a teary redhead, in public no less, he didn't bolt for his car as fast as possible. In fact, he was extremely solicitous, taking my hand and passing me a napkin to wipe my nose. Sweet and practical. "Hey, it's okay, Ally. The pie's not that good." He tried to lighten the mood. I gave a slight chuckle. "Listen," he continued, "are you in trouble somehow? Ally, I promise I'll understand—I've been there myself—and I'll help you."

I managed to control my tears enough to say, "Oh, God, Jack, I'm not on drugs or anything. I haven't committed a crime of any sort." He looked at me while still rubbing the back of my hand with his thumb. "And I am absolutely not pregnant."

"Well, that's a relief. I haven't experienced that last one. I could help you with the first two, however. Come on, Ally. What's going on with you?"

What on earth was I going to tell him? I remembered Grams' dictate that outsiders shouldn't know about our "family gift," but I couldn't lie to him anymore. Maybe it went back to the feeling I've had all along that there was more to Jack than met the eye. I decided to try to tell him the truth, realizing that this was probably the end of our very short relationship. "It's just that I have to tell you something that sounds insane and kinda like science fiction."

He was still rubbing his thumb across my knuckles. How was I supposed to concentrate with him touching me like that? I felt it tingling all the way to my toes.

"I promise to listen with an open mind," he said.

I took a deep breath a dove in. "All right. Here goes. Ever since I was a little girl, I have known certain things about people. Things I shouldn't have any way of knowing. This kind of thing actually runs in my family. And yesterday, I had an extremely clear vision in the middle of English about Veronica Albluth. I know for a fact that she's pregnant, which won't come as a shock to anyone, but today, a little while ago, I had another vision of her being smacked around by some guy and called some very bad names. And I really don't think it was her boyfriend, Daniel. That's all. Except I'm really scared and freaked out by all this. And, oh, yeah, you can ask Tara if you don't believe me. Or my grandmother. Or my mom." I finally stopped to take a breath, afraid to look at him, afraid of what I'd see in his eyes.

He stopped rubbing my knuckles and sat back in his seat. "So, wait a minute. You're telling me that you're having some sort of ESP visions? That you're, like…a psychic?" He laughed once, disbelieving.

I withdrew my hand from his and looked down at the table, making designs in a drop of cold, spilled coffee with my finger.

"Holy shit. You are telling me you're a psychic. Wow. Okay." He sat back in his seat, running his hand through his black hair.

I didn't know what to say, so I took another bite of pie and looked anywhere but at Jack. There was a guy working on his laptop at a nearby table and a woman eating by herself at another table. I did a double take when I realized that the woman was actually a man in drag. The Adam's apple gave it away. The pie in my mouth seemed to have doubled in size as I tried to swallow it down my throat, which was trying to close up. I kept chewing and chewing. I had a horrible feeling I resembled a cow.

"Ally?" Jack reached over the table, turning my chin gently to make me look at him. "So, can you read minds, or what?"

I shook my head. "No," I whispered, finally managing to choke down the pie. "I just get these visions, I guess. I've had two of them now. It sounds pretty crazy, huh?"

"Yeah, it does." He touched my face again. "But it also makes sense."

I stared at him. "What do you mean? In what universe does this make sense?"

"Well, it makes sense because we've ruled out most everything else, except maybe a brain tumor. Do you think that could be your problem?" His smile told me that he was teasing.

I tried to smile back, but it was a half-hearted attempt. "I don't think it's a brain tumor. Do you believe me, Jack? Really?"

He smiled that wonderful smile I was becoming addicted to. "Yeah, which makes me crazy too, I guess. But I do believe you, Ally. How could I not? So, Veronica Albluth is pregnant by some guy who's smacking her around? That's not right. We need to figure out who he is."

And now I started crying in earnest. Great big heaving sobs. Wonderful. I was starting to attract unwanted attention, so Jack, sweet, wonderful Jack, stood up and slid into my side of the booth. He put his arm around my shoulders, pulling me to his side, shielding me from the rest of the coffee shop patrons, while handing me more napkins with his other hand. "Shh. Don't cry. It's okay." He stroked my hair as I continued to sob messily.

"You believe me? I can't believe you believe me. Jack, I can't tell you what this means to me. Why do you believe me?" I pulled away to look at him. "My story is completely unbelievable. You shouldn't believe me. It sounds like something from Harry Potter or some other fantasy." I was out of dry napkins so Jack got up and fetched a few from the refill counter.

As he slid back into his side of the booth he said, "Well, for one thing, your grandmother and Tara seem like pretty reliable people, your grandmother's ancestral tea set aside. I haven't met your mother yet, so I can't speak for her. In addition, I've been watching you all year long in two classes every day and you don't seem given to drama of any sort."

Wait a minute—he'd been watching me all year? What?

"So, what's up with the dizziness and that crazy heat you give off? That's happened both times, hasn't it?"

"Yeah, it has. I don't know why it happens." I shook my head and blew my nose in what I hoped wasn't a disgusting way. "Grams is looking into it, doing some family research. It's pretty darn inconvenient, if you hadn't noticed."

"It's fine, Ally. I don't think anyone else really noticed it was you. It's none of their business, anyway. You said this runs in your family. So does your grandmother have any powers? Like maybe knowing when people are coming over or something? Hmm?" He gave me a rather pointed look. He was apparently a pretty smart guy.

I finally was able to smile for real. "Yeah, she

46

can touch stuff and tell things about the owner. She goes through my stuff all the time. Kinda sucks, not gonna lie."

"So that explains the tea party. What about your mother?"

"She finds things. It definitely comes in handy. We never lose our car keys or the remote." I couldn't believe he was so understanding. "Doesn't this freak you out at all?"

He appeared to think about it. "Not so much. I knew there was something special about you. You know, more than meets the eye? Plus, my grandmother is a curandera, so maybe I'm predisposed to believe in the paranormal."

I had thought the same thing about him, that there was more to him than was readily apparent. "What is a curandera?"

"It's a form of healer. She uses herbs and contacts the spirit world, stuff like that. I've seen some pretty freaky stuff that can't be explained by science."

I looked down at the pie and was surprised to see nothing but crumbs. "Please tell me I didn't wolf down all that pie. Oh, my God, I'm so embarrassed."

"I'm saying nothing. Besides, you needed it. I'm sure those visions cause some kind of hypoglycemia or something. That's probably why you get dizzy and weak feeling. Well, on top of eating nothing but a few vegetables for lunch." He placed a tip on the table. "Let's get going. I've got to get to class and I bet you didn't call to tell your grandmother you'd be late."

"Shoot, you're right." I pulled my cell phone out of my back pocket and texted her an apology while we walked out to his car. When he dropped me off, as he walked me to my door—such a gentleman— he stepped very close to me and said, "I'm really glad you told me, Ally. I swear I'll keep it to myself. I hope we can figure out a way to help that girl. No one should have to put up with that."

I looked up into his beautiful ebony eyes. His eyelashes were so thick. How fair is that? And he smelled so good. "Thanks, Jack. I really appreciate that. And thanks for the pie. Sorry I ate it all."

He laughed and opened the door for me.

CHAPTER FOUR

"Once you eliminate the impossible, whatever remains, no matter how improbable, must be the truth."
–Arthur Conan Doyle

Grams spent Friday evening and all day Saturday sequestered in her room. When we asked what she was doing, she would only say "research." Mom and I were surprised, because she nearly always has a Friday date and often a Saturday one as well. The statistics for single women versus single men after age 55 are definitely in her favor. And my grandmother is hot. I know that sounds weird, but it's true; she's tall, slim, and dresses with style. Plus she's a lot of fun. I want to stop thinking about the ramifications of that last statement immediately. Ewww. Anyway, I felt bad because I knew she was spending all that time researching my issues with these visions I was suddenly having. So late Saturday afternoon, I rapped on her door, balancing a tea tray with one hand. I figured she needed some sustenance since she hadn't been out for a regular meal since she got home Friday after work.

I entered Grams's bedroom to find her typing busily away on her laptop, her bed covered in papers. "Here's some tea and a sandwich, Grams. You need to take a break. Where should I put this?"

"Oh, thank-you, sweetheart, that's very thoughtful. Set it there on the dresser. I'll get to it in a minute." She continued clicking her keyboard.

"Grams," I said in my sternest tone. "You need to take a short break. That email will still be there when you've eaten a bit."

"Yes, ma'am," she capitulated meekly and stood up to stretch. "I get so caught up." She was wearing sweats and slippers, which told me, more than anything else, how serious she was about this research. She usually pays much more attention to her personal appearance.

The fragrance of bergamot filled the room as I poured us each a cup of Earl Grey and set a plate with a cheese sandwich and some sliced fruit in front of her. "How's it going? Have you found out anything yet?"

As we sipped our tea, she began to tell me how she was attempting to find records of the women in our family dating back to the 15th century. "As I've told you before, the gift of the Seer runs in our family through the women. All the women have it to some extent, but it's most often a very mild form of shall we say, *enhanced* intuition. My ability to touch an object and see something about its owner is really rather unusual in its strength. Your mother's ability to find lost items is far more common."

"But then, if it's always mild why I am having these really vivid vision-type things? This is way more than enhanced intuition! Is it going to go away?" I asked hopefully.

"Well, Ally, I wish I had better news for you, but from what I've discovered every once in a great while, maybe once every 3 or 4 generations, a very powerful Seer comes along who has a gift that is most powerful and unusual. Our gifts usually begin to develop around the time we begin to reach maturity—16 or 17—and settle into their final form by the time we reach our 18th birthday. I think we're going to have to wait and see how your gift develops as you get a little older. It may settle down, or it may get even more powerful."

"Oh, great. I just want to graduate high school without attracting too much attention. Is that too much to ask?" I whined. "Grams, you said that this 'gift of the Seer' is in all the women in our family? Is this one of those Irish legends you've told me about all my life? Does this happen in any other families?"

"Well," she began, "the Moran family dates back to the 14th century in County Mayo in northwest Ireland. There are some indications that this gift was given to an ancestor by a druid priestess in gratitude for sheltering her from Oliver Cromwell's soldiers during the English Civil War."

"How does a priestess 'give' a power to someone?" I asked skeptically.

"Well, I don't know, but I'm sure it involved sex. I've heard those druids were quite the lusty set."

"Wow, Grams. Thanks for that mental image."

"Oh, Ally, don't be such a prude. You surely didn't get that from me."

Surely. "So, let's recap," I said. "I may or may not be a powerful Seer whose powers may or may not have come from an ancient druid booty call. I might continue to develop some really freaky vision power that is of no practical use to anyone—" but then I remembered the vision of Veronica getting hit by some guy and stopped.

"What is it, sweetie?" Grams put down her teacup and looked closely at my face. "What did you see that's bothering you?" I hadn't had a chance yet to tell her about yesterday's vision; when I finished, she looked at me and said in a very serious tone, "A Seer's powers, if they are true, are always for the purpose of helping someone. Power is never given or meant for mere profit or fame. I think you have a mission to help this young woman. She sounds like she's gotten herself into a situation that she can't find her way out of on her own. You're being called to help her."

Well, crap. That's really inconvenient because I kind of despise Veronica and everything she stands for. Why can't I be called to help somebody nice who deserves it? No, I have to be called to help someone who's a total slut and who hasn't had a nice word to say to me since elementary school. I hate my life. "Grams, how the heck am I supposed to help her? She got herself knocked up because she couldn't figure out how to use a condom. She is such a bitch!"

"Aletheia Grace! I am ashamed of you." Yep. That's my full name—you always know you're in trouble when you get both your full first *and* your middle name. Aletheia means truth in Greek. You are picking up on the irony of this, aren't you? "Are you forgetting that your own mother is 'someone who got herself knocked up because she couldn't figure out how to use a condom'? There's always a story that the rest of the world isn't privy to. It's not our job to judge her. I certainly wouldn't want anyone judging me. Are you so sure you are above such judgment?" I've never seen her look so disappointed.

I have also never been more ashamed of myself. Where did all those horrible words come from? Being the mature person I am, I started crying messily, with big heaving sobs. "I'm sorry, Grams. I didn't mean it. I don't want to mean it. I don't know why I hate her so much. I don't want to be that kind of person!" I wailed.

She took me in her arms and held me close. "It's all right, baby. Let it all out. I know you're not that kind of person. We sometimes need a reminder to check our attitude. You're going to be fine. We'll figure this out." After a bit more crying and generally feeling sorry for myself, Grams had had enough. "All right, stop crying. Go wash your face and then let's figure out what our next steps are." Her day job as a family counselor gave her an advantage when it came to dealing with my issues.

I did as she ordered and then returned to sit on her bed. "So, how am I supposed to help this girl? I don't even talk to her anymore. She never even notices me except to give me dirty looks."

"Well," she began, "I think your first job is to try and talk with her. Have a nice conversation, get to know her again, get her to trust you."

I sighed. "I can try, Grams, but I don't think you understand how the modern high school social hierarchy works. I hate to tell you, but I'm pretty much a complete loser at school. I am definitely at the bottom of the food chain and Veronica is at the top. We have absolutely nothing in common and nothing to talk about. She's a cheerleader, for heaven's sake!"

"Oh, God, not a cheerleader!" she mocked me. "Ally, I know you think I went to high school wearing flapper dresses and rouging my knees in the 1920s, but I actually graduated in 1973, for God's sake. You kids have nothing on my generation for decadence and bad behavior. Think Woodstock. The stories I could tell." Oh, dear heaven, please don't. She started cleaning up our tea and sandwich things, stacking them on the tray. "Now, you need to find an opportunity to talk to this girl and get her to open up to you. You need to think beyond the ridiculous labels teenagers think are so all-important. A few years from now, what and who you were in high school won't even begin to matter. Now get out of here so I can get back to my research." She shoved the tray at me and pushed me out the door. Her comments made me think of what Jack had said earlier this week at lunch about not liking to label people. I don't know. It sounds really good to talk about not labeling people and to look deeper into who they really are, but the reality of a 21st century public high school in America is pretty brutal, let me tell you. *Not* for the faint-at-heart.

***

Sunday morning began, like all Sundays begin at the Moran house, with a top-to-bottom house cleaning. Mom says that Grams instituted this fun-filled little tradition back when Mom was in elementary school. Grams says that with three such busy people, there has to be a routine—which is rarely deviated from—so we don't end up living like a bunch of pigs. I wish we could get a maid. Or a house elf. I'm not picky.

While I was scrubbing the downstairs guest bathroom, I tried to plot how I would start a deep and meaningful conversation with Veronica tomorrow at school. I only have two classes, English and physics, with her so I needed to find a time where 1) she was alone—tough since she is popular and popular people tend to constantly hang out with other popular people—and 2) we would have at least a short amount of uninterrupted time. I finished the bathroom, for some reason whistling "Popular" from the musical *Wicked,* and moved on to the other two bathrooms in the house. By the time I finished I had a rather lame plan, but it was the only somewhat viable thing I could come up with.

Monday morning I headed toward the bus stop carrying my hot pink backpack as usual and an additional item: a gym bag with running shorts, a t-shirt, and my seldom-used running shoes. I planned to lie in wait for Veronica in the girl's locker room after she finished with cheerleading practice, but I needed a good excuse to be there, hence the running gear. I would happen to be changing back into my street clothes at the same time as Veronica after a healthy run after school. Hey, it's the best I could do. As plans go, it really wasn't that bad, but it didn't quite work out like I hoped.

I got done with school and reluctantly refused a ride home with Jack. He looked at me a bit strangely when I told him I was going to do some laps around the track after school. I guess I don't give off the athletic aura. I took him aside and told him what I was really up to. He was skeptical but wished me luck as he headed off to his CNM classes. When I realized I was spending too long staring at his jean-clad rear end while he walked out to the student parking lot—what can I say?—I reluctantly gathered up my backpack and gym bag and made my way to the locker rooms.

I hadn't been there since freshman year P.E. as New Mexico only requires one P.E. credit to graduate. Somebody really needs to investigate the correlation between so little physical education and high obesity rates in New Mexico. I wrinkled my nose as the humid, sweaty aroma of generations of female athletes enveloped me. There was a heavy note of chlorine as well, since my school has an indoor pool. Hmmm, maybe I should have brought my suit and done some laps instead of running? I really don't like running. Oh, well, next time. I made sure I followed Veronica into the locker room, but at a bit of distance. I needed to choose a locker in the same row as her, but I didn't want to look like a creepy stalker, which I kind of was, but for a good reason. I managed to slip into her row as she was pulling a sweatshirt over her yoga capris and bandeau bra top. Really? She might want to consider a more supportive garment for cheerleading practice. I mean, all that jumping around was going to give her sagging boobs when she was older. But then, so was childbearing. Or so I've heard. Gross. I'm never having kids. "Hey, Veronica, how's it going?" I decided to hit the conversational ground running.

She turned to me in surprise and—I kid you not—she looked me up and down. "Uh, fine," she said, turned back to her locker, closed it, attached the combination lock, and left without another glance. I never knew two little words could be infused with so much snottiness—and one of them wasn't even a real word! I cannot express how close I was to saying, "forget this" and leaving. But then I remembered what Grams said to me and simply sighed and changed into my running clothes. I put everything into an empty locker, secured it with my hot pink Master Lock combination lock left over from my freshman year, and set out for the track that ran around the football practice field. The cheerleaders were already gathered in the center, but the actual football team was nowhere to be found. I wanted to be where I could see Veronica so I could catch her maybe when she took a break. If need be I would follow her back to the locker room and try to talk to her again there. I *was* starting to feel a bit stalker-ish. I pondered the mystery of the missing football team while I did a warm-up lap. I don't know anything about high school athletics except for what I've picked up by osmosis, being trapped in a building with them for nine months every year. There were a few other joggers utilizing the track, including some older ladies "power walking"; you know, pumping their arms like crazy, wearing brightly-colored velour jogging suits. I tried to picture Grams doing this and had to chuckle. I'm nearly certain Grams could out-run me, not to mention these ladies. The cheerleaders went through a series of stretches and then they all hit the track for a few laps. My warm-up lap had about done me in, but these girls sailed around the track and headed back to the center of the field without even appearing out of breath. I admit to some grudging respect for their athleticism.

By about an hour into their practice I was bored and cold. That's the thing about Albuquerque weather—you never know what it's going to do. It's really unpredictable. It had been unseasonably warm for early November for the past few days, but this afternoon it appeared that a storm was beginning to blow in. The temperature had dropped at least 10 degrees since school let out. I was determined to do this, however, so I kept alternating walking and running laps. I must have looked ridiculous.

At 3:30 the mystery of the missing football team was solved as they came running onto the field in their practice gear. The cheerleaders moved to the sidelines. There was some very disgusting catcalling as the guys began to warm up. Ick. It was all so stereotypical. I will admit to some pride in the fact that I received a few catcalls of my own, a fact the cheerleaders did not seem to appreciate. I watched the football team warm up and I found myself a bit surprised by the way they looked. They were all so big and buff. I mean, I had been going to school with these guys for years and had never noticed all those muscles. It was like watching a bunch of bodybuilders work out. Oh well, I guess I've never paid much attention. I don't go for super musclebound guys. I like a guy to have a nice, defined chest and abs, but nothing too overdone. I found myself daydreaming about what Jack might look like without a shirt on. Judging from what he looks like with one on, he's probably exactly the way I like a guy to look. He has amazing arms, and I bet his chest matches nicely. But I digress. As I watched them begin practice, I was disturbed by how violent a sport football seemed to be. I admit to knowing nothing about it, but I was still surprised by how much anger seemed to be involved. There was actually one near-fight that the coach had to break up. Jeez.

Their practice and my running continued for another entire hour, by the end of which I was thoroughly chilled and yet sweaty. Go figure. I was so glad I wouldn't be seeing Jack in my current state. I mean, we didn't have that kind of relationship, but here's hoping. I really didn't know quite what to make of our relationship; were we just friends? It seemed like maybe that's all he wanted sometimes, but then I'd catch him looking at me in a certain way and I wasn't so sure. It would actually be fine with me—more than fine—if he wanted more than friendship. I mean, come on; he's totally hot! He's also really sweet and smart…and I almost missed the cheerleaders packing up and retreating to the locker room.

I sauntered after them casually, grateful to end my afternoon workout. Veronica was already stripping off her bandeau bra when I rounded the corner into our row. She gave me a dirty look and thrust her too-perky breasts a little higher. I tried to ignore her massive mammary glands as I made my way to my locker. "What the…?" I was gazing in shock at my open locker, backpack, gym bag and various articles of clothing spread on the floor. I looked closer and saw the ruins of my hot pink combo lock amongst the wreckage. "Shit," I whispered. I'm not usually much of a potty mouth, but my locker had been broken into! I think I'm entitled. "Shit, shit, shit…" I continued under my breath as I began to gather up my erstwhile belongings. "My wallet and my iPhone are gone!" I followed a trail of clothing into the showers and found my jeans, shirt, and jacket, wet and crumpled in a corner of the showers. Now that's just mean.

"Wow, that sucks." I turned quickly and found myself face-to-boob with Veronica's chest.

"Oh for God's sake, put a shirt on, " I mumbled as I pushed past her with my dripping garments in my hands. Great. What was I going to wear home? How was I going to *get* home? My bus pass was in my wallet. Shit.

I was standing in front of my locker, shoving the

few possessions I had left in my backpack. "I don't even know what to do. Do I report it?" I asked Veronica.

"I don't know. I've never had that happen," she replied.

"Do you think any of the coaches are still around? Maybe I should find one," I wondered, half to myself.

"No!" Veronica surprised me by nearly yelling. At least she finally had her shirt on. It's unnerving talking to someone who's topless. You can't not look. I'm not a perv or anything, but the eyes are drawn to the boobs. "I think they've all gone home. Yeah, they all go home pretty early. I think you should report it tomorrow at school. That's what you should do." She was nodding so hard I thought her head might bob off. Weird reaction, but I had other worries currently.

"Yeah, okay. Can I use your phone real quick? My bus pass got stolen so I need to call and see if I can get a ride home."

"Um, sure. Here." She shoved it in my hands. "I'd offer you a ride, but I'm getting a ride with my boyfriend and he only has two seats." I'd seen him tearing out of the parking lot in his Corvette. Some people have way too much money.

"Thanks. That's fine. I'm sure I can get my mom or my grandmother." Only I wasn't able to reach either of them. I knew Grams had late office hours tonight so she was probably with a client and I suddenly remembered my mom had said she had a PTA meeting and that I was supposed to warm up leftover spaghetti for dinner. I tried to call Tara and even Travis, but no luck. I need more friends. What the hell good are cell phones if you can't get someone when you really need them? I handed the phone back to Veronica and decided I'd better get started walking the two miles home. I know it's not *that* far, but remember: I just finished running for, like, two hours, *and* I was going to be wearing shorts and a t-shirt and a thin sports bra courtesy of some inconsiderate thief. *And* it was getting really cold outside. Shit.

"Well, good luck," said Veronica. "It really sucks that your stuff got stolen." Yeah, you said that. "Well, bye." She waggled her fingers as she left.

I finished gathering up my stuff and headed out, prepared for the long, chilly walk home. It wasn't too bad until I emerged from the neighborhood surrounding the school onto the extremely busy Wyoming Boulevard, one of the major north-south thoroughfares in uptown Albuquerque. It was now around 5:00 p.m.—I guess. My cellphone was missing, remember? Nobody wears watches anymore—and the heavy northbound traffic from Kirtland Air Force base was humming along. Dusk comes early in November, which added to the chill. I had managed to get myself fairly wet when I picked up my clothes from the shower, so I was especially chilly in the wind that was now whipping around the more open boulevard. I think I also looked like I had been competing in a wet t-shirt contest. Shit. I want to make it known that the tears beginning to make their way down my cheeks were tears of anger. How *dare* someone break into my locker and steal my stuff! I felt so violated! I was so immersed in stewing in my own rage, that I was startled to hear my name. I turned, and life suddenly got a little bit better.

CHAPTER FIVE

"Truth without love is brutality, and love without truth is hypocrisy."
–Warren W. Wiersbe

"Ally!" It was Jack, now jogging up to me. I could see his car, headlights still on, driver's door open, parked in front of the Acapulco Taco Stand. I turned and he could see the tears, the wet t-shirt—yikes—and probably the goose bumps. "What the hell? Why didn't you take the bus? Where are your clothes?" He was taking off his jacket as he spoke and wrapping me in it.

"My wallet and my iPhone and my bus pass got stolen and my clothes got thrown in the showers and I tried to call everyone I know on Veronica's phone but nobody answered so I had to walk home," I babbled through chattering teeth.

"Come on." He picked up my bag and guided me to his car. "I've got the heater on. We need to get you warmed up."

I sank gratefully into the warm passenger seat,

pulling his wonderfully soft leather jacket around me. I could smell him on it, the delicious warm, spicy scent and, I'm sorry, but I've got to say it— *man*. He rooted around in the trunk, coming back a minute later with a blanket.

"It's got some dog hair on it," he apologized as he tucked it around my legs. "But it will help you get warm." He shut my door and went back around to the driver's side to get in. "Now…" He turned to face me, taking my hands between his and beginning to chafe them. "What happened? How did your stuff get stolen?"

So I told him, more coherently now that I was beginning to feel my hands and cheeks again, how I had returned to the locker room after my run to find my locker broken into and my stuff gone.

"Do you still have the lock?" I nodded my assent. For some reason I had felt the need to pack it up with my other stuff. "Can I see it?" I bent down to the floor to fish it out of my bag and handed it to him. "Yeah, they popped your lock." I shot him a questioning look. "Well, these are pretty easy to break into. All you need is a table knife or a screwdriver and you stick the tip between the u of the lock and the locker handle and give it a good whack. It's actually pretty simple physics: levers, you know?" In response to my raised eyebrows he gave one of his little half-smiles. "My misspent youth, remember?" He reached down past me to put the broken lock back in my bag. "You should have called me. I would have come to pick you up." When he sat up his face was close to mine.

"I don't have your number," I said ruefully. We

stared at each other for a moment. He looked at my mouth and I really, truly thought—hoped—he was going to kiss me, but then he cleared his throat and sat back behind the steering wheel.

"Yeah, well, I'll make sure you have it from now on. As soon as you get a new phone." He put the car into gear and began to pull out onto the street. "Let me buy you a cup of coffee to get you warm faster. There's a McDonald's right up the street on Candelaria. Not the best coffee, but we can do the drive-thru."

We sat in the McDonald's parking lot with the car still running and the heater blasting warm air into the confines of the Mustang. The coffee was too hot to drink, but I held it between my hands, enjoying the warmth. "The paint job looks great, Jack." I had noticed the beautiful, shiny red paint as I got in.

"Thanks." He smiled and sipped his coffee carefully. "I finished it yesterday. Pretty much took up my whole weekend. Hey, was this afternoon a complete disaster or did you get a chance to talk to Veronica?"

"Jack, I'm still amazed that you actually believe any part of this crazy story," I said.

"Of course I believe it." He paused in the act of taking a sip of the too-hot coffee. "It's you, Ally." Like that explained everything. When I shook my head in disbelief, he reached over and put his hand against my cheek, turning my head to face him. "Don't do that," he said rather sternly. "Don't ever sell yourself short." In a movie this statement would be followed by a passionate kiss. In my life it was followed by him removing his hand and going back to trying to drink the fiery coffee. Maybe the sweaty stench starting to be noticeable now that I was warming up was holding him back. Shit. I really needed to stop cussing.

"Well, it wasn't a deeply heart-felt conversation, but she did let me use her cell phone to try to call for a ride." I must have looked confused or something following my statement.

"What?" He was searching my eyes. "What did you just think of?"

I told him how Veronica had sort of freaked out when I suggested trying to find someone to report the theft to. "It was kind of weird, that's all. So, no great conversation, no deep, dark secrets revealed, but I did talk to her. At great personal cost to myself, no less," I ended ruefully.

"Yeah, that does, indeed, suck," he commiserated.

"So," I began hesitantly, "you seemed to know a lot about breaking a lock. Did you ever do anything like that?" I couldn't even look at him. He was always so closed-mouth about his past, but I was growing increasingly curious.

He gave a big sigh. "Yeah. I did a lot of stupid stuff when I was younger. Stuff I'm not proud of, stuff I'm still paying for now."

"Would you be willing to tell me about it?" I dared. "I mean, you don't have to, but I thought, you know, since we're friends and all…"

"Yeah, sure," he said dejectedly, running his hands through his hair. I hated to do this to him, but I really felt it was an important step in our friendship. "What do you want to know?"

"I guess...what happened to you? I mean, you seem so nice now, and so mature. I can't picture you as a hell-raising juvenile delinquent," I said as I tried to lighten the mood.

He gave a half-hearted chuckle in appreciation. "Well, I was a good kid all the way through elementary school and most of junior high. The trouble started when I was in 8th grade. My mom was hit and killed by a drunk driver on her way back to Taos from a business meeting in Santa Fe. She was an attorney."

"Oh, God, Jack." I was horrified. "I'm so sorry. You don't have to tell me."

"No, it's probably a good idea to tell you. You can decide if you want to even mess with me. I may not be worth the trouble." He smiled as he said it, but I could see through the veneer.

"Hey!" I turned in my seat to face him. Now I was the one putting my hand against his cheek. "Don't *ever* say that. You are definitely worth the trouble." He took my hand in his and held it loosely while he told me the rest of his story. How his father had spiraled downward after his mother's death into severe depression and alcoholism, leaving Jack and two year old Megan to fend for themselves. How he started getting into trouble at school, although he had previously been a good student. As a freshman his behavior had gotten worse: suddenly he was involved in a gang, painting graffiti, breaking and entering, fighting, ditching school, and both using and selling drugs. "I was on a really destructive path," he finished.

"What happened? How did you get out of that lifestyle and here to Albuquerque?"

"I got arrested. My dad didn't even come to bail me out." He rubbed his hand over his face. "I had to spend three nights in the county lock-up. You do a lot of thinking in jail. I thought about how disappointed my mother would be and I thought about how I wasn't there for Megan. They were really close to taking me and Megan away from my dad and putting us into foster care."

"But they didn't? What happened?"

"My auntie and uncle drove up there to Taos and bailed me out." He laughed, once. "My uncle looked me straight in the eye and told me to get my head out of my ever-lovin' ass and shape up. What kind of an example was I setting for my little sister?"

"So, that's your Kryptonite, huh? Megan?"

He chuckled. "Yeah, I guess so. Anyway, my aunt and uncle saw what was going on with my dad and packed Megan and me up and brought us back to Albuquerque. Manny told me that I had one chance. He gave me a job at his body shop and told me that I had to go back to high school and graduate. He and my aunt took us in, fed us and clothed us, gave us each our own bedroom. Their kids, my cousins, are mostly grown and gone. I wanted to drop out and get my GED because I was so far behind in my credits, but they said that was a deal-breaker. I needed to set a good example for Megan. I had to serve ten months in juvenile detention before I got to live with them, but at least Megan had a good home. I got out this summer."

He stared out the front windshield. "Man, I owe them so much."

"Hey," I squeezed his hand. "I think you owe yourself some credit too. You have really turned things around. That can't be easy."

He wrapped his hand around mine. It was a wonderful feeling; his hand was so warm and rough from his job at the body shop. "Thanks, Ally. You're a really good person. Does my story scare you away? Still want to be friends?" He looked at me hesitantly.

I squeezed his hand. "Of course I want to be friends. You have a great ride." I made a last attempt to lighten the heavy mood and change the subject.

He chuckled appreciatively. "Let's get you home so you can get changed. Then, if you want, I can take you to pick up a new cell phone."

"I would love that, thanks. Isn't it amazing how dependent we are on a piece of technology? How did our parents' generation get by without them?"

"Payphones, I think," he said as he backed out of our parking spot. "My Aunt Trina talks about always having to have a quarter in her pocket when she was younger. Can you imagine?"

"Do they even have payphones in real life anymore? Hey, there's something I've been wondering about. Why don't you ride a motorcycle?"

"What do you mean? I have a car," he replied, stating the obvious.

"I *know* you have a car, but it would totally fit your badass image, you know, with a tattoo and a leather jacket, and that dangerous look you have."

"Badass image?" He laughed. "You're crazy. Nobody thinks I'm a badass. Nobody thinks about me, period. Why would they? Most people are too busy thinking about themselves, at least in high school." He paused and looked over at me. "So, you noticed my tattoo, huh?"

"Well, at least *some* people aren't too busy thinking about themselves." I tried for a superior tone, trying to cover my embarrassment at having been caught out on the tattoo comment.

He spared me a glance with more than a little smirk in it. "Do you like tattoos? Do you have any?"

"I like them on some people. And no, I don't have any. I'm only 16 and my mom would *never* even consider giving me permission to get one, unlike Veronica's mother."

"You're only 16?" I'm pretty sure I heard him swear under his breath. "So, when do you turn 17?"

"Next month. I'm one of the unlucky few that has a Christmas birthday. Why? Does it matter? Do you have a rule against hanging out with 16 year-olds?"

"No, I don't have a rule against it. I just thought you were older. You seem older." He drove in silence for a few minutes. "I'm 18, Ally, almost 19. And I'm on probation. Listen, I know we're not dating or anything, but it still doesn't look too good. I have to be careful. The next time I'll be tried as an adult."

"Oh," I said in a small voice. "I don't want to get you into trouble or anything."

"I know." He sighed and reached over to take my hand. "It's okay. None of this is your fault. I need to be extra careful because my next probation hearing is coming up in a couple weeks. I'm really hoping this will be my last one and I'll be done."

I gripped his hand tighter. "God, Jack, that would be great. What can I do to help? Can I talk to anyone, tell them how great you are or anything?"

He gave me one of his wonderful half-smiles. "How about you don't do anything that would make you seem like you're having your morals corrupted? Like don't go getting a tramp stamp like Veronica."

Why was he noticing that tramp's tramp stamp? "Gross. I would never do anything that trashy." I took my hand out of his and pointedly looked out the side window.

"So, you think I'm great, huh?" he teased.

I continued to look out the window and crossed my arms in front of my chest. "Yeah, well that was before I knew you were scoping out Veronica's ass."

"Hey," he defended. "I can't help noticing when she sits down and her jeans ride down and those stringy underwear are showing along with her tramp stamp. What do you call those things?"

I chuckled in spite of myself. "You mean thongs?"

"Yeah, thongs. You never have those showing above your jeans."

I turned and punched him on the arm. "I would never wear a thong. And you shouldn't be looking at my ass, either." Of course, I was lying and was secretly flattered. And I might have a secret thong or two hidden in my underwear drawer, courtesy of a shopping trip with Tara. But Jack certainly didn't need to know that.

"Oww! Jeez. Besides, what you ask is physically impossible. But I will never look at Veronica's ass again. Pinky swear," he said as he held out his pinky to me.

I really couldn't tell if he was being serious or teasing me some more, but I wrapped my pinky around his. He didn't let my hand go as we continued to drive to my house.

Later that night, as I sat on my bed doing homework—which the thief had not stolen, unfortunately—I got a text on my new iPhone from Jack. He had made sure to program his number into it before we even pulled out of the Verizon parking lot and then made me call his phone to make sure it worked.

Jack: Hey just wanted 2 make sure ur OK. Sick or anything?

Ally: I'm fine. That's an old wives tale that getting cold gives you a cold.

I have a thing about proper grammar and spelling in my text messages. I don't have a problem with other people using shorthand, as long as I don't have to look anything up, but my messages will be written with correct spelling and punctuation, thank you very much.

Jack: Yes ma'am

Ally: Thanks for rescuing me today. You seem to be doing that a lot lately.

Jack: My pleasure. Any time. C U 2morrow

As I lay back on my pillow staring at his text messages, I realized I needed to face the truth: I did indeed have a major crush on Jack Ruiz. No more denials. No more self-lies. In the span of about a week and a half we had gone from being two strangers who had a couple classes together to a friendship of sorts. And tonight there had definitely been some flirting going on. Okay, fine. There had also been some rather unattractive jealousy on my part. I admit that too. Happy? I sighed as I realized I had probably totally tipped my hand to Jack. He probably knew now that I was feeling very friendly indeed toward him. All right, calm down. Let's take a moment to analyze the situation. On the plus side, he had not run screaming into the night. Instead, he had driven me to pick up a new cell phone—we had insurance, so it didn't cost anything. My mom says that not buying the insurance for a teenager's cell phone is insane. He had also made sure we now had each other's numbers. On the minus side, he had totally backed off when he found out I was only 16. Now, so you understand, an 18 year old dating a 16 year old is *not* illegal in New Mexico. I googled it to be sure. But there was still the issue of his probation, about which I couldn't find very much information online. I fell asleep still pondering this conundrum.

***

The rest of the week was fairly uneventful. Jack and I continued to work together in physics, he ate lunch with Tara, Travis, and me, and we sat next to each other in English, but there had been very little progress made in the *relationship* department, if you know what I mean. By Friday, I was beginning to think I had imagined any flirting on his part. Tara was sympathetic yet practical, figuring he had backed off because of the age difference.

"But it's not even a full two years' difference," I complained as I gathered books from my locker before school.

"Yeah, but he's 18, which means he's a legal adult and you, little missy, are still 16 for another month. You're jailbait, sweetheart, and he's already got trouble with the law. Why don't we find you a nice, safe 17 year old guy around here, huh?"

"I don't want a nice, safe 17 year old." I slammed my locker with more force than strictly necessary. "I want Jack."

"Well, then..." Tara gave me a look up and down my entire body. "Stop whining and do something about it. Maybe we could start with a makeover so you don't look quite so much like an eighth grader. I mean, my God, Ally, are those the same jeans you wore in middle school? I know you haven't grown since then."

"Remind me again why you're my best friend."

"Because I'm not afraid to tell you the painful truth?" She hugged me to her side briefly. "Come on, it'll be fun! You need him to look at you as a woman, not a little girl."

"Fine," I said. "But you need to show some restraint. I don't want to look like I'm playing dress up. And absolutely no heels! I have to be able to walk. And I can't pull off a ton a of makeup, either."

"Yay!" she squeaked. Tara loved nothing more than playing dress up with me, but it had been quite a while since I had been a willing victim.

"You really think he'll look at me differently?"

"No, I think he's already looking at you in the naughtiest way possible, but I'm going to make you irresistible. His inconveniently noble character will be no match for my deviousness," she said proudly and marched off to her first period class.

The other major issue in my life, the whole psychic vision thing, also seemed to be giving it a rest. There was, however, one positive outcome of Monday's afternoon adventure and that was that Veronica was now speaking to me. It's not like we were suddenly BFFs or anything, but she did say "hey" to me on Tuesday as she sat down in English. And on Wednesday, she said, "What's up?" as she passed me in the hallway, only it sounded more like "wuz up." On Thursday she asked me if she could see my homework. See? We were really working at a quality relationship. At least she wasn't glaring at me anymore. She still seemed nervous and edgy, though. I hadn't had a vision in more than a week and I was starting to wonder if I'd lost my touch.

Things changed during 4th period physics on Friday, but not exactly in the way I had been hoping. Jack and I were working on a new lab, trying to figure out the velocity of a series of matchbox cars we were sending down a track, laughing when the car ran off the side. The classroom door opened and a student aide walked in with a pink slip, which he gave to Mr. Chiszowski.

He called out, "Jack, you're wanted in the office. Take your stuff." Jack's shoulders slumped and I could see his jaw flexing.

He packed up his notebook and pencil saying, "Sorry. See you at lunch, okay?" As he left the classroom, I could see there was a man waiting for him in the hallway. I had a hard time concentrating during the rest of the period. Who was that guy? Why did Jack look so grim?

Toward the end of the period, I was startled out of my thoughts by Veronica's horse-like laughter at the lab table next to ours. I looked over to see what was so funny and was immediately swept into the most vivid vision I had ever had. One second I was seeing Veronica's bright red mouth gaping open, laughing, and the next I was seeing Veronica crying, mascara running down her cheeks.

"Please stop, Nick. I don't want to. You're too angry and you're scaring me. No!" She was backed against a table of some sort and the huge man I still couldn't see clearly was roughly squeezing her breasts.

"Now you don't want it, huh, slut?" He pulled back and slapped her. "Shut the hell up and take what's coming to you. You trap me by getting pregnant and now you won't put out?" He roughly turned her around, shoved her face down on the

table, and reached under her short skirt to pull down her underwear.

Oh, God, I couldn't believe what I was seeing! This man was actually raping Veronica! He undid his belt, stepped close to her, and began. She cried out in pain and sobbed all the way through the violent act. He called her names that I never imagined a man calling a woman. When he was finished, he stepped away from her, fastened his pants, and then grabbed her roughly into his arms, soothing her, smoothing her hair, and kissing her face.

"Baby, I'm sorry. You know I love you. You just make me so mad sometimes. Why do you make me punish you?" Veronica continued to sob.

I felt sickened to my very soul by what I had seen. He claimed to love her? That violent act had nothing to with love!

As the vision faded, all I could hear was the buzzing in my ears and the classroom floor rushed up to meet me as I passed out. I came to very quickly, but Mr. Chiszowski was completely freaked out and insisted I go immediately to the nurse. Surprisingly, Veronica volunteered to escort me, which was actually a good thing since I was clammy and shaky, and had a difficult time walking unassisted.

In a few minutes I was resting on the cot in the nurse's office with a cold compress, trying to calm down after the horrifying vision I had seen. The nurse was trying to talk to me but Veronica kept interrupting with such thinly veiled questions about prenatal care that I'm sure the nurse wasn't fooled for a minute. I knew Veronica was dumb, but really? And I'm the one who passed out; could we focus on me for one tiny minute? And yes, I did feel bad for thinking those things about her right after seeing a vision of her getting raped.

At that moment, Jack burst through the door. "Ally, what the hell happened? They said you passed out!" He knelt down beside the cot and took my hand, brushing my hair out of my face with his other hand. Just looking into his concerned eyes had a more calming effect than the compress. "You okay?" he asked quietly. I looked past him and could see that the same strange man who had been outside of the physics classroom was standing in the doorway.

Before I could say a word, the nurse came to my bedside and said quietly, "She's fine. Are you the father?" she whispered. Well, maybe the nurse wasn't as sharp as I'd given her credit for. She apparently thought Veronica had been asking about prenatal care on my behalf.

"The what?" Jack practically shouted. I noticed the man suddenly looked very interested.

"She's not pregnant!" Jack, Veronica, and I all said at nearly the same time, only I said *I'm* and Jack said, "she's not *pregnant!*" while Veronica said, "*she's* not pregnant!"

The nurse looked dubious, but at that same moment Grams walked in the door looking every inch the consummate professional in her business suit and heels, saying sternly, yet calmly, "She's not pregnant. Now, may I have a moment of privacy with my granddaughter?" I admired the way she took control of the situation, shooing the nurse, Veronica, and the man out of the room. "Jack, I'd like you to stay, please."

"Grams!" I cried. She came towards the bed and I stood up and threw my arms around her. She soothed my hair back from my face and told me to start at the beginning. I told both of them about the horror of the vision, how I'd seen the whole vile act, but never the face of Veronica's attacker.

"Son of a bitch!" murmured Jack as he paced the room, his hands running through his hair in agitation. "You shouldn't have to see that kind of stuff! What kind of a 'gift' makes you watch sick stuff like that?"

"Jack." Grams put her hand on his shoulder in a soothing gesture. "I know this seems very disturbing, but imagine how it must be for that poor girl." She motioned toward the door. "Ally is much stronger than you give her credit for. She's going to have to be, since it appears that she has been given an extremely powerful gift. I've never heard of anything like it."

"Grams, I'm scared. I don't know what to do."

"I know, sweetie." She came over to sit beside me on the cot. "We'll figure this out. I have a few ideas. Now." She stood up and smoothed out her skirt. "If you, Jack, would be so kind as to help Ally get her things together, I would like to take her home for the day. Meanwhile, I'll step outside and have a little chat with your probation officer and assure him that not only are you *not* about to become a father by a 16 year-old girl, but that you have actually become a rather upstanding young man." She winked at him and left us alone.

I swung my legs over the edge of the cot and stood up, rather wobbly at first. I hate passing out. The last time it happened was when I was 13 and had cut my finger all the way to the bone while I was trying to peel an orange, and when I saw some gross white stuff that looked like a little worm coming out of the cut, I crumpled to the floor. Luckily, I didn't land on the knife and gut myself. This time, Jack was right there, holding me up. No, I wasn't faking just to get him to touch me! As if.

"Hey, take it slow. Did they give you any juice or anything?" His arm around my back, supporting me, was insanely warm and hard.

"No, the nurse hadn't got around to it yet. Veronica was talking her ear off, so she didn't get a chance."

He said another bad word under his breath, sat me back down, and began rooting around in the mini-fridge on the counter. He found a small bottle of orange juice, shook it, unscrewed the cap, and handed it to me with an imperious look. "Drink."

"Yes, sir," I muttered and took a sip. "So, that was your probation officer?"

He sat down next to me on the cot with a sigh. "Yeah. He shows up for these fun-filled, unannounced visits occasionally."

"What for? I mean, just to check up on you?" I continued sipping the orange juice, which was helping. I was beginning to feel more normal.

"Yeah, he wants to see if I'm actually at school, for one thing. Then he escorts me to the bathroom and watches me pee in a cup so he can do a drug test. Then he searches my backpack for any contraband or weapons or whatever and looks through any recent discipline reports. Really makes my day."

I reached over and took his hand. I love holding his hand. I love touching him in any way. "Hey." I gave him a little smile.

He squeezed my hand and asked, "How did your grandmother know who he was? Is it that obvious? And how did she get here so quickly? When did you call her?"

"I didn't call her. And no, it's not obvious who he is, at least not to me. That's just Gram's gift. Remember the tea party?"

He chuckled. "Oh, yeah. How could I forget?" He became serious for a moment. "Ally, are you going to be all right, you know, after what you saw? That's some pretty heavy stuff to deal with."

I nodded, but I couldn't look him in the eyes. The scene ran through my head again and I felt my chin tremble and tears behind my eyes.

"Hey, it's gonna be all right. Shh." He pulled me into his arms. "You know, what you saw? That's not what it's supposed to be like. Don't let it mess you up, please?"

I didn't let myself dissolve; I hung on and simply breathed in the scent of aftershave and soap and felt myself calming down.

He gently disengaged and stood up, shouldering my bag yet again. "Come on, I'll walk you out to your car."

CHAPTER SIX

"The truth is incontrovertible. Malice may attack it, ignorance may deride it, but in the end, there it is."
–Winston Churchill

On Saturday morning Grams took me out to breakfast to The Range Cafe. Over Huevos Rancheros for me and fruit and oatmeal for her, she told me that she'd set up an appointment with a friend of hers for later in the morning.

"Cassandra McTeague is an old friend of mine who, I think, might be able to give us some help and advice," Grams said over a final cup of tea.

"What does she do? Why would she be able to give us advice?" I wondered as I sopped up the last of the red chile sauce with a tortilla. Huevos Rancheros is a real farm-hand kind of breakfast, one that my slender grandmother would never consider indulging in, but hey, I might as well enjoy my teenage metabolism while I can.

"Cassandra is a very powerful Seer, and although

I had my doubts about it when she started, she has set up shop as a sort of fortune teller. I can't really approve, but she seems to make it work."

I pictured a toothless old woman, swathed in scarves, waving her hands over a crystal ball. Or maybe she was a gypsy, reading people's fortunes in tarot. Maybe we would have to cross her palms with silver. Which is why I was surprised when my grandmother pulled into a parking spot in front of a newly renovated, ultra-modern office building in downtown Albuquerque. I had fully expected us to head to one of the skeezier areas of town, like along Central Ave. I gave Grams a surprised look; she shrugged and got out of the car. I followed her inside to an office suite labeled *McTeague and Associates Lifestyle and Wellness Coaching* in burnished silver lettering. I could swear Grams hmmphed as we entered. A gorgeous blond young man greeted us as we approached the reception desk.

"Good morning, how can I help you?" He had one of those phone headsets on and looked very official. He was wasting his talents here; he should clearly be a model. Grams informed him that we had an appointment with Ms. McTeague. "Please have a seat. It will be a few minutes."

We sat on one of the plush grey couches that furnished the waiting room. "Grams," I whispered, "why did you bring me here if you don't like this lady?"

"Not like her? Who says I don't like her? I like Cassandra very much! She's one of my oldest friends."

"But," I sputtered, "you said she was a fortune teller and you didn't approve."

"That doesn't mean I don't like her, dear. We don't always approve of everything our friends do, but Cassandra is very gifted." At that moment, the beautiful receptionist—I'm sorry, guys *can* be beautiful, and this was one beautiful hunk of man—called us to follow him back for our appointment. He ushered us into a large, well-appointed office.

"Adele, how are you, dear?" An attractive black woman in her maybe mid-to-late forties rose from behind a desk and gave my grandmother a hug, kissing both her cheeks. "You look wonderful! And this must be Alethiea." Her voice was pitched low and smooth.

"Cassie, it's been far too long," said Grams. "The new office space is lovely, much better than that musty old space in Nob Hill."

"Yes, well, this recession has actually been good for my business. So many people are desperate to reinvent themselves. Now, both of you have a seat and let's see what we have."

She sat beside me on one of the couches while Grams sat in an armchair. I waited for the questions to begin and was therefore surprised, yet again, when Cassandra took my hand and began rubbing it between hers, closing her eyes in apparent concentration.

"Umm," I began.

"Shh," Cassandra soothed.

I raised my eyebrows at Grams, who shook her head slightly. Cassandra continued rubbing my hand for several more minutes while Grams and I sat quietly, waiting.

At last she sighed, set my hand in my lap with a pat, and sat back on the couch, saying, "Wow."

"Cassie?" Grams sounded worried.

"Adele, your granddaughter has a great amount of power coursing through her mind right now. I can literally feel the electricity humming through her veins."

I didn't like the sound of that at all. "Ms. McTeague, you can tell that just by touching my hand?"

"Please, Ally, call me Cassie. Yes, my gift comes through touching another person. I can tell a lot by touching you. If you will concentrate now on one of the visions your grandmother told me about, I'll be able to see it through you."

"Are you kidding me? That's incredible! And scary."

Both Grams and Cassie laughed.

"I'm serious. This stuff is freaking me out," I cried.

Cassie took my hand again, soothing it between her warm palms. "Ally, it's all right. I know this is disturbing, especially what Adele has described to me. I can help you make sense of it all. Close your eyes and concentrate on your first vision."

I closed my eyes and let my mind wander back to the first vision I'd had of Veronica in English class. I saw her leaning against her bathroom cabinet, then looking at the pregnancy test and dissolving into tears. I felt her sink down to the bathmat.

I opened my eyes when Cassie put my hand back

in my lap with a soft pat.

"These visions are so unusually strong," Cassie said, surprised. "I thought you must be exaggerating, Adele. I've never heard of a Seer having such clear visions. And she *hears* what is being said. That is exceptionally rare."

"So, she is a Seer?"

"That is not yet known. It certainly appears she is headed down that path, but she's young; much can happen before her 18th birthday." Now she sounded like a fortune teller. "Her prophetic gift is quite astounding."

"But these visions aren't of the future. These things have already happened," I interjected.

"Yes, that's true. But I'm using the word 'prophetic' in a general sense, for an uncovering of the truth. How do *you* know the visions have already happened?" Cassie asked me.

"I don't know how, I just *know*. Cassie, I don't know what to do with these visions. Grams says they're always meant to help people, but I don't know what to do. I don't know how to help Veronica." I could feel tears welling up, but I willed them back; I had cried more in the past few days than in the past few years.

"I don't have all the answers, Ally. I do know that your grandmother is correct; a true Seer is always called in a time of great need. You need to listen and be open to what these visions are trying to tell you. The path will be revealed." More fortune teller speak.

"But I passed out yesterday when I had a vision. That's going to be very inconvenient."

"Now, there I can help you. I can teach you some 'tricks of the trade' that could help you learn to cope with these visions and eventually control them. If you continue on the path of a Seer, you may well begin to experience other types of powers."

Grams looked at her sharply when she said this. "Cassie?"

"Adele, I think she should be prepared," Cassie said quietly. Grams continued to look at her for a moment, then nodded slightly.

"Now," said Cassie, "let's set a time for me to see Ally privately, perhaps later this week, to begin her lessons." She scribbled something on a pad. "Give this to my receptionist. He'll get you scheduled. Now, if you'll excuse me, I have some paying clients to attend to."

As we drove home, Grams seemed unusually quiet and lost in thought. "Grams," I ventured, "what was all that about 'the path of the Seer'? I gotta be honest, it sounds pretty crazy."

"I know, honey," she sighed. "Most people would think we *are* crazy. That's why true Seers tend to keep it to themselves. The ones who advertise themselves as psychics and the like rarely have any true power."

"So is that why you disapprove of what Cassie's doing? The life-coaching gig?"

"Oh, I don't know." She shook her head. "It seems a bit dubious to me. I love her dearly, but I can't approve of making money with a gift of this sort."

"Well, you called her a fortune teller, Grams. I was picturing something you'd find at a carnival, not that sleek set-up she has. That was totally impressive."

"Yes, well, I admit she seems to have done well for herself. And I'm sure she doesn't pull out a crystal ball for her clients. At least I hope not," she finished with a mutter. "But I digress. You asked about the 'path of the Seer.'"

"Yeah. Cassie said 'if' I follow the path. Is there a choice?"

"Of course. There's always a choice, Ally. Always remember that."

"So how do I follow the path? What happens if I decide not to follow it? And how do I know what the right choice is?"

"Whoa, slow down. Cassie will be able to help you figure all these things out, which is why your mother and I decided it was time for you to see her. This has gone beyond either of us."

"Grams, I'm scared by all of this. I didn't ask for it. I don't think I can help Veronica."

She reached over and patted my hand. "It will all turn out to be all right, you'll see. Now, why don't we talk about something different? Why don't you tell me how things are progressing with that young man of yours?"

"He's not 'my young man,'" I protested. "I don't even know what that means. We're friends. I think. I mean, I've only really known him for a couple weeks. I hope we're friends."

"Of course, you're friends. Anyone can see that. A more discerning person, like myself, can see that there's more to it than mere friendship though, don't you think?"

"I don't know, Grams." I dropped my head back on the headrest and closed my eyes. "Of course I hope there's more to it, but I don't think he agrees."

"You don't see what the rest of us see," Grams said.

"I wish that were true. But Grams, he has *issues*. He thinks he's too old for me because he's 18. And he's on probation."

"Yes, well, he's managed to turn himself around. Be patient with him, Ally. Give him some time. He has a good heart. I can tell." She gave me a secretive smirk, which for some reason both of us found hilarious.

***

The next week at school was fairly uneventful as far as Veronica was concerned. We did nothing more than exchange the barest of greetings. At this rate we would be graduated before I was able to figure anything out. Equally concerning, at least to me, was my relationship, or lack thereof, with Jack. Was it my imagination, or did he seem to be cooling off toward me? Last week we had been laughing, spending time texting, and talking at lunch. This week he seemed more distant. We still worked together in physics, but he seemed to sit farther away from me. In English he didn't lean forward near as often to crack a joke. And worst of all, he didn't text me in the evenings. There were no offers of a ride home in his newly painted Mustang. What had I done? Did he decide I was too freaky? Had he found someone he liked better? Someone maybe closer to his own age, like some skanky senior girl? The possibility of a *nice* senior girl was, of course, impossible.

Thank goodness for Tara. She patiently listened and made all the appropriate noises and gestures. She had been there for me two years ago during the Travis fiasco and I had always been there for her when her heart was broken. Tara had a lot more experience than I did when it came to dating, but was currently single. My experience with Travis—you try being dumped for another *guy*—had put me off the whole dating scene. Well, that and my total lack of popularity. It's not that I lack any attractive qualities; I can be objective enough to admit that I have a few. I have fairly nice features, no giant nose or anything, and I have nice skin. I'm not at all fat, but I am pretty short—really short, like 5' 1''. And the red hair is definitely an acquired taste. I was really hoping that Jack had acquired it. Tara, on the other hand, is tall and model-thin, yet with nice curves, broad shoulders and a flair for making whatever she happens to throw on look amazing. I hate her sometimes. She never seems to pine for a guy; if she likes him then of course he likes her. Why wouldn't he? She totally goes for it, even asks a guy out if she wants to. And the guys always accept.

"So, just ask him. What's the big deal?" Tara asked while painting her nails with my new light blue nail polish in my bedroom.

"I don't know." I flopped back on the bed. "I can't! It's not like that."

"It's always like *that,* Ally. Ask him already. If

he's not interested, then move on. But I think he's interested." She blew on her nails to dry them.

I sat up quickly. "What? Why? What did he say?" I grabbed for her hands.

"Hey! Watch the nails!" She pulled them out of my reach. "He didn't *say* anything. At least not to me. I can just tell. It's the way he looks at you. The way he's always rescuing you, whether you need it or not."

I flopped back down. "Yeah, well, that's all done with. He barely talks to me anymore." I grabbed my pillow and hugged it.

"Well, I think you should confront him about it. This is the new paradigm, Ally. We are women! We don't have to wait for the guy to act anymore." Easy for her to say. "Loser!" she taunted. I threw my pillow at her. "Hey, watch the nails!"

"Okay, okay. I'll talk to him about it. Probably. Maybe." Definitely not.

"First though, you promised me I could give you a makeover. Remember, we need to make you irresistible before you confront him. I think his parole officer must have scared him off after that whole pregnancy fiasco last week. He probably told Jack to stay the hell away from you," she said in entirely too off-hand a manner.

"It's probation, not parole. Don't make him seem like more of a criminal than he is," I muttered.

"Sorry. Hey, he's not a criminal. I really like him and I think you two will be a great couple, which is why I'm so willing to help you snag him. You simply need to put yourself into my oh-so-capable hands so I can make you look older, slightly sultry, and totally do-able."

"Do-able? Yikes, Tara. Could we focus on him asking me out on a first date?"

"Dream big, sweetie. It's good to have a concrete goal in mind." She blew on her nails. "Now, let's discuss when this makeover is going to take place. What's your schedule like next week after school?"

"Well, since Jack stopped talking to me, my schedule is wide open," I said as I hugged my stuffed dog.

"Perfect. We'll go after school, maybe Wednesday. I need to check my rehearsal schedule. Hey, how is your campaign to talk to Veronica going? Have you had any more visions?"

"No, not since that last awful one. Jeez, Tara, I never wanted to see anything like that. And talking to her is going very slowly. We're still pretty much on the one-word conversation level."

"Could it possibly be because she's a dumb bitch?"

"Tara! God, you're mean," I said. The thing is, I used to agree with her before I started getting my own personal Veronica-cam. Now I didn't quite know what to think about her.

"I tell it like it is. My nails are dry, so let's go raid your kitchen and then watch a movie. I brought over several and I'll let you choose. We can either watch Channing Tatum take his shirt off and save the President, or Brad Pitt save the world from zombies. Nothing like some hot eye candy to get your mind off that horrible vision."

"How am I supposed to choose between such hotties? You have to stay long enough to watch them both."

She laughed. "I can probably swing that. Hey, have you been thinking about the whole 'Nick' thing? Veronica calls the guy in the visions Nick. Do we know anyone named Nick? Anyone at school?"

"Yeah, I've been thinking about it, but I really don't think it's someone our age."

"Well, what about a teacher?"

"Eww, gross. I don't know, I guess we could start looking into teachers' first names. How many teachers do you think we have?" I gathered chips and salsa and diet sodas.

"At least 40, and that's not counting assistants or coaches or anything. Do we know anyone who's an office aide? That would really help."

"Nope, and I have no idea if it's even someone at school. It could be anyone she knows."

"Well, that's great. Sounds kind of like a dead end, at least for now. Come on, let's watch the movies."

***

My first session with Cassie came later that week. I don't really know what I expected, but it certainly wasn't what I got. To begin with, we simply talked. That's right. She didn't use a crystal ball, do a séance, or even read tarot cards. When I asked her about this, she laughed and told me she occasionally used tarot cards for her clients, but only as a prop; she didn't need cards to see what people desired. She asked me to describe, in detail, the visions I had experienced, what I was doing right before them, how I felt during and after them.

"All right, Ally. The first order of business is to prevent you from passing out during these visions. You need to be able to have the experience and not attract extra attention, no matter how cute he may be."

I looked up at her sharply, amazement clearly on my face. She raised her eyebrows at me.

"Now, I'm going to take you back through your visions. You're going to focus on my pendant. Go ahead; stare at it and try not to blink too much."

I began to stare at the large silver pendant that hung on a chain around her neck. Of course, the second someone tells you not to blink, you can think of nothing else but your need to blink.

"Now, I'm going to touch your hand. The power of touch is very important in a Seer. When I touch you, I want you to think back to your first vision about Veronica. I want you to concentrate on it and don't be distracted. Don't worry about the temperature in the room or whether or not you'll pass out. I won't let that happen." She slowly reached out to touch my hand. Immediately I was transported in my mind back to the very first vision I had about Veronica. It was her red belt and *The Scarlet Letter* that had started it. Just like Hester Prynne, she had a secret pregnancy. And just like Hester, she was going to find it impossible to keep it secret for very long unless she did something more modern about it. More than anything, I could feel the intensity of her feelings, both the fear of her situation and her reluctance to end the pregnancy.

She was curled up on her bathroom rug, crying, but I knew what she was feeling. In a weird way, I was the one curled up on the rug, not Veronica. I had a hard time distinguishing whether it was Veronica or me in the vision. I kept reaching further; now I could feel/see her worry that this would end the relationship with her boyfriend, Danny, whom she had not, contrary to everyone's expectations, had a sexual relationship with. She knew she was running out of time. Hoping it would all go away wasn't working. I could feel her confusion about her feelings for this Nick person who had gotten her pregnant.

"Ally! Come back! Now!" Cassie removed her hand and I slowly fought my way back to myself.

"Wow, Cassie. That was clearer than anything I've experienced. I saw deeper into the vision than I did the first time. What was it like, I mean in the room? Did it get really hot?"

"It got a bit warm, but nothing too extreme or exceptionally noticeable. That's what we're looking for: you able to see clearly without the whole room knowing something odd is happening. Now, we have to get you to the point of being able to do it by yourself. The problem is how deep you went into the vision. I wasn't sure you were going to come back on your own. You can't ever let yourself go that deep."

"How do I do that? I didn't intend to go that deep. Great, I'm getting worse instead of better."

"It will come, Ally. Don't worry. Let's try it again, now that you know what's going to happen. Concentrate this time on controlling your reaction and how far into the vision you let yourself go." She took my hand again and immediately I was back in the same vision of Veronica. I could see just as clearly, but I really thought about still being present in the room with Cassie. I would lose it for a minute and hear Cassie urge me to get it back. I don't know how long this went on; keeping track of time was beyond me at this point. Finally, Cassie let go of my hand and I was back. "Much better, Ally. You're a quick learner."

"Cassie," I hesitated, "last time you said I might develop other types of powers. What did you mean?"

"Well…" She stood up and began pacing around her office. Was she nervous? "Adele has told you that Seers usually manifest only one type of gift, I assume?" I nodded my assent. "Well, that's almost always the case, especially in this day and age. In ancient times, Seers were much more powerful, but the gift has been much diluted through the ages as families have married outside of the ancient lines."

"Are you from the same family line as Grams and I?"

"No. My family line traces back to the McTeige line in County Donegal, Ireland. But obviously, there has been much dilution along the way." She gave an ironic smile, gesturing to her dark skin. "But every once in a while, a Seer is born who has the gift of the ancients. Your grandmother and I feel there's a strong possibility that you are such a person. We'll have to wait and see what else happens with your visions. They seem to be getting clearer each time."

I swallowed that bit of information down. "Do you have this 'gift of the ancients'?" I asked. "What about Grams?"

"No, our powers are much more limited than yours seem to be. I'm only able to touch a person and see what they see. "

"I'm not quite sure how I feel about that. Me being one, I mean."

"Completely understandable. For now, are you willing to follow the path?" Cassie looked at me hard.

I swallowed again and nodded.

"Good. Then let's try something different. I want you to touch an object and see if you can sense anything about where it came from."

"Like Grams?"

"Yes, like your Grams." She walked to the shelf behind her desk and picked up a small, iridescent glass ball from a stand. She carefully placed it in my hands. "Now, stare at the ball."

It was beautiful, with pink, blue, and green streaks running across it. At first nothing at all happened. I felt stupid staring at a ball. Then, as I continued to focus, the streaks seemed to dance before my eyes. I stared harder. Suddenly, the ball became fuzzy and I began to see a crowd of people, chattering in what sounded like French. I could now tell that it was a gift shop, in a museum of some sort. Cassie was standing next to an extremely handsome black man, who was paying for the glass ball. They were laughing and he leaned down to kiss her. I could see the name of the shop, Musee D'Orsay, on the bag as he handed it to her with a smile. 'To remember our dream trip,' he said.

I opened my eyes and smiled up at Cassie. "You got this in Paris, at the Musee D'Orsay gift shop. A very handsome man gave it to you."

She clapped her hands together in front of her mouth. "That's wonderful, Ally. On the first try! Amazing! Do you realize that this means you have two powers already? I haven't heard of that since…" she trailed off.

"Cassie? Who is he? The guy in the vision?"

She appeared to give herself a mental shake. "Sorry, sweetheart. I got caught up. That man is my fiancé, Gregory, and, yes, he's very handsome. I'm no idiot." She said as she smiled slyly.

"When are you getting married?"

"We're planning a traditional June wedding. I'd rather elope to Vegas, but he insists." She said it fondly, and I wondered how much she had protested. "All right, that's enough for today. You must be beyond exhausted. Go home and get some rest. As I was leaving to go catch my bus, she said, "And I agree with Tara. You should ask Jack why he's giving you the cold shoulder. You don't ever have to be afraid to talk to him."

"How did you…?" I began.

"Ally, he's all over your thoughts. Stop obsessing and start talking to him."

Jeez. Everyone thinks they know what I should do. Okay, so Cassie *is* psychic and probably knows what she's talking about, but still.

CHAPTER SEVEN

"Three things cannot be long hidden: the sun, the moon, and the truth."
–Buddha

I couldn't stop obsessing over whether or not I should talk to Jack about our relationship. Or our lack thereof. Whatever. But that's what we teenage girls do: obsess over boys we like. We can't help it; it's hardwired into our DNA or something. So I tossed and turned for quite a while that night, thinking about how Tara and Cassie both thought I should confront him and find out what the deal was. I wasn't so sure. I remembered how Jack had talked about the fact he was 18 and on probation and it didn't look too good, even though we weren't dating or anything. That last bit was the part that really got to me. *Even though we weren't dating or anything.* Not "I wish we could, but this stupid age difference and my criminal history is the only thing keeping me from kissing you passionately." Nope. Not even close.

I finally fell asleep around two. Yikes. I was going to look less than spectacular in the morning. Maybe Jack would take one look at me and think, "Whew, dodged a bullet there!" This was not one of my best moments. As a result of my sleepless night, I was less than pleasant to my friends the next day. I snapped at Tara on the way to school when she asked if I had considered talking to Jack about 'you-know-what.'

"Just leave it, Tara."

"Jeez. Kill the messenger, why don't you?" She sounded a bit offended.

"Sorry." I immediately felt horrid. "I didn't sleep well last night. I shouldn't take it out on you."

"Hey, it's okay. That's what best friends are for. Now that I know, feel free to bitch away," she said breezily.

"No, that's not fair to you. It's just that Cassie told me I should talk to him too." I had filled Tara in over the phone last night about my session with the psychic. Well, I certainly wasn't busy texting or talking to Jack, who seemed to have forgotten my phone number. "I know I should talk to him, but I mean, what if it ruins what little we do have?" I whined.

"What is it, exactly, that you think you have?"

"Ouch. I thought I was the one allowed to be bitchy."

"Touché. But I'm serious. You're barely more than acquaintances right now. It sounds to me like you have a whole lot more to gain than lose," she said.

"I know, I know," I muttered. "I need time to

think."

"Whatever," she derided. "You're going to 'think' yourself right out of a perfectly hot boyfriend."

Physics was plain brutal that morning. Sitting by him, working with him, yet barely communicating with him was awful. Every conversational volley I started fell flat when he answered with as few words as possible. I was distracted from my misery and gloom by Veronica and her current coterie cackling over something. She may be going through hell in her private life, but on the surface she was as obnoxious and loud as ever.

"I know," Veronica was saying in a stage whisper. Seriously. A stage whisper. You'd have to be stone deaf not to hear her. "She can't do *any* of the stunts anymore. She doesn't have a sense of balance at all anymore." More giggles. "But we're totally screwed! We lost our best flyer!"

It seemed they were blathering on about cheerleading. Boring! I went back to my misery and gloom with Jack. So much better. Cold, formal politeness always beats inane chatter.

"Pass me the calipers, please."

"Sure. Here you go."

See what I mean? To make it worse, he made a completely lame excuse about having to take a make-up quiz for pre-calculus so he had to skip lunch and would see me later.

"Enough," said Tara as I moped over my salad. "Meet me after school. We're taking this to the next level. Today is D-Day for Operation Makeover. I don't have rehearsal and I got permission from

Grams for you to use your credit card for some much-needed wardrobe updating."

"Oh, I don't know, Tara. I need to…"

"I know: think. Enough thinking already! It's time for action, if you're ever going to get any."

"Oh, ha ha. Whatever."

"All right. It's happening. Now, I have great news," Tara announced.

"What?" I asked warily.

"I have a great idea for how you can get close to Veronica! It's brilliant!" She fished in her bag and came up with a crumpled flyer, which she handed to me.

Cheerleading Tryouts
Flyers/Tumblers Needed
Friday 3:00 p.m. Main Gym

"What on earth are you thinking?" I asked, dumbfounded.

"Apparently Tricia Barnes' boobs grew into gigantic melons over the past few months, or she got implants or something. Anyway, she completely lost her sense of balance and has been relegated to the bottom of the pyramid. You will try out for the team or squad or whatever they call it. They need a flyer—one of those girls they throw around and who gets to be on the top of the pyramid. You'll be perfect! You used to be in gymnastics and you're so small, you'd be a great flyer! And once you're on their little team, you'll have to spend all sorts of time with Veronica, which sucks because she's a completely vapid excuse for a human being, but that's just my opinion."

"I can't think of anything in the entire world I want less than to be a cheerleader, and that includes root canals. That is lamer than lame!"

"Tell me, Ally," she said in her superior tone. "And how successful have you been in getting close to Veronica and finding out about her little secret? Hmm?"

Ouch. She was right.

She wasn't finished, apparently. "The best way to get her to open up to you is to become part of her crowd. You need to go undercover with the In Crowd. You need to infiltrate their ranks. You need—"

"You need to stop watching Nikita on Netflix. Seriously, Tara? I can't be a cheerleader. I'll never make it on the squad. Why would they choose me?"

She went in for the kill. "Well then, there's no reason not to try out. Nothing to lose. Prove me wrong."

I knew I shouldn't fall for it, but heck, I'd been falling for it for years. It's my weakness. I can't resist when Tara issues what is basically a double-dog dare. Crap.

"Fine." I snatched the flyer out of her hand. "When are the stupid tryouts? I'll go and try out and they'll laugh me out of the gym. Will that make you happy?"

"Yes," she said smugly. The bell rang. "Remember, meet me after school. After your makeover, we can go to Starbucks and make our plan of attack."

I made my way through the hallways after school

to meet up with Tara, thinking how awful it had been to sit through English knowing Jack was behind me, but never said a word. All I got was a curt "see ya" as he skirted around me to leave the classroom at the last bell.

Tara was waiting for me by her car, a Jeep Cherokee that had been her mother's before she traded up for an Infiniti. Not that I'm jealous or anything. I have a driver's license and I'm perfectly capable of driving. It's just that the actual act of driving is truly frightening to me. I was in a fairly minor fender bender right after I got my license this summer. And, yeah, it kind of freaked me out. I may have had a teensy weensy panic attack and refused ever to drive again. So this is why I'm a gold card member of the Albuquerque Metro bus pass of the month club.

"So, after you dress me up, let's go to the Starbucks in Barnes and Noble. I can drown my sorrows and get a new book at the same time," I suggested as I got into the Jeep.

"No," she replied a bit too quickly. "They don't take coupons. We'll go to a different one, if you don't mind?"

It was proof of my extreme level of distraction that I wasn't more suspicious. After we stopped by Victoria's Secret so Tara could get her free panty— of course she was on their mailing list and of course she picked a lacy thong—she dragged me into Hollister. "This would be so cute on you, Ally. Try it on." Before I knew what was happening, she was shoving me into a dressing room with several outfits. I don't know how we've managed to stay best friends for so long when she loves this kind of stuff and I usually shop on Amazon.com while sitting on my couch in my pajamas. She was a woman on a mission, and in very short order had me dressed in a new outfit, which I had to admit was cute and made me feel attractive. She picked out a short plaid skirt with black leggings and a teal sweater that she said looked really good with my hair color and showed that I actually had boobs. She even found black flats. I told her I had some at home and didn't need the shoes. That's when she broke the news that I was wearing this outfit home and couldn't possibly do so in my tennis shoes. She had the clerk cut off the tags and bag my jeans and hoodie and then she bullied me into changing into the new clothes. She then whisked me off to Sephora, where it turns out she had made an appointment for me to get a mini-makeover. Again, I know I should have been more suspicious, but she didn't give me much time to process what was going on. She said it was a great chance to try out my new look before debuting it at school. By the time we had finished and she let me finally look in a full-length mirror, it was pushing 4:30. I was shocked by my appearance. She was behind me, taking out my ponytail and smoothing out my hair with her brush. She hugged me from behind.

"You're gorgeous, Ally. You need to permanently give up your middle school jeans and t-shirt look and let me start picking out your clothes. This is so fun! I've made you look at least four years older. Jack won't be able to resist you! Wait 'til he sees this!"

"Let's go. I'm dying of thirst. And I need a marshmallow treat in the worst way," I whined. I was secretly pleased with what she had done. I did look older, and the makeup was subtle enough that I didn't freak out. The artist at Sephora had given me what she called 'smoky eyes' and it looked good without being too much.

I was surprised and somewhat annoyed when we didn't head to the Starbucks right across from the mall. There truly is one on every corner.

"I want to go to the one on Lomas," Tara said in answer to my 'hey you just drove by Starbucks' comment. "I saw a really cute guy there last week. I want to see if he's there again."

Now I was finally suspicious. When we reached Lomas and I could see the Starbucks about half a block away, she pulled into the parking lot of an auto body shop and put the Jeep into park, engine still idling.

"Ally, you know I love you. This is for your own good. This is where Jack works. Now get the hell out of this car and go in there and talk to him." She hit the unlock mechanism and looked at me expectantly.

In shock, I tried to sputter my refusal. "You set me up!"

"Of course I did! Just do it. Meet me at the Starbucks when you're done."

I got out and she drove away. I guess I could have sat there in the passenger seat refusing to budge, but I wouldn't put it past her to walk around and pry me out of the Jeep in a very undignified manner. I squared my shoulders and turned around to face the auto body shop. Jimenez Auto Body. I had to hand it to her for her research skills. She had found out when and where Jack worked, which was more than I had done. I had absolutely no doubt he was currently inside. Tara would have made sure.

Well, let's get this over with. At least you'll know.

***

I mentally pulled up my big girl panties and walked inside the auto body shop. There was a small reception area, with a young, pretty dark-haired woman at the desk and a small seating area.

"Can I help you?" asked the woman as I entered.

"Um, yeah," I practically whispered as I approached her desk. "I, uh, I was wondering if I could talk to Jack. Um, Jack Ruiz, for a minute. If he's here. And not busy."

"Jack, huh?" she said. "Let me see if he's available." She picked up the phone to apparently page him. I could swear she was trying to keep a smirk off her face. "Hey, Manny, can you ask Jack to come up to reception for a minute? He has a visitor. Thanks." She hung up the phone. "Have a seat," she said, not unkindly. "He'll be right here."

Oh, god, oh god, what have I done? What on earth am I going to say to him? I worried on like this for several minutes.

And then he was coming through the back door, wiping his hands on a towel. He was wearing a uniform of sorts: dark blue work pants and a matching shirt that had "*Jack*" embroidered on the left breast pocket. It was odd seeing him in a context other than school. He looked completely wonderful. And very grown-up. Crap. "Hey, Shelly. Manny says I got a visitor? Who…" He didn't need to finish as Shelly pointed to where I was nervously sitting on my hands.

"Hi, Jack." I stood up and nervously wiped my hands on my skirt. I stood there, awkwardly, wondering what on earth I could possibly say to him.

"Ally!" His eyes widened in shock. "What are you doing here?"

Well, what did I expect? "I, uh, I was wondering if you had a few minutes. I, uh, wanted to talk to you about something. You know, about our English project," I said for Shelly's benefit, realizing that accosting him at work might not be such a brilliant idea. I didn't want to get him in trouble or anything.

"Huh?" He stared at me and didn't seem to be picking up on my oh-so-subtle subterfuge.

I stared back at him hopefully. "You know, the paper?"

"Um, yeah, sure. Hey, Shelly, tell Manny that I'm taking a break. I'll be back in a few." He stuffed the towel in his back pocket and gestured for me to follow him. "Come on. We can go to the kitchen. Nobody's there."

He led me down a hallway, past restrooms, to a small kitchen with an old-fashioned dinette set that looked like a cast-off from some grandmother's 1970s kitchen. "Have a seat." He motioned to one of the cracked vinyl chairs and opened the refrigerator. "Would you like a Coke or a Sprite or something?" he offered, still seeming confused to see me in his place of employment. I accepted a Sprite. He sat down opposite me and opened a can of Coke for himself and took a sip, all the while still staring. "You look…different."

Well, great. "Different?"

"No, I mean you look…good," he ended on a whisper. "Is everything okay? Did something happen?" He looked up from his soda.

I took a sip of Sprite. "No, everything's fine." I looked down at the scarred tabletop. Well, this was going brilliantly.

"*Shit*," I heard him mutter under his breath. "What's going on, Ally? Why did you come here, to my work?" he asked quietly.

"I'm so sorry, Jack. This was a mistake." I got up to leave, mortified at what I'd been about to do. I planned to slink back home and never leave my room.

He put his hand on my arm to stop me. "No, it's fine. I'm sorry. I was just surprised to see you. What did you need?"

I sat back down. "I wanted, um, I just wanted to know…" I couldn't finish.

"Hey." He rubbed my arm gently. His touch, light as it was, felt so incredibly good. "It's okay. Tell me."

Finally, the dam burst. "Jack, what did I do? Why won't you talk to me?" I couldn't keep the tears from forming. Blast! Crap. Well, I was in all the way now. "What happened to us? I thought we were friends, but you've been really distant lately. You barely talk to me anymore."

"Aw, jeez, Ally." He moved from his chair to kneel in front of mine. He reached up to wipe the tears that were starting to make their way down my cheeks. I hoped the eyeliner and mascara that the girl at Sephora had coated my eyes with wasn't running. "You haven't done anything. It's not you, it's me."

Oh, well. That makes it all so much better. That classic line. I started crying harder.

"Hey, hey. Come here." He lifted me out of the chair and into his arms. Well, this was better. I had wanted to be in his arms for quite a while. It felt so good, so right to be held by him. "Shh. Don't cry. We can figure this out." He held me close, stroking my hair.

This gave me hope. I pulled back and looked up into his handsome face. "What's going on, Jack? I miss the way it was. I miss you."

"Yeah," he sighed. "I miss you too. But I thought I was doing us both a favor. I told you it wasn't a good idea for an 18 year old on probation to hang out with a 16 year old. My probation officer had a fit when he saw us together. That whole thing in the nurse's office with the pregnancy wasn't good for my report."

"I'm so sorry, Jack. I never meant to get you in trouble. I just want to be friends."

"Friends, huh?" he replied. "I'm not sure it's a good idea for us to be friends, Ally."

I drew away from him, appalled. So he had been trying to back away from me and it wasn't only my imagination. He wasn't interested in being friends or anything else. The disappointment flooded through me, filling me with heaviness. Oh, God, I needed to get out of here! "Oh, okay. I just thought…I mean…but if you don't want—" I started to back away.

"No, I mean"—he reached for me. "Jesus, Ally. Of course I want…ah, screw it. Of course we're friends. I'm sorry I was such a jackass."

I threw myself back in his arms. "Oh, thank God. I thought you didn't want anything to do with me."

He 'oofed' a little at my enthusiasm and slowly wrapped his arms back around me, stroking my hair once or twice before pulling back and tipping my chin up with his finger. "It's that important to you, Ally? I didn't think it would matter that much." He looked vulnerable as he stared into my eyes.

I nodded and laid my head back against his hard chest. "Yeah, Jack. It's that important."

"Okay. I'm sorry I didn't talk to you. I was trying to do what's right for both of us. I don't think I'm good for you, Ally."

"Being friends is right for us," I whispered against him. "You're definitely good for me, Jack."

We stayed like that for a moment, holding each other. At length he let me go and said, "Listen, I gotta get back to work. Manny's going to wonder what happened to me. How did you get here? Do you need a ride home?"

"No, Tara dropped me off. She's waiting for me at the Starbucks."

"So, Tara was in on this, huh?"

"Oh, it was completely her idea. She kidnapped me, dressed me up, drove me here, and practically pushed me out of the car," I explained.

"Oh, great. Wonderful. I'll have to thank her in person," he muttered sarcastically. "So, uh, can I call you tonight?" he asked hesitantly.

"Of course."

"And can I drive you home from school tomorrow?"

"Well, that won't work. I, uh, I actually have, uh, cheerleading tryouts after school tomorrow." I couldn't meet his eyes.

He choked on the Coke he had been in the process of sipping. He began coughing violently, so I moved around to whack him a few times on his back. If I got in a few caresses, well, that's nobody's business but my own. "That unbelievable, huh?" I asked sardonically.

"No," he protested. "I just never pictured you as the cheerleader type. But whatever. I'm sure you'll make a great cheerleader."

"I'm sure I won't make it on the squad. I've never cheerleaded? Cheer-led? In my entire life. Tara thinks it will be a great way to get close to Veronica and find out what she's hiding."

"So, another one of Tara's brilliant ideas, huh? Well, I, for one, am looking forward to seeing you in one of those short little skirts." He earned a light punch on the arm for that.

"Hey, don't you have to get back to work? If I get you fired, your probation officer will not approve." I grabbed his hand and said, "Come on. You can walk me out."

When we emerged into the reception area again, Shelly was talking to an older man wearing the same sort of uniform as Jack. His said "*Manny*" on the pocket. He glanced at us, down at our locked hands, and then back to Jack's face, the question written clearly on his face. "Hey, Jack. I was wondering where you had disappeared to. Now I see. And who is this?"

I dropped Jack's hand and stepped forward, my hand now outstretched in greeting. "Hello, sir. I'm Ally Moran, a friend of Jack's from school. I'm sorry I distracted him for so long. I needed to check on something we have to do for physics."

"I thought it was for English," said Shelly with a smirk. She was so off my Christmas list.

Jack stepped in at this rather awkward point. "We just needed to talk. Ally, this is my uncle, Manuel Jimenez, and this," he gave a *look* at the young woman, "is my cousin, Shelly, who should mind her own business." She laughed and came around the reception desk to greet me.

"Hi, Ally, so nice to meet you." She gave me an exuberant hug and whispered, "good job, girl."

Wow. I'm not much of a hugger, but she seemed nice. Maybe back on my Christmas list.

"Call me Manny. Nice to meet you, Ally," Jack's uncle said. Both of them stared at us expectantly. Awkward.

"Well, Jack," I suddenly didn't know where to put my hands. "I need to let you get back to work. I'll, uh, talk to you later."

"I'll walk you over to Starbucks. Manny, I'll be right back."

"Sure, take your time," Manny seemed unconcerned. Maybe he was playing it a little too cool.

"Yeah, take your time." Shelly said with a snicker. I'm pretty sure Jack shot her the finger as he ushered me out the front door. I could hear her cackling as we left.

"I am so sorry about that," Jack began.

"Don't worry about it. It was very sweet. It was less awkward than a tea party." I raised my eyebrows at him.

"Only slightly. Hey, I have an idea. Why don't I pick you up after your tryouts tomorrow and we can take Megan out for dinner and a movie? Or is that too lame?" It was cute to see him unsure of himself.

"It's perfect. Just the sort of things friends would do." I should have let it be, but I couldn't resist reaching up on tip-toe to kiss his cheek. "See ya tomorrow. Thanks." I left him standing in the Starbucks parking lot.

I was halfway to the door when he called out, "Hey!"

I turned back around expectantly.

"Tara did good. You look great!"

Tara was about halfway through a venti caramel macchiato when I joined her at the table. "Success? Judging by the look on your face," she guessed.

I told her about our conversation while she had an insufferable 'I told you so' look on her face.

"So, you guys are playing the 'we're just friends game'? Kinda lame."

"I don't think he'll try to take it any further until he's off probation. He's so damn noble," I groused. "If he even wants to take it farther."

"He does. Trust me on that. And in the meantime, you can enjoy torturing him," she advised.

"Tara! That's awful." I thought for a moment. "Torture him how?" I asked slowly.

"Well, keep kissing him on the cheek, for starters. You should have seen the look on his face when you turned around to come in here. It was priceless. BTW, 'just friends' don't typically go around doing that, you know. Unless the guy is gay."

"Been there, done that, remember?" I interjected.

"Yes, I remember. That asshole. Why are we still friends with him?"

"Because we've known him since middle school. And he's basically a good guy. But I can't believe I wasted my first kiss on him."

"Nuh uh, doesn't count," she stated emphatically. "That absolutely does not count. You get a do-over."

"Oh, good. I want it to be Jack. I hope I don't have to wait till I'm 20."

"If you play your cards right, he could be your first *everything,* bow-chicka-wow-wow." She waggled her eyebrows up and down suggestively.

"Wow. You had to go there. Not talking about this. Let's go. I've got stuff to do and Jack said he'd call me tonight."

CHAPTER EIGHT

"Rather than love, than money, than fame, give me truth."
–Henry David Thoreau

Why is it that when you're dreading something, the time seems to fly by? I mean, seriously. I found myself in my last period English class the next day with shocking speed.

"Hey," Jack tapped me on the shoulder. "You all right?"

"I'm fine," I snapped. He sat back in his seat abruptly and I felt like a jerk. I wrote a brief note on a half-sheet of notebook paper and turned around and set it on his desk.

I'm sorry. I don't mean to be such a bitch. I'm just nervous—dreading these stupid tryouts.

I could hear him scratching a reply. He leaned forward and tossed it on my desk.

117

You could never be a bitch. Don't worry about it. Remember how good you're going to look in that skirt.

He had drawn a pair of pom-poms after the words. Quite the artist.

I wrote my reply under his.

I will not hesitate to kill you.

I could hear him chuckling as he read my reply. He scratched another reply.

Wait for me after class. I have a present for you.

When the bell rang, way too soon in my opinion, he gathered up his stuff, shouldered both our backpacks and said, "Come on. I'll walk you to the gym." I followed like a prisoner on the way to the gallows. "You know, I could stay and watch. Be your moral support and all that," he offered.

"Absolutely, positively not," I assured him. "I do not need anyone witnessing this debacle."

"Nice SAT word. I was only teasing." He pulled me into a deserted hallway and fished around in his backpack, pulling out a small, badly wrapped package. "Here. A good luck present." He handed it to me.

"Jack, you didn't need to do this," I began. I pulled the wrapping off and found a new lock, the kind Veronica had used last time I was in the locker room. I started laughing. "Thanks. I was so wrapped up in my misery that I didn't even think to get a new lock. I really appreciate it."

"Well, we can't have you getting your cellphone stolen again. This kind of lock is really hard to break into. I can personally guarantee that," he said with a knowing look.

This was so touching I had to hug him. Yeah right. But I wanted to. I always want to. He hugged me back for far too short a moment and then pushed me away with what sounded like a groan.

"You are going to be the death of me," he breathed. "Now, come on. You don't want to miss your tryout." I followed along, trying to hold in my triumphant smile.

When I got to the gym, I signed in and joined the other soon-to-be rejects on the bleachers. I looked around at my competition and my heart sank. There were some very pretty, very athletic-looking girls here. Wait, why was I disappointed? Did I really want this? Nah! It must be my competitive nature peeking through. I couldn't possibly truly have a desire to be a *cheerleader,* could I? Inconceivable, to quote *The Princess Bride.*

It turned out that this was only an informational meeting and there would be a clinic after school Monday through Wednesday where we would learn a routine and the actual tryouts would be Thursday, in groups of three. We would be judged on our knowledge of the clinic dance, sideline, jumps, and tumbling. *What the hell was sideline?* On tryout day we would be required to wear red shorts, plain white shirt or tank top, hair in a high ponytail, and all jewelry out. The decisions of the judges were final and would be posted on the auxiliary gym doors by 9 p.m. Thursday evening. They handed out a bunch of paperwork we were also required to complete prior to the tryouts. Then the coach launched into the financial obligations involved and fundraising opportunities. I had no freaking idea being a cheerleader was so expensive! I nearly walked out right then, but managed to stay put through the rest of the lecture on draconian cheerleading in the 21st century.

***

By the time Jack picked me up at 4:30, my head was spinning. I sank, exhausted, into the passenger seat of his beautiful red Mustang, my hands full of paperwork.

"Ally!" Megan squealed from her car seat in the back.

I turned to greet her. "Hey, girlfriend. You ready for our hot date?"

She giggled in response. "Jack, she said it's a date!"

"Yeah, I heard." He gave me a smile as he closed the door for me and went around to the driver's side. "So, how's the newest OGHS cheerleader? When do I get to see that skirt?"

"Ha, ha," I said. "Turns out there's a lot more to it. Today was just an informational meeting to give us all this." I waved the paperwork at him. "There's a clinic next week to learn the routine, then the tryouts are Thursday."

"You're a cheerleader?" Megan breathed in worshipful awe.

"Not yet, sweetie. I still have to try out." I turned back to Jack. "I don't know about this. These people are really serious. I thought I'd go in, wave some pom-poms, say 'ready, okay,' and be on my way. And it's mondo-expensive. I had no idea."

"I want to be a cheerleader," Megan continued, unabashed by my negativity toward her revered sport. "Will you teach me, please, Ally?"

"Well, if I make it, I will teach you whatever I learn, but I don't think I've got a very good chance of making it." To Jack I said quietly, "I don't even know if I'll go back."

Jack reached over and touched my hand, rubbing his thumb over the back of it. Can I just say that I love it when he does that? "Do you believe this cheerleading thing will help you find out what you need from Veronica?"

I thought for a minute. "Yeah, I guess I do. I hope so."

"Then," he continued, "you will go back and try out. And you will make it."

"How do you know?"

"Because I know you. You do what needs to be done."

I squeezed his hand. How did I stumble onto such a sweet guy? If I could only get him to get over his ridiculous, noble idea that he wasn't good for me. "Thanks," I said quietly.

"I really need to see you in that skirt," he teased and put his hand back on the steering wheel.

I gave him a mock disapproving look and turned

back to Megan. "So, girlfriend, what movie are we going to see? Sci-fi, horror, or does your brother want to see the latest chick-flick?"

She giggled again. "We get to see a cartoon." She named the latest Pixar movie to hit the big screen. "Is that okay? Do you like cartoons?" she asked worriedly.

"I love them! I have every Pixar movie ever made on Blu Ray. You can come over to my house and we'll have a movie marathon."

"Wow," she whispered. "Can I, Jack? Please?"

"Sure, squirt. Sounds fun." He reached to squeeze my hand again.

We got to the movie theater and Jack bought our tickets. I tried to pay for mine since we were 'just friends' and all, but he simply gave me a disgusted look and continued paying. "Come on. Let's get some popcorn." We decided to get a large bucket and put Megan between us with the popcorn on her lap. Jack stopped to get a booster seat for her on our way into the theater. I realized that Jack acted more like Megan's father than her older brother, perhaps because of their age difference or perhaps because her real father was out of the picture. I also realized we probably seemed more like a young family out for the evening to the people around us in the theater. To my surprise, I found this didn't bother me in the least. We got settled as the previews started. Jack opened the box of candy he had bought for Megan and she commenced feeding pieces to each of us. She seemed to delight in Jack's monster noises when he pretended to bite it out of her hand. I was seriously falling for this guy. He had to have some faults, didn't he? Any at all? Well, he did have a tendency to be bossy and take over sometimes, but even that could be filed under 'sexy confidence.'

Previews over, we settled down to watch the feature. Megan turned out to be a good theater patron, laughing in all the right places, but not talking or being disruptive any other time. About halfway through the movie, she poked me and motioned for me to look at Jack. He was clearly asleep, slunk down in his seat with his head resting against the back, mouth open slightly. We both smiled at each other.

"He always falls asleep during movies and T.V.," she whispered. "Auntie Trina says he works too hard and takes too much classes at CNM." Only it sounded more like 'cinnamon'. She was completely adorable.

As the credits began to roll, he woke up with a confused look around. "Wha...? Where's Megan?"

Megan giggled. "I'm right here. You took a nap."

"Yeah," I agreed. "A $10.25 nap."

Jack smiled sheepishly. "Money well spent. I'm starving. You guys ready for some dinner?"

"Can we go to El Patron? Please, Jack?" Megan begged.

"Well, let's make sure that sounds good to Ally. You need to check with her," Jack replied.

"Ally, it's really fun. They have music and dancing!" Megan enthused. "And tacos. I love tacos! Do you want to go?"

"Music and dancing? What kind?" I have to

admit I was picturing a bar. It was the only place I could think of that would have music and dancing, but I couldn't visualize Jack taking his little sister to a bar.

"Tell her, Jack," Megan tugged on his hand.

"You've never been? It's that big place over on Montgomery; used to be a Garduños?" he asked. At my headshake in the negative he continued, "It's pretty decent Mexican food, and they have a two-man band in the back room and people dance. It's really kind of a senior citizen-thing, but Megan loves it." He shrugged. "We can go somewhere else if you want."

"No, of course not. This is Megan's date and it sounds fun." To the little girl I said, "Does Jack dance with you or do you just watch?"

"He dances with me! He loves to dance!" Jack was rolling his eyes. "But he'll dance with you too. So will I."

We drove a few miles to the restaurant, a sprawling adobe behemoth that had opened in the last year. I had never been and was looking forward to trying a new place. Also to maybe having an opportunity to dance with Jack. And eat with him. And look at him. And smell him. I had it so bad for this guy.

As we entered the front lobby, Jack said, "Why don't you and Megan go grab a seat over there"—he nodded toward the fairly crowded waiting area—"while I get us on the list. I'll try to get us a seat in the back with the band," he assured Megan.

I watched him approach the reception podium where an attractive young woman, probably in her early twenties, was taking names. I couldn't hear what they were saying, but I could tell she was more than amenable to trying to accommodate Jack's request for special seating, if her admiring glances and coy smiles were any evidence. I truly don't think Jack was attempting to schmooze her, but I also don't think he was aware of how truly good-looking he was. I knew from experience that he simply needed to smile down at her from his nearly 6-foot height, and she was putty in his hands. I chose to be amused rather than annoyed since he seemed unaware of the undercurrents. He came to sit down by us with one of those little plastic pagers that lights up when your table is ready.

"She said she'd try to get us a table by the band," he assured Megan. "What?" he asked as he noticed I was trying not to laugh.

"Oh, nothing. I'm sure she's gonna try *real hard,"* I said with a smirk, nodding my head toward the girl, who had watched him walk away, eyes never leaving his backside. I can't blame her at all since I, myself, had enjoyed the same view on numerous occasions.

"Huh?" he asked in a clueless manner that was really kind of cute. "She was really nice. I think we'll get a good table."

"I'm sure we will," I replied quietly. He gave me a quizzical look.

Megan got up from her seat and plopped herself on Jack's lap, leaned against his broad chest, and yawned. "Hey, now. Don't you go falling asleep on our date." He brushed her long, dark hair out of her face and then tickled her.

She giggled and said, "Like you did?"

He tickled her more and said, "Yeah, like I did. What a boring old big brother, huh?"

She snuggled sleepily against him. "You're not that old."

"Oh, but I'm boring, huh? Is that it?" He tickled her some more.

Just then the plastic pager lit up, notifying us that our table was ready. The hostess, after a last, longing look at Jack, handed us off to a waitress, who led us in a labyrinthine path through the restaurant to a table very close to the two-man musical group.

Jack said to the sleepy little girl in his arms, "Is this good? Close enough for you?" She smiled shyly and nodded.

In very short order we had chips and salsa in front of us, which seemed to revive Megan. As soon as we had placed our order, she hopped down from her seat and tugged at Jack's hand. "Dance with me," she ordered.

He looked at me with amusement. "Well, at least she'll never be a wallflower. Excuse us for a moment? Come on, Princess." He took her hand and led her to the small area set aside for dancing. There were several other couples already dancing, and Jack had been correct; they mostly consisted of the 60 and up crowd. The musicians played oldies, most of which I didn't recognize. Jack and Megan drew many amused glances from their fellow dancers as he attempted to lead her through basic steps from his much greater height. She clearly had a good sense of rhythm and was enjoying herself immensely, judging by the wide grin on her face. At the end of the song, they came back to the table and Megan climbed back in her seat and drank thirstily from her Sprite.

When Jack attempted to sit down, however, she said, clearly appalled, "But you have to dance with Ally now!"

"Sorry, how I could I be so silly?" Jack stood back up with a half-smile at me. He approached me and held out his hand. "May I?"

I put my hand in his and we took to the dance floor. "I'm not nearly as good as Megan," I said. "She really has some moves."

He laughed softly and replied, "Well, you have other attractions." He pulled me into his arms and we began to dance to some old-timey jazz song. I really haven't done much dancing in my life, but Jack made it pretty simple. I tried to follow, enjoying being close to him, touching him.

"What's this song called? Do you know?" I asked.

"'The Girl from Ipanema,'" he replied. "They play it every time we come here." He began humming along. I was amazed at his level of maturity; he seemed unembarrassed about dancing with his little sister or knowing a classic jazz song. Most guys his age would be more worried about not appearing "cool" or whatever. I stared up at his clean, strong jaw line, noticing he had a slight five-o'clock shadow and wanting very badly to reach up and run my hand or lips along it and feel how scratchy it was. What would it feel like to be kissed by him? Would his whiskers leave red marks on my fair skin? I was dying to find out. "Hey," he interrupted my reverie softly. "Song's over." I belatedly realized the music had stopped while I was staring up at him like a love-struck idiot.

"God, sorry. I zoned out for a minute." I stepped abruptly away from him and headed back to our table. I felt his hand on the small of my back and smiled to myself. 'Just friends' indeed. Well, not for long, if I had any say in the matter.

Our dinner arrived almost as soon as we sat down; tacos for Megan, of course, beef enchiladas with green chile for Jack and cheese enchiladas with red chile for me. I made sure they didn't use meat in their red sauce. I actually prefer green, but it is nearly always made with chicken broth in restaurants, which is a total turn off to a vegetarian.

"So, how long have you been a vegetarian?" Jack asked.

"What's a vegenarian?" asked Megan, her mouth full of taco.

"Vege*tar*ian. Don't talk with your mouth full," Jack admonished gently. "It means she doesn't eat meat."

Megan swallowed obediently and said, "Ever? What about turkey on Thanksgiving?"

"Nope, not even turkey on Thanksgiving," I acknowledged. "I've been a vegetarian since I was 12 years old but I'm kind of embarrassed to tell you why I decided to go meatless."

"What? You can tell us. We promise not to laugh, right?" he looked at Megan for confirmation. She nodded her agreement.

"Fine, but don't judge me. I became a vegetarian

because I was reading *The Princess Diaries* and the main character, Mia, was a vegetarian and I wanted to be just like her." I looked at them rather shamefaced. "Silly, huh?"

"I have that movie," said Megan.

"So, why are you *still* a vegetarian?" Jack wanted to know. "Still following in the heroine's footsteps?" he teased.

"No," I said, jutting my chin proudly. "Now, I'm a fully conscious PETA cardholder who is against overt cruelty to animals. I don't eat anything with a face."

"I'm only teasing," said Jack. "I totally respect you for living out a belief so strongly. I don't think I could do it."

After Megan managed to finish one of her tacos and about half her beans and rice, she was ready for more dancing. Since Jack wasn't finished eating, I volunteered to dance with her. "You sure you don't mind?" he asked, sounding relieved.

"Of course not. Come on, Megan. Let's go shake our groove thing, girl." We danced to two fast songs and then Megan wanted to go back to the table for sopapillas. As she bit the corner off the pillow of fried bread and poured honey in the middle, Jack took my hand and led me back to the dance floor. They were playing a slow song as he pulled me into his arms and I gladly fit my body against his. With my head against his chest, I inhaled his wonderful scent: slightly spicy aftershave mixed with whatever detergent his aunt used on his clothes, and the clean and wonderfully male smell that was Jack himself. It was intoxicating. We fit together so well, in spite of our height difference. Why was he so determined to declare us "just friends"? It was clear we were more, and part of me wanted to call him on it; the other, saner part of me said to leave it alone, let it take its course. Pushing might push him away again, and that was completely unacceptable.

"I think our little third wheel is about to give up the ghost." He nodded his head toward the table where Megan was literally falling asleep as she ate. "We better get her home."

We worked together to get her cleaned up, Jack dipping an edge of the napkin in a water glass and wiping the sticky honey off her hands and face. "Ahh, Jack. That's cold," she complained sleepily.

"Sorry, Princess. If I don't, you'll stick to your car seat and have to spend the night in the car," he teased. He wrapped her jacket around her and picked her up. "Come on. I'll carry you." As we were pulling out of the parking lot a few minutes later, he glanced at my profile and said, "Do you mind if we drop her off before I take you home? I mean, it's still pretty early. We could go grab some coffee or something?"

"That sounds good," I said casually. There was no way in the world I was going to turn down more time, especially time alone, with Jack.

When we got to his house, Jack carried the sleeping girl inside, and introduced me to his Aunt Trina, who offered to take the child from him.

"No, I want Jack and Ally to tuck me in. Please?" she whimpered. He gave his aunt an amused look and carried her to her room. I followed him upstairs to a small pink and white bedroom, where we again worked together to get the limp child into her pajamas and tucked into bed. "Jack, sing me my song, please."

He rolled his eyes and tried to weasel out, "Oh, come on, Meg. Don't make me sing in front of Ally," he begged.

"Oh, I don't mind at all," I said virtuously. Jack gave me an evil look that promised retribution.

"Please, Jack?" Megan wheedled.

"Fine," he sighed and began to sing a soft lullaby in Spanish. He had a beautiful, deep voice that quickly lulled Megan to sleep.

I was enchanted. I reached over to brush the hair out of the little girl's face, but as I touched her skin, I immediately felt intense heat crawl along my skin and her face was replaced with a vision.

Megan was wiggling one of her front teeth with her tongue and it was extremely loose, moving back and forth in a disgusting way. She reached up with her fingers and the tooth suddenly came out. She stared at it with a comical look on her little face and then held it up triumphantly to Jack and his Aunt Trina. They both laughed and Jack hugged her, telling her to be sure to put it under her pillow that night so the tooth fairy would come.

I gasped and pulled away suddenly. As visions go, it was pretty mild—nothing truly shocking about it. Oh, yeah. Except that I know for a fact that Megan still has both front teeth because I had watched her chowing down on tacos all evening, biting into a crunchy shell with two intact front teeth. Apparently I had just had a vision of the future.

CHAPTER NINE

"There's a world of difference between truth and facts. Facts can obscure the truth."
–Maya Angelou

Well, of course Jack noticed that something was wrong. There seemed to be no hiding anything from him. Within a very few minutes he had me back in my jacket, a brief goodbye said to Trina, and then we were sitting in his car in the driveway, heater blasting, and he was chafing my hands between his. I couldn't seem to stop shaking.

"Damn it," Jack muttered. He let go of my hands and wriggled out of his jacket with some degree of difficulty and wrapped it around me, then continued to rub my hands. "You're shivering."

I stilled his hands. "Jack, I'm fine. It's okay." I turned to face him. "I just had a shock. I'll be all right."

"Tell me," he said. "Did you see something about Megan? Was it bad? Please tell me."

"No, Jack," I put my hands on his face. "She's

133

fine. I saw her losing a tooth. That's all. She was pulling out her front tooth and she showed you and she was so proud. It's all right. She's fine. Really."

"Are you sure?" At my nod, all the tension drained out of his body and he pulled me close. "Oh, my God. Okay. She's fine. Sorry. I kinda freaked out for a minute. But you were only seeing when she lost her..." He realized what the real issue was, why I had freaked out. "Ally, she hasn't lost her front teeth yet. My God! Did you just see the future?" Now he was the one with his hands on my face, looking intently into my eyes. "That's never happened, has it?" I shook my head. "Jesus, Ally. I don't even know what to say." He pulled his hands away and sat back in his seat, shocked.

My heart sank. So this was it. I was too much of a freak for him, finally. "No, it's fine." I moved back from him, suddenly cold once again. "Can you take me home, please?" I folded my arms tightly in front of my chest, tears close to the surface.

I could tell he was staring at me. "What? What are you talking about?"

"I get it. It's fine. I need to go home. Now."

He stared at me. "Ally? What's the matter? Do you think...? God, do you think I'm...I don't even know...disgusted or something?"

I couldn't help it. I really couldn't. I started crying. And not quietly or prettily. Real sobs. Hey, I make no excuses, except, well, can I simply say that I've been under a lot of stress lately?

"God, Ally," he said as he slid over and pulled me into his arms once again. "I think I might actually be offended. Do you honestly think this would put me off? You idiot," he said. He held me close, rubbing my back.

"I thought maybe this was too much," I hiccupped. "It's kind of too much for me."

"Yeah, I can see that." He said softly. "Hey, we'll figure this out. When do you see Cassie next?"

"On Monday. Jack." I sat back and looked into his face. "What's happening to me? I don't want this—this power. I want to be normal. I don't want to be able to see people's deep, dark secrets and I sure as hell don't want to be able to see the future. I don't want to be a freak."

"Listen to me, Ally," he said as looked intently into my eyes. "You are not a freak. You are a beautiful, strong, confident young woman who has been given a great gift. You're going to figure out what it's for and what to do with it. I have never met a stronger person than you."

"You think I'm beautiful?" I breathed. I was feeling much better now that I knew he wasn't going to bolt.

"Out of that whole speech, that's what you got?" He kissed me on the forehead and slid over to his side of the car, putting it into gear and backing out of the driveway. "Now let's get out of here before my aunt comes to investigate. I'm sure she thinks we've been making out in her driveway."

I would have loved to be engaged in making out with Jack in any driveway. I wanted to state that for the record.

"Let's get some coffee. I could sure use some. I think there's some tissue in the glove box if you want to, uh, you know, clean up."

I gave him an evil look as I began to root around in the glove box. "I thought I was beautiful," I muttered. "Hey, do you think Barnes and Noble is still open? I need a book and they have a coffee shop."

"I think they may be. Let's give it a try."

"Jack, would it be all right if we tabled the whole psychic thing for the rest of the evening? Please? I'd like to pretend to be normal for a little while."

"No problem. Normal it is."

Twenty minutes later, we were ensconced in the café at Barnes and Noble, drinking coffee with a new book apiece on the small table between us.

"So," Jack said, turning my book around to face him. *The Ultimate Guide to Cheerleading*? Looks like quite a page turner."

I rolled my eyes at him over my coffee cup. "Yeah, well, the coach was throwing around some terminology that was completely unfamiliar. I figure I better study up this weekend if I'm going to have any chance at all. I am going to be the world's worst cheerleader."

"Nah, you'll be the world's cutest. Ally." He grabbed my hand again on the top of the table. "Can I ask a kind of personal question?"

He could pretty much have anything he asked when he said my name like that. "Hmmm. Do I get one in return?" I countered, attempting to keep my mushy feelings to myself.

"Sure. Knock yourself out," he challenged. "Mine first. When you were paying for your book, I noticed that you have a driver's license. But I've never seen you drive or even talk about driving."

"Uh, yeah," I began. "Well, I do have a license. I actually had to get a new one when my wallet got stolen. But I don't like to drive."

"Why not?"

"Well…" I blew out a breath. "I actually got into an accident my first week driving. Of all the luck, huh? I haven't been able to drive since."

"Really? That sucks, but what about 'getting right back up on the horse' and all that?" he asked.

"I don't know." I shrugged. "I guess I got really freaked out. The thought of getting behind the wheel again terrifies me."

"What if I helped? I could take you out driving, you know, and get you used to it again. I'm a really good teacher."

"Oh, I don't think so," I said, shaking my head. The offer was tempting, especially the thought of spending more time with him, but the thought of driving freaked me out too much. "I'm really not ready for that. But thanks. Maybe someday. Okay, my turn. What was the song you sang to Megan tonight?"

He chuckled. "That's your question? Kinda seems like a waste."

"Yeah, you're right. I reserve my right to any follow up questions directly related to the original."

"Oh, that's not how this game is played," he argued.

"Yes, it is. Now, what's the song?" I tried to look very stern.

He laughed. "Fine, I bow to your interpretation of the rules. The song is called 'Duermete mi Niña.'

It means 'go to sleep my child.' My mom used to sing it to me, and to Megan, but I'm not sure she remembers that."

"Do you speak Spanish, Jack?"

He gave me that wonderful little half-smile. "Yeah, I do. My mom was bilingual, but my dad only spoke Spanish when they met in Mexico City. She was down there on an exchange at the university, working on her law degree. He was a literature professor. So, I was raised bilingual. It comes in handy at the shop. Any more follow up questions?"

"Yeah," I said softly and turned his arm over on the table. I was still wearing his jacket. "Tell me about your tattoo." I gently rubbed the image of the compass rose with dates swirling around the edge of it.

"I don't think that qualifies as a follow-up." He was quiet for a moment before he continued. "It's for my mom. In her honor," he spoke as softly as I, as if what he was saying was sacred, not for the ears of those around us in the coffee shop. "She loved roses. She had a beautiful garden at our house in Taos. She spent hours out there. I would help her, carrying buckets with the petals and rose heads in them. She would dry the petals and stuff. Make potpourri and I don't know what else." He pointed to the two dates. "This is her birthday: 4-22-67. This is the day she died: 10-15-08. I got it the day I got out of jail. I knew a guy who would do it without parental permission 'cuz I was only 15. I swore that day I would never let her down again. This reminds me to stay on the right path."

When he dropped me off in front of my house an hour later, he of course walked me up to the front door. I can't imagine Jack ever doing something like dropping a girl off at the curb. I hugged him tight and whispered in his ear, "Thanks for telling me about your mom. You're not letting her down."

***

Tara came over the next day to help me study for cheerleading tryouts. I do realize how weird that sounds, but it's true. I didn't know anything about cheerleading. We read most of the book, watched endless YouTube videos, and ended the evening in our pajamas, popcorn between us, watching *Bring It On.* Neither of us had seen it before, it not being anywhere near the genres we usually chose. At the end of the movie, I turned to Tara and said, "Shoot me now, please." She laughed and said that I would do fine on Monday.

Monday came, no matter how hard I wished it not to. Jack walked me to the auxiliary gym for the clinic before he headed to his CNM class.

"I'll pick you up from Cassie's office at 6." Even with his busy work and community college schedule he tried to minimize my reliance on the city bus. "Maybe we could grab a bite on the way home so I can hear all about the clinic and your session with Cassie?"

"That would be great, Jack. God, I'm dreading this," I sighed.

"Get in there and give 'em hell." He waved as he walked away.

I made sure to get a locker by Veronica and tried to engage her conversation while we changed, but the results were disappointing. I don't think she was going to have the time of day for anyone but a fellow cheerleader. Ugh! Why couldn't she be a member of the chess club?

The clinic itself was exhausting and mind numbing all at the same time. I was not a huge fan of the dance they were trying to teach us, nor was I any good at it. It was full of sexy moves that I felt ridiculous attempting. It was not until the last half hour that we finally got around to something I could shine at: tumbling. I was a competitive gymnast until my freshman year, when it became clear I didn't have what it took to be world class. But I sure could tumble. I made the rest of the girls look really lame. Hey, I'm not bragging. I'm also not layering on a lot of false modesty. I had put in hundreds of hours of work to learn the round-offs and back flips that I was, admittedly, showing off. But this was the only area I had the slightest chance in. I was never going to make it with my dance moves.

I was a sweaty, disgusting mess by the time I had changed back into my street clothes and headed downtown to meet with Cassie. I so wished I could take a shower before I met Jack for dinner, but I was running late and there was simply no time. Having to live by the city bus schedules was brutal sometimes. Yikes, he'd take one whiff and head in the other direction for sure.

In Cassie's office, she led me through a few more of the exercises we had done before. I like to think I made some progress. She did the object exercise again, this time with a decorative pillow that I saw her shopping for at Pottery Barn. Admittedly not the most exciting vision ever, but hey.

That exercise turned out to be a warm up for what she had planned next.

"Ally, I want to take you back to the other visions you had of Veronica. The more disturbing, violent ones. I'm sorry, but I think we need to revisit them."

I sank back into the cushions of her couch. "Yeah. I'm not looking forward to it. Especially the last vision. I passed out, you know."

"I know, sweetheart. I won't let that happen."

She took my hand and we went through the vision of Veronica getting slapped by her...what to call him? Her lover? Her baby-daddy? Her personal sadistic bastard? I favored the last one. As I went deeper into the vision with Cassie's assistance, I could actually *feel* the slap.

As she helped me re-surface from the vision, she said, "Ally, you're doing so much better today. You put off very little extra heat and came out of it very well. What's wrong?" She noticed that I wasn't sharing in her excitement.

I stood up and began to pace. "I don't want to do the next vision, Cassie. I won't. I felt him slapping her. I don't want to, I can't feel what he does to her in the next vision. I don't care about the passing out! I won't do it!"

"It's all right, Ally. We don't have to do that right now. I understand. Calm down, please?"

I sat back down and tried to get my breathing

under control.

"Now, why don't you tell me about the next vision? We don't have to go into it."

I told her about it; how the man raped Veronica and then apologized and held her. She was as appalled as I and encouraged me to keep trying to see the man's face. He needed to be in jail, hopefully before he could hurt Veronica any further. After we talked about that vision for a while, I finally got a chance to tell her about my vision of Megan and her tooth. Her reaction was not at all what I expected.

"Did you tell anyone about this?" she asked sharply, grabbing one of my hands. She held it so tightly that it kind of hurt.

"No, I didn't tell anyone. Oww, Cassie. You're hurting me." I tried to pull my hand away.

"What aren't you telling me?" she demanded. "Don't try to keep anything from me!"

"Cassie, you're scaring me. Let go."

She finally let go, a look of shame on her face. "Ally, honey, I'm sorry. I didn't mean to scare you. Are you all right?"

"Yes." I rubbed my hand, still looking at her somewhat suspiciously. "What's the deal?"

"Again, I'm sorry, but a vision like that, of the future, is really quite rare. It wouldn't be a good idea for anyone else to find out about it. Even your grandmother," she said sharply.

I laughed ruefully. "Cassie, I didn't tell her, but do you think I can keep anything from her? She'll know."

"You might be surprised," Cassie said rather

mysteriously.

"Um, Cassie, I didn't tell anyone else, except Jack. He was there when it happened. He knows about it. He saw me have the vision and thought it was something bad about his little sister. I did tell him. I'm sorry."

"Hmm. I don't know. I really don't know." She wasn't speaking to me. She was pacing around her office, mumbling to herself.

"Cassie?" I asked, at a loss.

She finally stopped pacing and addressed me. "Ally, I need to think about this. Why don't you go home? I'm sorry I upset you. I'm sure it's nothing. I need to look into a few things."

I gathered up my things and left gladly. Jack was waiting in the parking lot for me.

"Hey, how did it go?" he asked as he got out and opened the door for me.

"Jack." I laughed. "I can open my own door occasionally."

"Yes, but while I'm here you don't have to. Now tell me about your afternoon."

I told him about the strenuous clinic while we drove to The Cube, a BBQ place that has delicious homemade sides. They serve a mean grilled cheese, my personal vegetarian favorite. If you have never tried a grilled cheddar-provolone sandwich with a hint of bleu cheese, well, I urge you to indulge. As we waited for our order to be delivered, I told Jack about reliving the vision where Veronica got slapped and how I was so deep into the vision that I actually felt the slap myself. When I told him I refused to go into the next vision, the one in which

Veronica was raped, he went a little crazy.

"So Cassie actually wanted you to go through with that one? What the hell is wrong with her? It was bad enough you had to see it even once! No way am I going to let you go through it again, especially if you would feel it yourself! Goddammit! What's her number? I'm calling her right now!" He pulled out his phone.

"Jack, it's okay. Calm down," I put my hand over his phone. "No, she didn't want me to. She didn't know how bad the vision was. It's fine. I only had to tell her about it. She won't make me experience it again, promise."

He looked at me intently, seemed to realize that I had it under control, and finally put his phone back. I was flattered at his concern, but also frustrated. At times like these he seemed like he thought of me as much more than just a friend, but there was no action towards a more romantic relationship on his part. Ever.

"Sorry, but I remember how you were right after that vision, when you fainted. God, Ally, you were so pale. You looked like death or something. I'm glad you refused her. It should be up to you whether or not you decide to block something like that out."

I waited until we had our food in front of us to tell him about the bizarre reaction Cassie had to my future vision.

"Jack, I'm not gonna lie. It creeped me out a bit." I paused to take a bite of homemade mac-n-cheese, licking a stray bit off my bottom lip. I know, grilled cheese *and* mac-n-cheese? What can I say? I have a great metabolism. Tara is always insanely jealous that I can eat whatever I want, while she's constantly dieting. My mom warns me that it will catch up to me some day, and then my cheese-on-cheese days will be over.

"Jack? Earth to Jack!" He was staring at my mouth while I was chewing my food. *Oh, great. I probably have cheese sauce on my chin. Not only do I stink, now I can't feed myself properly. Maybe I can spill my drink to round out the disgust factor.* I wiped my face with my napkin, but it actually seemed clean. Hmm. *Maybe he was disgusted by how fast I was shoveling food in my mouth.* I made a concerted effort to slow down.

"Sorry." He couldn't seem to meet my eyes. He cleared his throat. "Yeah, it does seem a bit weird, because you actually handled the vision of Megan pretty well. I mean, you fell apart afterward, but I think you're starting to get some control."

I threw my wadded up napkin at him. "Thanks a lot. Yeah, I think so, too. About the control, that is. I figured she would have been glad to see my progress, but she kind of flipped out."

"Well, when do you see her again?"

"That was kind of weird, too. She didn't set a new appointment. She said she'd call me when she was ready to see me again."

"Yeah, that is weird," he agreed. "You ready? I've got a ton of homework I need to get started on." He picked up the check and prepared to pay.

Suddenly, I was tired of the double standard he was imposing on our relationship. He apparently didn't want to date me, but in so many ways he behaved like I was his girlfriend, like always picking up the tab for whatever we did together. I grabbed the hand with the check. "Why don't you ever expect me to pay?"

He looked blankly at me for a moment. "Uh, I don't know. It doesn't seem right. The guy should pay."

"That's terribly unenlightened of you, Jack. We're just friends, right? Friends should take turns paying, right?" I raised my eyebrows innocently at him.

He swallowed. I swear I could hear it. "I, uh…" he said in a truly urbane manner.

I swished the check out of his hand. "That's what I thought. I'll get this one, I think." I pulled out my wallet and counted out bills, leaving a decent tip. I can't stand bad tippers.

"Ally, come on," Jack complained. "Let me pay. You don't even work. This isn't cool."

I gave him a sugary sweet smile as I paid the bill. I got up and went to his side of the table and held my hand out for him. "Ready?"

"Jeez. You're so stubborn. I would have ordered something smaller if I knew you were paying."

"I know. That's why I waited until we were done."

When we got to my house he put the car into park and got out, ordering, "Stay put and let me open your damn door for you. Leave me some pride."

"Thank you, Jack," I said with mock sincerity. "You are such a gentleman."

I'm pretty sure he muttered something like "I'll show you gentleman" as he walked me to my door.

I stood on tip-toe to torture him a little more with a kiss on the cheek, but he surprised me by looping his arms around me and pulling me close in a hug.

I loved it, but felt compelled to say, "Jack, I haven't had a shower. I must smell terrible."

"You smell amazing," he breathed, his head tucked on top of mine. That earned him an extra squeeze from me as well as the kiss. God, this was killing me.

CHAPTER TEN

"Say not, 'I have found the truth,' but rather, 'I have found a truth.'"
–Khalil Gibran

The next two days of the dreaded cheerleading clinic sped by with unwarranted haste. Before I knew what was happening, it was Thursday and I was facing the actual tryouts. I had managed to acquire the requisite red shorts and white tank top, divested myself of all jewelry, and scraped my curly red hair up into a high ponytail, which made my head ache. Ugh! Did I mention that I hate this?

Jack and Tara both walked me to the gym after school. I felt like I was heading to a firing squad. I started to bite a nail. Tara slapped it out of my mouth and turned me around to yank my ponytail even tighter.

"Enough, Ally! This is nothing! Get in there and show them what a tough bitch you are! You will make the team...squad...whatever the hell it is!"

"Oww! Leave my poor hair alone. Okay, fine.

I'm a tough bitch. I got it, " I said, rubbing my scalp.

Jack took a gentler approach. "You've totally got this. I'll see you tonight at 8:45 so I can drive you back here and see that you made it." He bent down to kiss my cheek, but at the last minute seemed to change his mind and brushed my lips ever so briefly with his. "Now get in there and give 'em hell."

Well. I met Tara's equally surprised gaze. I turned and walked into the gym in a daze.

We tried out in groups of three, going through our routine, sideline cheers—thanks to *The Ultimate Guide to Cheerleading* I now knew what these were—and tumbling in front of the group of judges consisting of the coach and upper classmen cheerleaders, including Veronica. I did well on the routine, messed up a bit on the cheers, but truly gave 'em hell with my tumbling. Being so small, I can really get some nice height on my backflips. As soon as my group finished we were allowed to leave. Yikes. It was only 3:30. I had five and a half hours to wait for the results. There was only one spot to be filled with a reserve of three going to the junior varsity squad. I had no plans to accept if I only made JV, since I didn't want to be a cheerleader in the first place; I was only doing this to get close to Veronica. I kept trying to tell myself this.

I spent the intervowing hours doing my homework, cleaning my room within an inch of its life, grooming Mr. Wickham within an inch of his life—he finally got disgusted with me and stalked away to curl up in a warm spot by the heating vent—and preparing a really nice dinner for my mom and grandmother. This is how they could tell how nervous I was: I rarely cook voluntarily. I also found myself going back over the ever-so-brief kiss Jack had given me before tryouts. Yeah, it was short, but it was on the lips. That, in my humble opinion, crossed the friendship line. It gave me some slight hope that I was getting to him and maybe he would make his move soon. If he ever planned to make a move. Sigh. I wished I could be more like Tara and go after what or who I wanted and damn the consequences, but I had used up all my bravado the day I confronted him at work.

By 8:45, when Jack finally pulled into my driveway, I was a complete mess. I met him at the car, not even able to wait for him to come up the path and ring the bell.

"Let's go," I said tersely. He wisely said nothing, but simply put the car into gear and took off. When we got to the school, he prepared to get out of the car and walk with me to check the results. "No!" I exclaimed. "I don't want you to come with me. Wait here. I have to look by myself." He nodded, trying not to smirk or laugh, and kept the car running.

Nobody else was there. I guess I had expected a crowd of girls, but it was empty. In my mind I had created a total *Legally Blonde* moment—you know, when Reese Witherspoon goes to check whether she made it onto Victor Garber's legal team and when she sees her name she's like, "Yes. Me!" Then she tells her ex-boyfriend how much better that was than being in a hot tub with him for four hours.

Yeah, this was nothing like that. The path to the front doors of the gym had never seemed longer and I could barely make out a white piece of paper taped to the right hand door. I didn't allow myself to look directly at it until I was right on top of it.

Varsity Cheer Squad:
Ally Moran
JV Cheer Squad:
Hannah Gorman
Janie Soto
Mercedes Saavedra

I had done it. I mean, I had done it! I didn't know whether to be excited or devastated. This would be a game changer. I would now have to actually hang out with these girls and their social set sometimes, and to be honest, I wasn't too keen on it. Hopefully it would allow me to get closer to Veronica, although it seemed like a high price to pay. I walked slowly back to the car and got in.

"Ally?" Jack asked hesitantly. "You gonna be all right?" He must have misinterpreted my stoic, shocked face and thought I didn't make it.

I turned to him and said matter-of-factly, "I made it. I did it. Shit."

He burst out laughing and pulled me into a hug. "I knew you would!" He held me away and looked into my eyes. "You don't seem happy. What's wrong?"

"I don't know. It's just that…now it's *real,* Jack. I'm a cheerleader. Now I have to actually be a cheerleader. And raise a crap ton of money for my uniform. And hang out with the in-crowd. Ugh!"

He laughed again. "Well, don't go dropping your truly cool friends for this new crowd."

I punched him on the shoulder.

"Sorry. Oww. Of course you would never do anything lame like that." He rubbed his shoulder.

"No, I won't. But God, I probably have to go to some of their lame parties. I hate that kind of party." I turned to him. "You will be attending with me. I don't care what kind of probation you're on. I'm not going by myself," I declared fiercely.

"Yes, ma'am. I like it when you get bossy. Feisty!"

"Shut up and take me out for some damn ice cream."

"Yes, ma'am," he said again, chuckling.

***

And so my new life began. I now had cheerleading practice every day after school. Jack was able to pick me up a few times a week and we would usually go out to eat, often with Megan, or to one of our houses. I met his dog, Sodapop, and it was love at first sight for both of us even though I tend to be more of a cat person.

I had also begun thinking about something Jack had said after my last meeting with Cassie. He had been glad that I refused to go deeper into the awful rape vision, afraid that I might have to feel and experience what Veronica had felt. In addition, he had told me that I should have the choice whether or not to block something like that out. I'm sure he was talking about blocking out visions during sessions with Cassie, but I started thinking about other possibilities. What if I was able to block out a vision when I felt it happening? I mean, if I'm now passing out at really horrible visions, maybe I should try blocking them out while I'm having them. It would give me a much greater sense of control over my life, something I was desperate for right now. It wasn't like I was any help to Veronica; I wasn't even able to see the face of who it was that was hurting her. I was also not very successful in my attempts to befriend her in order to get her to confide in me. Maybe I could concentrate on blocking out the visions entirely. I'm not very proud of these thoughts in retrospect, but it's how I was feeling at the time.

One evening in mid-November, as I was sitting on Jack's couch French braiding Megan's hair, Jack paused in his channel surfing, looked up at me from his spot on the floor at my feet, and asked if Cassie had called lately. Sodapop, curled up beside me, snorted in his sleep and stretched.

"You haven't mentioned anything about her for a while," Jack said.

"No," I replied, concentrating on the intricate hairstyle. "Grams said she's overseas. Has been for a week or so."

"Hmm. That's kind of weird, that she hasn't even called." He met my eyes over the top of Megan's head. He knew that I had continued to have more visions of Veronica, as frustrating as the first few. I would see her, hurting, as some man I couldn't see brutalized her. I was getting somewhat better at controlling my reactions when I had these in class, but I was still afraid of having another violent vision that would make me pass out; hence the idea of blocking them out altogether.

He also knew I was making extremely limited progress in trying to befriend her. She seemed wary of me. We'd talk some while changing for practice, but she hadn't really warmed up to me yet to the point of sharing anything personal.

"So," Jack was apparently changing the subject. "It also occurs to me that I have not yet had the opportunity to see you in your cheerleading outfit. When is this going to happen?" Again with the flirting and no follow through. Sigh. One of these days I was going to break and grab his face and start kissing the crap out of him. But perhaps not when his little sister was with us.

I flushed and replied, "We have a pep rally on Thursday for all the winter sports, so you'll get to see it then. The first game is Friday night. Are you going to come?" I tried to sound nonchalant.

"A basketball game? Hmm, I don't know. Basketball's really not my thing. I'm more of a football guy," he said, offhanded, continuing to flip through channels.

"Oh," I said, trying not to sound disappointed. "Oh, okay. That's fine." I kept braiding hair mechanically.

He got up and carefully maneuvered himself so he was sitting behind me on the couch with me between his legs. "Scoot over, buddy," he said to Sodapop. The blue heeler groaned and went back to sleep. Jack wrapped his arms around my middle and whispered in my ear, "I'm totally kidding. Tara, Travis, and I have had tickets for days. I wouldn't miss it for the world."

I was at a point where I couldn't let go of Megan's hair, so I leaned back into his warmth and said, "I will punish you for this." He laughed silently; I could feel the vibrations against my body. "I know. You can take me to Veronica's party Friday after the game."

"Oh, God, no—not a party!" He flopped back on the couch. "That's cruel and unusual punishment. Can't you pull my fingernails out or something?" He sat back up and hugged me again. "Why don't we go to your house and watch movies?"

"I would love that," I sighed, breathing in his spicy scent. I could imagine cuddling on the couch with him. Maybe more than cuddling, if we're being totally honest here. "But I need to go to this wretched party for a little while, and I did warn you that I wouldn't be going to any of them on my own. That's too much to ask." I turned my head into his delicious smelling neck. "We don't have to stay very long; only long enough for me to get in good with Veronica. I wish I could like her, but she drives me crazy."

Way too soon he unfolded himself from behind me and returned to his seat on the floor. "Fine. I can do maybe fifteen minutes at a stupid party."

***

Thursday morning I woke up early enough to fuss with my hair and makeup as required by the cheerleading Nazis. I never wear very much makeup, but there were even rules about that! Acceptable amounts and colors were outlined in our cheer contracts. As I put on blush, sparkly eye shadow, and lip-gloss, I thought about how I was not cut out for all this über-girly crap. I had been dressing better lately, thanks to Tara's tutelage, but this was over the top. We were told to wear our cheerleading warm ups to school and change into our skirts and shells right before the assembly. I fastened the puffy red bow around my super-high ponytail. Checking myself a last time in the mirror, I rolled my eyes and went downstairs to meet Tara.

"You look like *Bring It On* exploded all over you," she said after giving me a once over.

"One more comment from you and I'll smother you with my pom-poms, I swear to God, Tara! Let's not forget whose idea this was." She laughed. "I should have made you join cheerleading with me. Maybe there's still time," I threatened.

"Hell no. I have to devote myself to my oboe. I have no time for shaking pom-poms."

I walked into fourth period physics and noticed Jack sitting at our table, texting on his phone and looking irritated. I walked up behind him and touched him on the shoulder. "Hey, what's wrong?"

He looked up and smiled, the irritated look clearing away, when he saw it was me. "Aww. Where's the short skirt?"

"Don't be a pig," I said as I handed him a set of calipers. "We're not allowed to wear them during classes. Apparently all that bare leg would turn all these high school boys into slavering beasts. I'll change before the assembly."

"As a member of the slavering beasts, I get it. But I'll be sure to get to the gym early and get a good seat with an unobstructed view. "

I mouthed "pig" at him. He gave a wolfish grin.

We were on a special schedule for the pep assembly, which was right after 4th period, right before lunch. When I left early to change into my uniform, Jack gave me a wink and a lascivious grin. *I wish,* I thought. *Too bad he doesn't put his money where his mouth is. He'd find me a completely willing participant.* Sigh. All this flirting, hugging, and almost-but-not-quite kissing was starting to get on my nerves. Don't get me wrong, I loved it, but I wondered where we really stood in our relationship. I was ready to dive in, but he was still holding back, keeping it mostly light, friendly, and on the surface.

The cheerleaders were warming up when they started allowing the rest of the students into the main gym. The basketball team was also warming up, shooting a few practice throws, although I have no idea why since this was simply a pep rally. They were probably showing off. I couldn't help overhearing some of the girls talking and giggling about the boys on the team, several of who were every bit as muscular as the football players I had noticed a couple weeks ago. One of the girls was cracking a joke about a "big man with a really little man" that I didn't understand. Judging from the way the other girls laughed, it was a crude joke. I felt really young and naïve at that moment. Maybe I would ask Tara or Jack about it later. I spotted them, sitting together with Travis about halfway up the bleachers. I saw Tara point and then Jack spot me. His jaw dropped in a flattering way when he saw me—the skirts are *really* short, but have these things called bloomers that cover our underwear—and he put his fingers in his mouth and let out a shrill whistle. Veronica, who was stretching beside me, noticed and said, "So are you guys together, or what?"

"Or what," I sighed and continued stretching.

"He's hot," another cheerleader named Lina inserted herself into our conversation. "He's got that whole bad boy thing going on. If you don't want him, I may jump on that."

My eyes narrowed into slits as I looked at her. "He's taken." Lina and Veronica snickered.

"Fine," said Lina. "You might want to make sure to stake your claim, though, or I'm going to consider him fair game." She sauntered away.

"Bitch," I muttered.

"Bitch who's after your man," Veronica added.

Perfect. All I needed was competition for Jack. Great.

We did some lame cheers to get the crowd excited and then did a dance routine to 'Move, Shake, Drop'—a clean version so the administration would not have kittens—by Pitbull. The climax of the routine came when I was standing straight up on Devonne's hands and he threw me up in the air and I came twirling down sideways to land in his arms. It looks pretty spectacular, but is actually a pretty easy stunt. Devonne's really strong and is able to throw me pretty high, and I tuck everything in on the way down so I spin really fast—thanks for the physics tip, Mr. Chiszowski. He then kind of throws me out of his arms and I do a series a backflips into drop splits. Hey, I did say I was a decent gymnast. Seriously, Jack doesn't know what he's missing. Kidding, jeez. I'm not that kind of girl. At least I don't think I am.

Jack and Tara were waiting for me after the assembly. "So, how'd I do?" I asked anxiously. They were the only ones I cared about impressing.

"You were great, Ally!" Tara gushed. "I'm glad you're finally putting all your years in gymnastics to good use." She hugged me.

"Well?" I stood in front of Jack, who had his arms crossed and looked a bit moody.

"You were really good," he said reluctantly. "But my heart about stopped when you were flipping around in the air. You should have warned me." He uncrossed his arms. "And why does that guy have to have his hands all over your ass? I'm not loving that part. It seems a bit intrusive and personal. Is that why you got into cheerleading, so you could have guys put their hands all over you in public?"

Wait, what? He was supposed to be proud. I had no words. What a jerk! Why would he say something so mean? I was so mad I could only stare at him, fuming, trying not to let him see the tears that were trying to escape. He stared right back. I was seriously contemplating punching him in the face when Tara stepped in.

"Okay, lover boy. Why don't we go to the cafeteria?" Tara grabbed Jack's arm and began pulling him away. "Ally, go get changed and meet us there. Maybe you both will have cooled off by then."

I turned without a word and stomped off. How could he? I never even wanted to do this stupid cheerleading! He had been all encouragement up until now, but then he goes and has a complete cow the first time he sees me actually cheer! Ugh! I expected a little more support from him! I angrily ripped my skirt off and put my warm-ups back on. I was trying to keep the angry tears from overflowing, but it was a losing battle.

"Hey," it was Veronica. "You're ruining your eye makeup. Here…" She approached me and began dabbing at my eyes. "Stop crying. He's not worth it. Men are pigs. Accept it. Don't let him see that he made you cry. There." She stepped back to check her repair work. "You look great." She gave me a brief hug. "You also did great out there. You're the best flyer we've ever had. I never even thought you'd be interested in cheerleading. Who knew?" Who knew, indeed? "You are coming to my party tomorrow night, aren't you? Bring your boyfriend, if you've forgiven him by then."

"He's not my boyfriend," I objected, but she was already gone, leaving a whiff of perfume behind her. I shrugged and gathered up my cheer bag and headed to lunch. I had no intention of going *anywhere* with Jack Ruiz. You don't treat me like that! I would show him a thing or two.

Jack was waiting for me in the hallway, leaning against the wall outside the cafeteria. I paused when I saw him, but then squared my shoulders and prepared to walk right past him without a word. He reached his long arm out and gently grabbed my hand. "Ally, please. Can we talk?"

I pulled my hand roughly out of his and said, "Fine. Talk."

He sighed, pushed himself off the wall, and took both my hands in his. I didn't pull mine away this time, but I refused to meet his eyes. "Ally, I'm sorry. I was a jerk. Tara pretty much let me know I was acting like an asshole."

"What did she say?" I asked, still not looking at him.

"She said 'Jack, you're acting like an asshole.'" Tara really never minces words. "Look, Ally, I'm so sorry. I saw you looking so amazing and sexy in that tiny skirt and then that guy was touching you in places that made me see red. I went a little bit crazy."

"Jack," I said, pulling my hands away from him in frustration. "We're just friends, remember? You have no right to be so insanely jealous." Inside, I was somewhat flattered that it was actually jealousy that caused him to act like such a jerk, but still!

"Ally, you know we're more than that!"

"No, Jack! I don't know that! How could I know that?" I cried.

We both stared at each other, chests heaving. Then, suddenly, I was sick of it all: sick of the guessing, the flirting, the backing off. I could see the hurt in his eyes and wondered if there wasn't more to this than he was telling me. This stupid fight wasn't important. It was really only my pride that was smarting. Props to Jane Austen for that little life lesson. Jack was what was important right now. I wanted more than friendship, but would take him on his terms for however long it took. I got one of my feelings that there was indeed more to this than what was on the surface, so I stepped forward, put my arms around him, and buried my head in his hard chest. I heard him mutter *'shit'* very softly before his arms came around me and held me tight.

"Jack, what is it? It's not only this, is it? Is something wrong?"

"Yeah," he sighed against my hair. "I got a call this morning. My probation hearing has been moved up. It's this afternoon. I guess I'm just freaking out. I was doing fine, holding it together, until I saw that guy's hands all over you. I'm sorry."

"I want to come with you," I stated as I pulled back to look at him, instantly putting our fight aside.

"No. Absolutely not. I don't want you to have to hear all that crap about me, the stuff I did. No way. I'll call you when it's over." He set me away from him and turned away from me. "Let's go eat lunch, please?"

"Fine. I'll take the bus and meet you there. I'm sure Trina will tell me where to go."

He turned and exclaimed, "Goddammit, Ally! You are the most stubborn person I have ever met!" I stared at him with my arms crossed, my eyebrows raised, waiting. "I want to keep you separate from that part of my life," he tried again. Still I waited. "Fine," he sighed. "You win. Wait for me after school. I have to change clothes. You can ride with me. Maybe you'll finally realize why we shouldn't be together."

I smiled and stepped back into his arms. "I

seriously doubt it, Jack."

"At least tell me that guy who was fondling you is gay," he said into my hair.

"Nope. 100% heterosexual. He asked me out." I couldn't resist.

Jack didn't let go; in fact, he held me tighter. "And what did you say?"

"I said I couldn't possibly," I paused. "At this time."

Jack said a very bad word.

"See you after school." I gave him a last squeeze. And I walked away.

***

I waited for Jack outside the men's room after school. He walked out buttoning his dark suit jacket and my jaw must have dropped visibly.

"What?" he asked. "Do I look all right?"

"You look wonderful, Jack." He looked amazing, handsome, and about 25 years old. I stepped forward to straighten his collar.

He stilled my hands on his lapels. "I'm glad you're coming. I'm sorry about earlier. I'm really nervous. I hope this is my last hearing."

"Jack, you're 18. Can they really keep you on probation any longer?"

"My probation officer said that the judge could grant a six month extension if the court feels I haven't met the restrictions of my probation. He hasn't been real happy with me lately, so he may testify that I need a longer term. If the judge thinks I'm in danger of being a habitual offender, he could keep me on probation until I'm 21. God, Ally. I want to be done with all this."

"You will be. Just like you knew I'd make the cheerleading squad, I know for a fact that you'll be a free man tonight." I finished straightening his collar.

"Ally," he held my face between his hands. "You're going to hear all the charges that were laid against me. Please don't judge me. I've changed a lot since then." In spite of the grown-up suit, he looked so vulnerable in that moment. I'm pretty sure I tumbled the rest of the way in love with him right then.

"Never," I said and reached up on my toes to give him a soft, brief kiss on his lips.

He pulled me close and set his forehead against mine. "Thank you. You have no idea what this means."

The drive downtown to the courthouse on 2nd and Lomas was nearly silent. He turned the radio on to a classics station and said nothing, his hands gripping the steering wheel tightly. When we got to the courthouse, Manny and Jack's cousin, Shelly, were both there, as well as a bunch of other relatives I hadn't met. Jack introduced me to his grandparents and so many cousins, aunts, and uncles I knew I'd never remember them all.

"Manny," said Jack, looking worriedly around. "You didn't let Megan come, did you?"

"Don't worry, mijo. She's at home with your aunt. Trina is praying for you."

Jack relaxed slightly. "Good. She shouldn't be here." Through all the various introductions, Jack had kept a firm hold on my hand, our fingers intertwined, as if I were his lifeline. My heart was breaking for him. If the judge didn't end his probation I would probably launch myself at him and start pummeling. Well, then Jack and I could be on probation together, at least.

We entered the courtroom and I went to sit by Manny and Shelly, while Jack sat up front with his lawyer. The judge started by stating that this was a post-disposition hearing for Jackson Iván Ruiz. He detailed the delinquency charges against Jack, the most serious of which was distribution of a controlled substance. I cringed to hear all the charges, not because they disgusted me or anything, but because I could feel Jack shrinking in his chair with every separate charge. I knew that part of Jack's life was in the past, left behind as he learned to deal with his grief over losing his mother, and in every practical way, his father. He had been through so much and had emerged with a strong, steady character.

I didn't follow everything that was said, as so much of it was legal jargon. Jack's lawyer spoke for him, telling the judge that he had met all the requirements of his probation, had become an outstanding student both in high school and community college, was working successfully in his uncle's auto body shop, and had tested negative on every random drug test in the last two years. There were no school discipline reports in his file since moving to Albuquerque. He also said that Jack had completed court mandated drug and alcohol counseling and had also completed his mandatory community service. He had the support of a large and loving family. I held my breath when his probation officer spoke, but he simply reiterated what the lawyer had said: Jack had met all the requirements of his probation.

I watched Jack during the entire speech. His jaw was surely going to ache with how tight he was holding it. Finally, the judge asked Jack to stand. Shelly reached over and grabbed my hand, squeezing it tightly.

"Mr. Ruiz, I have reviewed all of your probation reports and official school records. It is the judgment of this court that, having reached the age of 18 and having successfully completed the conditions of your probation and rehabilitation, you are now to be considered free and clear of the NM State Juvenile Justice system." He looked sternly over the top his reading glasses at Jack. "Son, you've been given a second chance. Don't blow it. Next time you will be charged as an adult. You may file a petition to have your juvenile record sealed. Court is adjourned." He rapped his gavel softly and got up to leave.

I watched Jack sink down in his chair and put his head in his hands. It completely floored me to see a tear slip down his cheek. He wiped it away quickly and stood to shake his lawyer's hand. Then he turned toward me. I was in his arms in seconds, not caring who was watching or who was in my way. He held me as we rocked gently. "It's over," was all he said. I could only nod. We realized we couldn't stay like that, not with his family waiting. "Come on," he said and wrapped my hand tightly in his as we turned to greet his jubilant family.

Shelly gave us both a hug, her eyes streaming. "Damn contacts," she said as she turned away to wipe her face.

"Jack." Manny approached with a cellphone outstretched. "Trina wants to talk to you."

He took the phone with a smile. "Hey, Trina. Yeah, I am, thanks. Um, yeah she is. Wait, I'll ask her." He took the phone away from his ear and looked at me. "She wants you to come to dinner. It's more of a command than an invitation."

I could hear Trina squawking from the phone, "It is not!"

I laughed. "Of course I'll come. Tell her thanks."

He picked up the phone again. "Let me talk to Megan, please." I squeezed his hand as I listened to him. "Yeah, mija. I'm done. No more probation. I love you, too." Another tear began to slide down his cheek. I reached up to wipe it away quickly before anyone could see. "See you in little while. Yes, I'm bringing her. Of course I'm bringing her." He smiled down at me.

Jack's extended family finally cleared the courtroom and began to disperse, heading to what was beginning to sound like quite the celebration at Manny and Trina's.

Jack loosened his tie as we walked to his car amidst the congratulatory well wishes of his relatives. I was dying for a few minutes of alone time with him and heartily wished them all to a very far-off island. We finally reached his car, parked on a different level of the downtown parking garage, and found a blessed moment of solitude. I waited for him to open my door for me as I had begun to become accustomed, but instead he turned me around and backed me against the side of his car, gently taking my face in his hands. My heart started beating crazily.

He looked intently into my eyes. "After everything you heard about what I've done, do you still want to be with me? I swear that part of my life is over, Ally, but I can't change what I did and I can't make myself any younger. I'm still two years older than you."

"Yes," I whispered. "I still want to be with you, Jack."

"Okay, then no more pretending," he whispered back. And then he was kissing me. He was kissing me with all the pent-up feelings of these last few weeks and I was kissing him back with every bit of longing and love I could possibly put into a kiss. Our lips moved against each other, our mouths opened and his tongue slipped into my mouth. I met him stroke for stroke, loving the taste, the feel of him. I couldn't get close enough. *Finally, finally,* my heart was beating against his. My hands were in his hair and his were making a wreck of my cheerleading ponytail. "God, Ally." His forehead rested against mine as we finally broke for breath. "Do you have any idea how long I have wanted, needed to do that? I don't want to be 'just friends.'"

I put my hands on each of his cheeks and looked as deeply into his beautiful almost-black eyes as I could. "Neither do I," and I kissed him again. This kiss was as soft and sacred as the last was frantic and frenzied. It was a promise, almost a vow, and I felt the last part of my heart click into place. We belonged together and I felt like so much of my life had been building up to this moment. We broke apart and I said against his lips, "Let's go. Your family's waiting."

***

I convinced Jack to swing by my house so I could change out of my cheerleading uniform and into regular clothes before meeting his family.

"You look fine, querida. You've already met most of them, anyway."

"Not as your girlfriend, Jack." I hesitated, unsure if I had assumed too much. "I mean, if that's what you—"

He laughed briefly and took my hand in his as he drove. "Of course you're my girlfriend, Ally. If that's what you want to be, I mean."

"Yeah, I do," I whispered. We looked at each other and smiled.

No one was home yet when we got to my house so I told Jack I needed about 15 minutes and left him on the couch with my cat. I rushed upstairs to change into one of the outfits Tara had helped me choose. As I looked through my closet, I pulled out the muted teal ruched t-shirt dress she had found for me on sale at Anthropology. Did I have the guts to wear the clingy jersey dress? Would Jack like it? Was it too much? I compromised by pairing it with black capri leggings so as not to look like I was trying too hard and added a sweater shrug since it was chilly outside. I brushed out my hair and removed the glitter from my eyes, trying to replicate the subtler 'smoky-eye' look that the magicians at Sephora had created. I wanted to look sophisticated for him, yet appropriate for his family. I added a long necklace and then headed downstairs to Jack.

He had removed his suit coat, loosened his tie, and rolled up his sleeves. Wicky was purring on his chest as Jack rubbed his ears. I stopped at the bottom of the stairs, hesitant, unsure of myself. He looked up, saw me, and put Wicky aside to stand up and walk over to me, never breaking eye contact with me.

"My God, Ally. You are so beautiful." Then I was in his arms and we were kissing again. Our height difference made it somewhat challenging, with Jack having to bend down quite a way, but we managed fine. I would never get tired of this.

When we paused to take a breath, I asked, "What does 'querida' mean? You called me that in the car."

He leaned back in to kiss along my jaw line, making my eyes flutter closed in pleasure. "It means 'darling' in English." He captured my earlobe gently between his teeth, which sent shivers all through me. "Is it okay to call you that?"

"To call me what?" I had completely lost track of what we were discussing. Why were we discussing anything? This was definitely *not* the time for talking. I felt him smile against my face and then his lips were back on mine, his tongue seeking entrance to the warm depths of my mouth.

We were so absorbed in each other that we didn't hear the door open. My mother clearing her throat finally penetrated and we broke apart, Jack still keeping his arm around me. In all the weeks we had been hanging out together, Jack and my mother had yet to meet. This was probably not the exact way I had pictured that meeting.

"Ally?" She stood there with her eyebrows raised, holding a bag of groceries.

"Hey, Mom." I resisted the urge to wipe my lips. "Um, well, this is Jack. My, um, my b-boyfriend," I ended weakly.

"Ma'am, it's a pleasure to meet you." Jack held out his hand to her. She held her hand out automatically.

"Jack? Well, yes. It's a, um…a pleasure to meet you too." How did one act in these circumstances, when one has walked in on one's daughter in an intense lip-lock with guy? Awkward doesn't begin to cover it.

"So, we're going to Jack's house. His aunt is having a party for him," I attempted to fill the silence.

"Oh, what's the occasion?" My mother wanted to know.

Well, this kept getting more awkward. "So, he's no longer on probation. Um, his aunt is having the whole family over. You know, to celebrate." It sounded so lame, saying it aloud.

"Oh, congratulations, Jack. Well, have a good time. Be home by curfew." We had never even discussed a curfew. It had never been necessary before.

"Yes, ma'am. Of course I'll have her home by then," Jack said.

"Yeah, Mom. Of course we will," I didn't even know what time this supposed curfew was. "Let's go, Jack."

We got in his car and sat for a moment, both of us still in shock or something. Then we looked at each other and slowly smiled. Then we started laughing.

"So," said Jack, still chuckling. "Do I know how to make a great first impression, or what? Please tell me my hands were not all over your rear end."

"I think they were fine. She was probably paying more attention to the fact that your tongue was in my mouth. That was incredibly awkward."

"So, what time is your curfew? I don't want any more black marks against me."

"I have no idea. I've never had need for a curfew before. I think she was as flustered as us and made that up on the spot."

***

The spread of food waiting for us at Trina and Manny's was impressive; it looked like everyone had brought something. This was no last-minute, thrown together party. They knew, like I did, that Jack would be finished with his probation today. There were many more friends and relatives here than had gone to his hearing, so Jack took me around, introducing me as his girlfriend, which thrilled me every time he said it. I was talking to Mrs. Flores, a long-time friend of the family, when Shelly approached, holding a baby in her arms who looked to be somewhere between 1-2 years old.

"Hey, Ally. You look fantastic tonight, by the way. Where did you get that dress? This is my son, Nathan. Can you say hi to Ally, son?" The little boy hid his face in Shelly's neck.

Jack turned from talking to Mrs. Flores. "Hey, little man," he addressed the baby, who looked up from his hiding place and stretched out his arms to Jack. Jack took him from Shelly and began tickling him, which Nathan apparently loved, judging by his giggles.

Shelly smiled at them fondly and put her arm around my shoulders, leading me away. "So, it's official now, huh? You guys are going out? I heard Jack introducing you as his girlfriend."

"Yeah. I guess so." I wondered where she was going with this.

"Well, it's about damn time. I never thought he'd grow the cojones to ask you out." She stopped and turned to me, serious for a moment. "I'm glad, Ally. You're good for him. He's been happier since that day you showed up at the shop. He even smiles once in a while. Come on, while I have a break from my son, let's get some food."

About an hour and a half into the party, after managing to eat part of a plate of food and visiting with more relatives than I could ever imagine, I found myself looking around for Jack. He was nowhere to be found.

When I asked Trina, she said, "I think he needed some time alone. This has been a big day for him. I think he went up to his room. He probably fell asleep. Poor boy hasn't been sleeping well for weeks. Why don't you go see if you can wake him up?" As I began to walk away, she touched my arm and said with a knowing look, "Don't be too long." Well, that's not embarrassing. My cheeks felt hot as I went to find Jack.

I opened his bedroom door carefully and found him lying on his back on his bed, his arm over his eyes. I stood looking around his room, this place where he slept, studied, and dreamed. Of me? Maybe. It was exceptionally neat, filled with mismatched, obviously hand-me-down furniture. A bookshelf overflowed with well-worn paperbacks, a mix of bestsellers and classics, evidence of how well-read he was. He seemed to favor thrillers and spy novels. His suit jacket was folded neatly over the back of a desk chair, his tie draped over it.

"I'm awake," he said quietly.

I quietly shut the door behind me and tip-toed over to the bed. I crawled up beside him and laid my head on his chest. "Are you all right?"

He put his arm around me. "Yeah. It got a little overwhelming down there. They mean well, but..."

We lay there for a few minutes silently before I raised my head to look at him. I smiled into his eyes and then we were kissing again, not as frantically or as intensely as earlier, but rather lazily, like we had all the time in the world. I could lose myself in his kisses. We broke apart and smiled at each other again.

"God, Ally. I am so happy right now. I can't believe that you're here with me like this, that you want to be with me."

"I love being with you like this," I said as I kissed him again. "I never knew kisses could be so different," I whispered.

"Am I the first guy you've ever kissed, Ally?" he asked, gently pushing my hair behind my ear.

"No, the second," I admitted.

"Who was the first? I probably need to kill him tomorrow."

I laughed softly, "I don't want you to kill Travis."

"Travis!" he exclaimed, sitting up. "The Travis that eats lunch with us? The guy is gay! Why the hell were you kissing him?"

"Well, apparently kissing me helped him decide to switch teams."

Jack called him a name I will not repeat here. "Well, his incredible idiocy is my gain. I can't believe that guy had you in his arms and ever let you go." He lay back down. We simply held each other, not kissing. After a while, Jack stirred and said, "We better go back down. I wouldn't want my aunt to walk in on us. That would be awkward."

"Been there, done that. Don't worry. I locked the door." I began kissing him again.

He kissed me back for too brief a time and then pulled back, saying, "Jesus, Ally. Don't tell me stuff like that. I don't have the willpower tonight to stop myself." He kissed me again. Then he rolled back onto his back, laughing ruefully. "And apparently I'm too exhausted to do anything about it."

I sat up and leaned over him, brushing his hair back, loving the feel of it, loving that I finally had the right to run my fingers through it. "Poor Jack. You've had a rough day. If it makes you feel better, I never had any intention of giving you my virginity with approximately 50 members of your extended family right downstairs." I gave him a last, quick kiss. "Come, on. Let's go mingle a bit more and then you can drive me home. I might even let you get to second base on my front porch."

CHAPTER ELEVEN

"Nobody ever sees truth except in fragments."
–Henry Ward Beecher, *Proverbs from Plymouth Pulpit*

I had never in my life been excited about a basketball game, but I was about this one, the season opener between the Oso Grande High School Bears and the Eldorado Eagles. Hey, I don't make up these names. The reason I was excited about this one had little to do with sports or cheerleading, although it would be the first game I had ever cheered at. It had everything to do with my boyfriend. That's right, I said it. I have a boyfriend. He is the handsomest, smartest, best smelling... I'll stop. I'm so excited to finally be dating Jack. Officially and everything. Last night, when he took me home, he insisted on going in the house and asking my mother and my grandmother if he could date me. If you thought my mother walking in on us kissing was awkward...

It was really sweet, but I sure could have skipped

the part where my grandmother laid down a few ground rules, including home by midnight on weekends and asking Jack if he carried condoms at all times. I could have died. Especially when she made it clear that it was not a rhetorical question. I stopped her as she was demanding to look inside his wallet. I'm not sure I was ready to know if he had condoms in his wallet. Oh, and before you get your panties all up in a twist, no, I did not let him get to second base on my front porch. Not that he tried, but I totally would not have let him. I'm nearly positive about that. Apparently, Jack is a true gentleman. Damn it.

Anyway, here I was at the first game of the season, the gym was packed, and my boyfriend and I were going to a party afterward. Well, neither of us really wanted to go to the party, but I was trying to get close to Veronica and find out who was hurting her and who had knocked her up. I'm pretty sure it was one guy who was doing the hurting and the, um, impregnating, and I'm even more certain that it was someone older than her boyfriend, Danny. Maybe it was one of the senior guys or maybe someone's older brother. Or maybe it was an adult. It was so frustrating to be able to see so much, but never his face. I felt completely useless.

This line of thinking made me remember an episode that had happened earlier in the day. Jack and I had been at my locker, right before lunch, talking and basically enjoying being with each other, when we were interrupted by an argument a few lockers away. It was a couple of the football players, whom I recognized from my ill-fated first attempt to talk to Veronica. They seemed to be in a violent argument and one of them seemed to be very angry with the other about some money that was owed to him. We were trying to ignore them when one of them slammed his fist into the locker, said a very foul word, and walked away.

"Well, that was weird." Jack looked concerned. "I wouldn't be surprised if that guy broke his hand."

Later at the game, I was cheering away on the sidelines and Tara, Jack, Travis, and his boyfriend, Dustin, were all in the bleachers cheering for me. At halftime, the cheerleaders again performed our routine to 'Move, Shake, Drop' by Pitbull, with me flying through several stunts in the middle. Jack was waiting for me outside the locker room after the game, which, sadly, Oso Grande lost.

"You were amazing," he said as I gave him a hug. Much better today in the compliment department, I noticed. It's amazing the kind of changes a day can bring. He did give Devonne a dirty look as we left, however. "I don't like that he can touch you in places even I'm not allowed," he grumbled.

"Well, if you say pretty please," I teased.

He laughed and pulled me into a dark corner for a kiss. "You're gonna kill me, girl," he whispered against my mouth. "You better watch what you ask for. I might not always be such a gentleman."

"I wish," I said and kissed him again.

We went out for pizza with Tara, Travis, and Dustin. I was starving after all that cheering and dancing and wolfed down more than my share of slices.

"Are you going to finish that?" I asked Jack, gesturing to a half-eaten slice of cheese pizza on his plate.

"Help yourself." He offered the plate to me.

"What?" I asked through a full mouth, as he stared at me while I chewed.

"I'm wondering how someone so small can pack away so much food. It's kind of a turn on, I'm not gonna lie," he said.

"I actually hate her," said Tara, who had limited herself to one slice and a small salad. She's not even slightly chubby, but complains that she packs on the weight way too easily. I personally think her tall, willowy figure could stand a couple more pounds, but what do I know?

"Hey, cheerleading takes a surprising amount of energy. I burned a lot of calories tonight."

"Yeah, and you need to replenish so you can burn more later, huh?" she said in a suggestive tone of voice.

"God, Tara, crude much?" said Dustin, who was holding hands with Travis under the table. Jeez, at least I hope they were only holding hands.

"What?" she said innocently. "I meant dancing. Why? What did you think I meant, perv?"

"Well," said Jack. "Ally and I do have plans later...for dancing," he said after a pregnant pause. We all laughed and I loved him for not being offended by my ridiculous friends.

"Let's all go back to my house and watch cheesy horror movies," suggested Tara. "I rented *Thankskilling* about a giant turkey who starts to kill everyone. It'll get us in the mood for Thanksgiving next week. Come on, it'll be fun."

"Oh, man. I would love nothing better. Maniacal turkeys are so much fun, but I'm dragging Jack to Veronica's party, at least for a little while," I explained.

"Oh, shit," said Tara. "I forgot you were torturing yourself like that. Well, do you want us to watch the other movie I rented, *Black Sheep,* first? It's about a genetic experiment gone bad and crazed sheep start killing people all over New Zealand. We could totally save *Thankskilling* for the late-night feature."

I looked to Jack for an opinion. He smiled wryly and said, "It really seems like Ally's got her heart set on the maniacal turkey, so I'm going to have to defer to my lovely lady here and say save *Thankskilling* for when we get there. I can personally guarantee that we will spend as little time at the popular kids' lame party as possible."

"That is the most romantic thing you've ever said to me," I replied in an over-the-top drama voice. "Oh, Jack, take me now," I suddenly had a southern accent as I laid myself across his lap, pizza crust still in my hand.

"Why, Miss Scarlett, I think I will," he said and leaned down to kiss me. Right before his lips were on mine he said, "Take you to the party, that is." He lifted me up and helped me on with my jacket. "If you can tear yourself away from your pizza, we can get this over with."

***

Veronica lived in a McMansion, of course. I've heard her stepfather is a high-priced divorce attorney, so that totally makes sense. I prefer older, more historic houses that have some character. Jack found a spot well down the street and we walked hand-in-hand into the house. The party was in full swing and was very well attended. There was loud music playing and dancing seemed to be the main activity, at least in the living room. Now, I don't want you to get the wrong idea about teen parties. This was not a scene out of a 1980's John Huston movie where sex-crazed teens completely trash a house. Everyone here seemed to be minding their own business and behaving themselves, at least on the surface. We walked through to the kitchen and found an impressive spread of snacks and soft drinks. Veronica was filling a chip bowl.

"Hey, Ally." She stopped to rush over and give me a hug. I met Jack's amused eyes over her shoulder. "You made it." She let me go and turned to Jack. "And I see you guys made up. Well, if you two want to be um, *private,* I'm sure you can find an empty bedroom upstairs. Food and drinks are right here; help yourself. There's goodies of all kinds out in the garage." She raised her eyebrows knowingly. "You want me to get you a beer, Jack?" she purred and sidled up to him.

"No thanks," Jack said coldly and moved closer to me.

Scratch my earlier comment. This was exactly like an 80's John Huston movie, only with fewer shoulder pads. I inserted myself between Veronica and my boyfriend, ostensibly to pour a Coke. I got a whiff of Veronica's breath as she laughed.

"Oh, my God, Veronica! Have you been drinking?" I put my hands on her upper arms and shook her slightly.

"What is your problem?" She tried to shake me off, but I was like a mongoose with a cobra. "It's a party! Of course I've been drinking. That's what you do at parties, except you guys, apparently."

"Yeah, but you're pregnant! You're not supposed to drink when you're pregnant! What the hell is wrong with you?"

"Shut up!" she said abruptly. "No, I'm not! God, why would you say that?" Her eyes began darting around nervously, seeing if anyone was close enough to have heard our conversation.

I decided to try a new tactic. I let her go and said softly, "Hey, it's okay, Veronica. I know. Remember in the nurse's office? You were asking all sorts of questions about prenatal care? I know about the pregnancy. It's all right, I won't tell anyone."

She looked at me with abject terror in her eyes. "I was talking about a friend. It's not me. I'm not pregnant. Get the hell away from me!" She turned and stalked out of the kitchen.

I looked at Jack, biting my lip. "Well, that went well."

He reached past me and finished pouring the Coke. "This party sucks," he said.

"Yeah," I agreed. "Come on, let's see if we can find Long Duk Dong here somewhere."

He chuckled, enjoying my *Sixteen Candles* reference. "You can be Molly Ringwald."

Twenty minutes later, Jack and I were slow dancing in the living room and making plans to blow off the rest of the party as soon as possible, when I suddenly remembered that I wanted to ask him about the crude joke the girls had been laughing about yesterday at the pep rally. "Jack," I said, looking up at his gorgeous face. "I need you to explain something to me."

"Sure. What is it?"

"Well, I heard something I didn't understand. It's probably dirty, but I felt really stupid not getting it." I told him about the 'big man with a really little man' joke I had overheard.

He smiled and pulled me back into his arms. "Oh, Ally. You are so beautifully innocent, sweetheart. I don't really want to tell you."

"Oh, come on, Jack. I don't want to feel like such a baby around these girls. Please tell me."

"Fine, but I feel like I'm ruining you or something. They were talking about the size of a guy's...well, dick. It's a kind of old wives' tale that really big guys have small...you know."

"Really? I've never heard that before. Is it true?"

He laughed. "I don't know. I certainly haven't asked any of the big guys I know. Nor do I plan to. I have heard that steroids can do that to a guy, though." We continued dancing quietly for a few minutes. "Does that satisfy your intense curiosity?"

"Yeah. Thanks for telling me. I hope I didn't embarrass you."

"Nah. Ally, I want us to be able to talk about anything. Even if it embarrasses us a bit. I want us to have a really strong relationship, querida." He leaned down to kiss me.

I reveled in his kiss for a moment, the way he caressed my jaw gently while stroking his tongue across my lips and into my mouth, but he soon pulled away and we just danced. As the song changed, I stiffened in his arms, suddenly swept into a vision I was completely unprepared for.

I was leaning against something, no, wait...Veronica was leaning against something. It was so hard to tell...I felt like I was there. She/I was opening a bottle of pills, but her hand was shaking so much she was having difficulty opening it. I tried to tell her no, not to do this, but I couldn't make a sound. She finally got the bottle open and shook a handful of little orange pills that had x's on the back. She started popping them into her mouth, washing them down with water as fast as she could. A few spilled onto the floor, but she didn't seem to notice as she sunk down to the floor.

"We need to find Veronica. Now!" I gasped. I was having a hard time staying on my feet; I needed to sit down but I knew I couldn't spare the time.

"What?" he asked, holding me by the shoulders, a troubled look on his face. "What did you see, Ally?"

"She took some pills. A lot of pills. We need to find her, fast!" I tried to remember what the room looked like that she was in, but I was in full panic mode and couldn't think straight. We checked the garage first, thinking that would be the logical place for her to take any drugs. All we found was a group of jocks, including Veronica's boyfriend, Daniel, who was smoking a joint. Seeing them there, sitting all together, it struck me again how huge they all looked. They were really muscular, with thick necks and bulging biceps. When had that happened? I had been going to school with all of them for years and had classes with some of them up until last year. None of them were in any of my classes this year, and they're not at all the type of guy I keep tabs on, but you would think I would have noticed these body builders walking around school. Something about this bothered me, but I couldn't quite put my finger on it. Nor did I have the time right now. "Daniel, where's Veronica?" I asked, waving away the sickly sweet smoke near him.

"Man, I don't know," he said, taking another hit. "She's probably off crying somewhere. All she does anymore."

Although I wanted to stay and give him a piece of mind and/or shove that stupid joint where the sun don't shine, I knew we didn't have the time. "Daniel, this is really important! Do you know where she might be?" He continued smoking the joint.

Jack stepped forward, a disgusted look on his face. "Dude, your girlfriend is in trouble! What is wrong with you?"

Daniel's reaction surprised us both, I think. His face turned absolutely purple with rage and he was actually trembling as he stood up, threw the joint down, and started for Jack. "What the hell is your problem?" he yelled, his fists balled up and the veins in his biceps bulging.

I quickly stepped in front of Jack, thinking...well, I really don't know what I was thinking. Danny was apparently not averse to hitting a girl, because he didn't even pause. If Jack hadn't pushed me out of the way and blocked Danny's fist with his forearm, I would have had a nice black eye, or worse. "Jack, no! Don't hit him! Danny, stop! We're not trying to start a fight! We're trying to find Veronica!" Both of them stood, tense and staring into each other's face, for a moment. Finally, Danny took a breath and visibly deflated.

"Sorry, man. I didn't mean it." He shook his head, as if he was confused by what he had done.

I grabbed Jack's hand, saying, "Come on. She's not here. Let's check upstairs."

We ran up the stairs and began checking in each bedroom we came to. Most were empty; couples were in a few. Gross—I saw way more of Todd Snelling and his girlfriend than I ever wanted to see. We finally tracked her down in the master bathroom. She was leaning against the jetted tub, knees to her chest, sobbing. A chill went through my entire body when I saw, lying on the floor at her feet, an empty prescription bottle. I turned to Jack. "Call 911," I ordered. He backed out of the bathroom to call.

"Veronica?" I crawled next to her. "Hey, um, are you all right?" Of course she wasn't, but I didn't know what to say.

She looked up at me through bleary, red eyes. "Ally? Why are you here? Leave me alone." She put her head back down on her knees, but the sobbing had slowed down some.

"I can't do that, Veronica. I want to help you. Did you take all those pills?"

She nodded.

"What were they?" I asked.

She shrugged. "Who cares? Probably some of my mom's sleeping pills. She takes them so she doesn't have to deal with my step dad. Makes me deal with him." Her face crumpled as she said this. "Well, I wanna sleep, too. I'm so tired. Tired of it all. I just wanna sleep." She slumped farther down, now lying fully on the floor. "Go away, Ally." Her speech was starting to sound slurred.

"Jack! We need that ambulance!"

He came back into the room, still talking on his cell. "Yeah, she's still conscious, but barely. You better hurry," he said.

I leaned over Veronica, her pretty face streaked with mascara. "How did you know?" she whispered. "I didn't tell anyone. How did you know?" I could barely hear her last whisper as she lost consciousness. I looked up at Jack, horrified.

"Look, she passed out," he said into the phone, holding it with his chin against his shoulder as he wet a washcloth from a basket on the counter and handed it to me. "They're here," he said, hanging up the phone. "I'm going to go down to meet them."

Within minutes, the paramedics were assessing her and loading her on a stretcher. Partygoers were crowding the hallway, making it difficult for the paramedics to get her out. Jack took command, clearing the way for them. I grabbed hold of Daniel's arm before he could follow her out and pulled him back into the master bedroom.

"What happened?" he asked, clearly freaked out.

"While you were down in the garage getting high, your girlfriend was up here trying to kill herself!"

"What?"

"She took a bunch of pills. Now you better figure out how to get hold of her parents and tell them to meet you at the hospital." He stared at me, obviously still feeling the effects of the weed. "Now!" I shouted. I watched while he fumbled with his cellphone, trying to find a phone number for one of Veronica's parents. I left him scrolling frantically through his call history and went to find my boyfriend.

"Let me guess," Jack said. "We will be foregoing maniacal turkeys for an ER waiting room?"

"I'm sorry, Jack. You can drop me off. I'll get my mom to come get me. I need to know that Veronica's going to be all right. I can meet you at Tara's."

He put his finger against my lips to shut me up. "That's not how this works. Let's go."

Two hours later, we were still in the waiting room with Veronica's parents, drinking bad vending machine coffee. I leaned against Jack, trying to keep my eyes open. He took my coffee, which was in danger of spilling out of my tired hands, set it on the table beside him, and pulled me against him. "Go ahead and sleep, Ally. I promise to wake you up when the doctor comes out."

I was dozing off when the doctor finally came out and asked for Veronica's parents. They had pumped her stomach and she was going to recover.

The doctor then pulled her parents off to the side, talking to them earnestly and quietly. I guessed he was informing them of their daughter's pregnancy.

"Let's go home, Jack. She's going to be okay. That's all I needed to know," I said.

We were sitting in his car in front of my house, heater blasting, holding each other, trying to process the events of the evening. "God, Jack. What if we hadn't been there? What if I hadn't had that vision?" I shivered, thinking of the consequences.

He held me tighter. "Shh. Don't think like that. You can't think like that."

I sat up and looked into his eyes. "Jack, she said something weird, that I can't stop thinking about." I told him what Veronica had said about her stepfather. "She said her mom leaves her to deal with him. She sounded scared, I think. Jack, what if the man in my visions is her stepfather?"

He pulled me back against him. "I don't know, Ally. What kind of sick bastard would do something like that to his stepdaughter?"

"I have to find out, Jack. I don't know how, but I have to find out. I have to help her. If this gift is good for anything, I have to figure how to use it to help Veronica. She may be vapid and selfish, but she doesn't deserve this."

"Hey." He held my face. "*We* will find a way to help her. You don't have to do this alone." He kissed me briefly and then changed the subject. "Ally, when you stepped in front of me earlier, you know in the garage with Danny? What in the sweet hell were you thinking, querida?"

I shook my head and looked up into his face. "I

have absolutely no idea! I was going on pure instinct. I didn't want you to get into a fight with that idiot. It was pretty stupid, huh?"

"Beyond stupid." He softened his harsh words with a soft kiss. "Please don't ever do anything like that again. You scared the living shit out of me."

"I'm sorry I scared you. I didn't mean to. I didn't want you hurt, Jack. Thanks for being there for me."

"That's my job now." He kissed me again and then sat back away from me. "I don't know that guy, Danny, very well, but there was something really off about him tonight, even before he completely lost it. Did you notice?"

"Yeah. I was really shocked by that whole group. They're so…big," I ended lamely. "I mean, they never used to be that muscular. It's really over the top."

"I agree. You know, I've been thinking about a bunch of things that have happened recently, and I think…well, I think those guys might be dosing." He looked puzzled and concerned.

"Dosing? With what? What does that mean?" I was confused.

"Taking anabolic steroids. It would explain a lot: how big they are, the jokes from the cheerleaders, Danny's irrational anger."

"Don't steroids have, like, massively bad side effects?"

"Yeah, like heart attacks. But I guess athletes will sometimes do stupid things to get an edge."

I had a hard time getting to sleep that night, worry for Veronica at the top of my list of things going through my mind over and over. I also couldn't stop thinking about what Jack had said, about the guys using steroids. It made sense and somehow Veronica was involved, but I had no idea how. I was glad that I'd had that vision tonight or it might have been too late for her.

CHAPTER TWELVE

"It takes strength and courage to admit the truth."
–Rick Riordan, *The Red Pyramid*

Veronica missed the next week of school. I visited her very briefly in the hospital, but barely got a chance to speak to her because her mother was there constantly. I finally got a few minutes alone with her when she sent her mom on an ice cream run to the cafeteria. The second she was out the door, Veronica was out of bed and in my face.

"What is everyone saying? What do they know?" she said frantically.

"I don't know how he did it, but Danny has managed to spread the rumor around school that you got food poisoning. Apparently you ate bad sushi right before the game and were barfing so much that you got severely dehydrated. Nobody knows about the pills."

She sank back onto the bed in relief. "Thank God. I could get kicked off the squad if the truth got out."

"Speaking of truth, Veronica, what about you being pregnant? I mean, are you still? Or did something go wrong? Sorry to be so blunt, but it's important."

She drew her knees up and put her head down on them. It reminded me of the night she had tried to kill herself. "Yeah, I'm still pregnant. Nobody knows about that, either. Except my parents. God, they are freaking out. Mom won't leave me alone for more than a second. Bit late for that," she said bitterly.

"What about Danny? Does he know?" I asked gently. She shook her head. I didn't know how to broach the subject that I really needed to ask about. I mean, I have no intention of telling her that I'd been having visions about her. This was a very delicate topic and I didn't want to screw it up. I also didn't have much time before her mother returned. "Veronica, I know it's really none of my business, You and I don't really know each other that well anymore, but, well..." I decided to jump in. "Danny's not the father, is he?"

She jerked her head up and stared at me, wide-eyed. "How could you possibly know that?" she whispered. Then she started crying.

I went to the bed to sit next to her and put my arm around her. "I don't really know," I explained. "I get the feeling from some of the things you've said. And trying to kill yourself is a really extreme solution to a fairly common teen problem."

She looked up at me, tears streaming down her face and said, "Danny and I have never even slept together. I know I have this really slutty reputation, but it's not true. I don't sleep around. How can I tell him about this? This has gotten so out of control. I don't know what to do."

"Veronica, who is the father? How did this happen?" Of course, at this crucial moment, her mother returned with the ice cream. Veronica wiped her face quickly, trying to hide her tears from her mom.

"Thanks for coming, Ally. I appreciate you bringing my homework. See you after Thanksgiving."

I left, frustrated. I had no clue how I was supposed to help her when I couldn't even get her to talk to me. Again I wondered what possible good this gift I have was. I see things that I have no control over and have no way of stopping. Why was I having these visions about her? What was I supposed to do?

***

I took the bus to Manny's shop to meet Jack as he was getting off from work. Tomorrow was our last school day before the Thanksgiving break and we planned to work on an English paper together that was due. We had finished *The Scarlet Letter* and were reading *Heart of Darkness*. I really didn't love the story, but Joseph Conrad is a great writer. I mean, the guy's first language wasn't even English! I find it very impressive that he chose to write an entire novel in what was like his third or fourth language. I can't even manage to learn Spanish and

I've been taking it since middle school. I will say that it helps a bunch to have a boyfriend who speaks fluent Spanish. When I get stuck on something in my homework, I give him a call.

He was actually speaking Spanish when I got to the shop, or rather *yelling* it. Jack seems to be a pretty even-tempered guy most of the time, but I sure got to see another side of him that afternoon. Shelly had sent me back to the garage area to find Jack. He was shouting at another employee, one I had never met, and gesturing to a grey, primered car they were apparently both working on. They were speaking so fast I didn't manage to catch much of what they were saying, but the gist of it was obvious.

"¡Qué pendejo estás! ¿No ves que se va a despintar cuando lo pintes? ¡Mi tío te mataría si le dieras algo así al cliente!" Jack yelled.

"No tienes idea de lo que estás diciendo," the young man replied. *"Yo he estado haciendo esto mucho más tiempo que tú. ¡Mi papa nunca se ha quejado de mi trabajo! ¡Parece que voy a tener que arreglar tu desmadre, pinche culo peludo!"*

Jack looked like he was going to launch himself at the other guy. *"Vete a la madre wuey..."*

Well. Jack was angry about something the other young man had done to the car and ended his commentary by calling him a dumbass. I'm fairly up on my Spanish curse words so I was able to keep up. The young man was not taking this lying down and returned fire, ending with a nice *culo peludo* (hairy asshole). Jack was in the process of telling him to go to hell, when the young man noticed me over Jack's shoulder. He stopped arguing and literally pushed Jack aside to come and greet me.

"Hi, how can I help you?" he approached me with a complete change in attitude from what I had seen when he was yelling at Jack. He was now oozing charm and graciousness.

Jack turned and saw me. The smile that lit up his face was gratifying, immediately putting me in a better mood. "Ally," was all he said as he shouldered the other guy out of the way, took my hand, and pulled me into his arms for a brief kiss.

"Ahh, this must be the famous girlfriend I've heard so much about," the guy said. "I can't believe Jack finally managed to get one. Well, she hasn't met me yet. Jack, introduce us," he commanded.

Jack rolled his eyes at me. "Ally, this is my cousin, Mateo. Manny's youngest son." I could definitely see the family resemblance. He was shorter and stockier than Jack, but had a very similar look about him. They could probably pass as brothers.

"Mat," he corrected, taking the hand I had extended for a shake and raising it to his lips, kissing the back of it. I raised my eyebrows at Jack.

"Knock it off, pendejo," Jack took my hand back from him. "Stop slobbering all over her."

"Nice to meet you, Mat." I laughed. It was obvious that he wasn't serious and that he and Jack were on good, brotherly even, terms. "I've heard about you. You've been visiting your great grandmother in Mexico?"

"Yeah, I was taking a break from CNM and decided to go see her. We're trying to get her to move up here, but she's being stubborn. I've heard about you too. Now that I'm back, you can stop wasting your time with Jack. You can go out with the handsome cousin."

I laughed. "Oh, I'm perfectly fine with this cousin, thanks. I think I'll stick with him. Are you about done, Jack? I can get a bus home if you need to work."

"No, I'm done for the day." He picked up a rag and wiped his hands. "I need to change. You can wait with Shelly if you want. I'll only be a couple minutes." We started to walk away.

"So, I'll fix this mess you made, okay, Jack?" Mat called after us, laughing.

Jack gave him the finger without turning around. Mat laughed harder. "Nice to meet you, Ally!" he called out after our retreating figures.

I started to turn around to wave and say good-bye, but Jack stopped me. "Don't encourage him, querida."

***

Jack ate dinner with Grams, Mom, and me. I loved how easy-going he was with them, able to take Grams' teasing and inappropriate comments without batting an eye. After dinner we settled in the living room to work on our papers. Grams had left for bingo at the senior citizens' center and Mom had an odd school night date with Brian, a guy she had been seeing for a few weeks. Hmm. That might need some looking into.

We had to write a minimum of three pages on

the role of obsession and ambition in *Heart of Darkness*. I finished before Jack and then quietly watched him while he worked, tapping away at his laptop. I was curled up in a corner of the couch with Wicky purring in my lap while he sat on the floor, leaning against the couch with his long denim-clad legs outstretched. He looked so adorable as he concentrated, black hair falling over his brow, eyes pulled together in a scowl. He highlighted a passage, read it back over, muttered, "shit" under his breath, and deleted the entire paragraph. I set Wicky aside and crawled up behind him, leaned over his shoulder, and said, "What's wrong?"

"Nothing. I hate writing conclusions. They always suck. I don't know how to end this effing essay."

"Undelete it. Let me read it," I commanded. As he did as I asked, I began to knead his shoulders with my hands. "God, Jack, you're so tight! You need to relax."

"You touching me is not exactly relaxing, Ally. Kind of has the exact opposite effect, in fact." He groaned in appreciation and laid his head back.

I gave him a quick kiss and said, "None of that right now. Work now, play later."

He kissed me back quickly and complained, "Such a task master! Here." He handed me the laptop with the restored paragraph to read. "It seems too repetitive."

I read it, typed in a phrase after the restatement of the thesis, and handed it back to him. "See what you think of that."

He took the laptop and without even looking at

the addition to the paragraph, pressed 'save,' snapped it closed, set it aside, and pulled me down onto his lap. "It's later," he said and began kissing me.

We had not had much time to be alone since we started dating, so we were both reveling in the luxury of being able to kiss each other at length. I loved the taste of him, the feel of him, the smell…I couldn't get close enough. If I could crawl inside his skin I would. I rearranged myself so that I was straddling his lap, facing him. He moved his warm hands all over my back, soothing and massaging. Then I felt him slip his hands under the edge of my shirt, caressing the flesh of my back. It felt so incredible. "Oh, God, Jack," I moaned into his mouth. I kissed his neck, working my way down and began unbuttoning his shirt. I slipped my hands inside and began to smooth them over the hot skin of his chest. I was discovering the crisp feel of his chest hair when he stopped me.

"Ally, sweetheart." His hands came up and covered mine, stilling them. "Ally, we have to stop."

I didn't even hear him. I was so intent on discovering…him…this…everything.

"Ally, stop!" he said more forcefully and pushed me gently away from him.

I blinked and looked at him in horror. "Oh my God! I'm sorry! I didn't…I don't…" I suddenly couldn't get off his lap fast enough. I was so embarrassed, I'm sure my face was bright cherry red. I stood up, preparing to run and lock myself in the bathroom out of shame.

He must have sensed I was about to run, because he caught me, and brought me back to the couch, setting me in one corner while he sat in the other and re-buttoned his shirt. "Oh, no you don't. You are not running away from this. If you can nearly seduce me, then you can stay and talk about it," he said sternly. "We need to be able to talk about anything, sweetheart," he said more gently.

I drew my knees up, put my head down on them, and cried, "I'm so embarrassed! You must think I'm some kind of sex-starved maniac! I've never done anything like that before. I don't know what got into me."

"Jesus, Ally," he said, reaching out and pulling my bare feet onto his lap. He began to rub them soothingly. "I don't think you're a sex-starved maniac. I know you've never done anything like that before. That's why we needed to stop. You were quickly pushing me to the point of no return."

Tears started rolling down my face. "I'm so sorry," I whispered.

He pulled me to him, putting his arm around me, wiping my tears away. "No, I'm the one who's sorry. I let that get way out of hand." He laughed mirthlessly. "I didn't realize you'd be so...responsive."

"I liked it so much," I said in a small voice.

He laid his head back on the top of the couch. "Yeah, me too." He sat up and turned to face me, seriousness gleaming from his eyes. "Look, Ally. We need to take this slow. You are a seriously sexy girl, and I would love nothing more than to make love to you right now, believe me, but it's not right.

That should be a decision we make together, not in the heat of the moment. I have no intention of taking your virginity on the floor of your grandmother's living room when she or your mother could walk in at any moment. Okay?"

I nodded. "I'm so sorry. I didn't mean to embarrass you or make you feel awkward."

He laughed and rubbed a hand over his face. "Believe me, what I'm feeling right now is not embarrassment."

"Jack," I continued, whispering, "You've done this before, haven't you? You're not a virgin, are you?" Some sick and twisted part of me needed to know.

He sighed and shook his head, sadness in his eyes. "No, I'm not. I'm sorry."

I couldn't help the little sob that escaped. I don't know why I was crying, why I should be surprised. I mean, how many 18 year old guys have never had sex? I guess I had hoped to be his first everything, like he was for me.

He pulled me back into his arms. "Shh. It's okay, Ally."

"I know." I sniffed. "It doesn't matter."

"Of course it matters," he said. "I was such a mess a few years ago, into drugs, stealing, a gang, and, yeah, sex. I did a lot of things I'm ashamed of. I treated the girls I knew with no respect."

"It's fine, Jack. You don't have to tell me anymore." I really, really didn't want to hear about the girls he had been with before.

"No, I think you need to hear it. I think you need to know the truth about who I was and what I did.

Maybe you'll finally realize you shouldn't be with me. Ally, I was in a gang. We spent our days stealing, breaking into houses, and selling drugs. Our weekends were for partying: it was all about getting drunk, getting high, and getting laid. I can't even tell you how many girls I've been with, because I don't remember."

I did not enjoy hearing that. But as I stared into his eyes I could see that the Jack I knew and had fallen in love with was not the person he had described. Yes, that person was a part of his past and would probably cause problems from time to time. I had a decision to make: I could either cut and run because I couldn't handle the things he had done before, or I could accept him as he was today and try to show him how much I loved him. I chose the latter and leaned in to kiss him.

He kissed me back so, so sweetly. "Ally, you are beautiful and pure and innocent. I absolutely don't deserve you. And I'm not going to mess up what we have by trying to rush you into a physical relationship." He smiled at me, kissing me on the nose. "And I'm not going to let you rush into something neither of us is ready for. Agreed?"

"Agreed," I sighed and settled further against his side.

He kissed the top of my head. "Someday, I hope to God I'm lucky enough to be the first man to ever make love to you, but now is not that time. I have to be able to look your mother and your grandmother in the eye. I have to be able to look myself in the eye." I smiled up at him. "Ally, what we have is special. Really special. You're special. You deserve the best." He finished this speech with a soul-searing kiss. "You are the best thing that has ever happened to me."

"Jack, you're the best thing that has ever happened to me too. I'll be honest: I don't love hearing about the things that you did in your past, but they are in your past. It's part of the man you are today, and I'm extremely fond of that man. I'm not running, Jack." I kissed him. This time it was my tongue seeking entrance to his mouth, although I kept my hands away from his buttons.

He groaned and pulled away. "Now, I'm going to go home and take another in the long line of cold showers I have been taking since we started dating."

I don't know if it's a sign of some new sort of maturity, but I had absolutely no desire to share what had happened with anyone, not even Tara, with whom I have previously shared every type of secret. I wanted to keep what had happened between Jack and me to myself.

***

Spending the first day of our break at the mall with Tara made it difficult to keep the juicier details of my newly activated love life a secret. She was persistent in her attempts to get me to spill.

"I want you to know you can come to me for advice, Ally. You know, if you any questions." She was trying to sound nonchalant, and failing, as we browsed the racks at Macy's.

"So, kind of like my own personal Dr. Ruth, huh?" I asked.

"Yes, exactly, but without the accent."

"And you think that you're the expert in all things love-related? You're not exactly the poster child for long-term relationships, Tara. What was your longest, like a month?"

"It's not the length that matters, sweetie. It's how deep you get."

"We are still talking about relationships, aren't we?"

She smirked. "Seriously, though, Ally. Do you have any questions, need any advice? Like, how far to let him go or how to tell him nicely to stop?"

"Tara, I'm absolutely not going to tell you how far Jack and I go or don't go when we make out. It's private and special." I held up a blouse against myself for her inspection.

She scrunched her face up and shook her head, nixing the blouse. "So, there are make out sessions, at least? You don't have to give me all the juicy details, although I wish you would. Please tell me that it's not a completely platonic relationship."

I laughed. "You're pathetic, you know that? Yes, there are make out sessions. Happy? It's definitely not platonic."

"So, Jack's got some moves, huh? Is he a good kisser?"

"He's an amazing kisser. And that's all you're going to get out of me. I'm not going to kiss and tell. Now help me choose an outfit for Thanksgiving with his family. I may not want your advice as it pertains to my love life, but I do need your fashion sense. I think I was born without one."

"I think so too. That color is disgusting," she

referred to the dress I had taken off the rack. "Here, you should try this one on." She handed me a dress I had overlooked. "You two are being careful, right? You're taking precautions?"

"Wow. I already got that speech from Grams, thanks. She actually tried to check his wallet for condoms. And then later, being the true feminist that she is, she bought me some to carry." I turned to look her straight in the eye. "I'm not having sex with Jack, nor do I plan to anytime in the near future. I still have my V-card intact. I keep it right next to the condoms in my purse."

She laughed. "Well, I still have mine too, but it's got a little more wear and tear than yours. So, he's not pushing you or anything?"

I laughed. "No, not at all. In fact, he's the one who refuses to let it get too hot and heavy. So, now that you've tricked me into telling you way more than I wanted to, let's go try this stuff on." I marched off toward the dressing rooms huffily. Tara followed behind gleefully.

***

Later that afternoon Tara and I were in my bedroom supposedly accessorizing the new outfits we had bought. She was actually lazing on my bed, staring at my bookshelf, when she suddenly leaped up and pounced on something lying on the floor.

"This is it!" She grabbed up my yearbook from sophomore year and began flipping through it.

"What? That's just my yearbook."

"Yes, and it lists everyone's first names, even the

teachers! And their pictures! We can look through it to see how many Nicks there are and if any of them could be the guy you've seen in the visions." We sat side by side and looked through, starting with the teachers.

"Here's one," Tara pointed to a picture. "Nicholas Chiszowski. Isn't that your physics teacher?"

"Yeah, but no way! It couldn't be him!" I argued.

"Are you sure? He's the only Nicholas I see in the teacher's section, unless there are new ones this year."

"God, Tara. He's so nice! I really don't want it to be him."

"Well, sometimes it's the guys that seem nice on the outside. He may be hiding a rotten soul."

"Rotten soul? You should be a writer, you know that? I'm in class with him every day and so is Veronica. Don't you think I would have picked up on some bad vibes or tension or something? Could she really sit there day after day and act be so normal?"

"I don't know, but we should at least keep him on our list. Let's look through the student section. This could take a while," she sighed as she flipped back to the beginning of the freshman section.

We found five guys named Nicholas, but only one of them seemed like even a remote possibility.

"Nicholas Grayson, junior. Which means he's a senior this year. He looks like a fairly big guy, huh? Do you know him?" she asked.

"Yeah, I kind of do. He's on the basketball team.

I've never talked to him, though."

"Well, it looks like we have two suspects: Mr. Chiszowski and this Nicholas Grayson. At least we have a place to start. I think you should start observing how they act. You could keep all your notes in a little notebook or something." She was really getting into this.

"Tara, I know you're dying to play spy, but this is serious. And we actually have three suspects: I'm wondering about Veronica's stepdad."

"Eww. That's disgusting. And hey, I know this is serious," she sounded slightly offended. "Fine. No notebook then. But you have to keep track somehow."

"How about I just remember? There are only two of them at school."

"Spoilsport," she muttered.

***

I spent Thanksgiving morning with Mom and Grams at the senior citizens' center, helping cook and serve a nice turkey dinner to old people who didn't have any family nearby. Several years ago we had decided that it was silly to fix a big fancy dinner for only three people, so we had made it our tradition to go to the center. Later that afternoon, I went with Jack to another one of his many cousins' house for their Thanksgiving feast. It was wonderful, but a bit overwhelming; the huge spread of food, including turkey and all the fixings plus tamales, enchiladas, and several varieties of empanadas. I was touched to see plenty of vegetarian choices. That, more than anything else, told me I was accepted as Jack's girlfriend. Mat was there and flirted as outrageously as he had when I first met him.

"Give it a rest, Mat," Jack warned when Mat cornered me by the dessert table. Jack came up behind me, wrapping his arms around my waist.

"I want the lady to know she has options, cousin. When you realize Jack is actually a boring stick-in-the-mud, you call me, Ally," he said.

"I'll keep that in mind, Mat. Thanks. Here, Jack. I got this pie for you, but I want a bite." I fed him a bite of pumpkin pie and whipped cream and then took a bite from the same fork.

"Oh, jeez. You're sharing silverware already? I'm gonna barf. You've really sunk your hooks into her, huh Jack?" Mat walked away, shaking his head in mock disgust.

"Ally," Trina called from the kitchen. "Are you coming with us tomorrow to cut a Christmas tree?"

"Um, yeah. I guess," I looked up at Jack, somewhat confused.

"Jack, you were supposed to ask her the other night," Trina scolded.

"Oh, shit, Trina. I forgot. Sorry," Jack apologized.

"Watch your mouth, young man," Trina scolded. "How are you going to like it when Megan starts copying your atrocious language? She practically worships you, you know."

Jack looked suitably contrite. "Sorry, Trina. I forgot to mention it to Ally the other night. I guess I was so wrapped up in writing that paper that it slipped my mind."

I nearly choked on my pie, remembering that what he had really been wrapped up in was my arms.

"So, querida, do you want to go up to the mountains with my family to get a tree? We go every year the day after Thanksgiving; it's a family tradition. There might even be some snow this year. Maybe I'll get to push you into a snow bank." He winked at me playfully.

I pointedly turned away from him and said to his aunt, "Thank you, Trina. I would love to." I turned back to Jack and took the last bite of pie for myself as I gave him a dirty look.

"Feisty!" he said, laughing.

***

Jack picked me up early the next morning, driving a slightly battered pickup truck pulling a flatbed trailer.

"What's this?" I asked as I got in, petting Sodapop, who was sitting in the middle of the bench seat. I got a generous doggy tongue bath in return.

"This is one of Manny's trucks. We need 4-wheel drive to get where we're going."

"Where's Megan? I thought she was coming."

"She's with Trina and Manny. There's no place for her car seat in here. Move, dog, my turn to kiss her," he said as he pulled me to him, pushed the dog out of the way, and began kissing me. After all too short a time, he set me back on my side of the cab. At my sulky look, he said, "Don't even go there, you little temptress." He tapped me on the nose and started the truck.

We drove about 30 minutes north of Albuquerque to a Pizza Hut parking lot in Bernalillo where we met up with the rest of his family. I counted four other vehicles full of various relatives and friends. Once everyone had arrived we began the hour-long trip northwest from Bernalillo to the Jemez Mountains, passing from dry, dusty desert to dense, high altitude forest. We stopped at the Walatowa ranger's station located on the Jemez Pueblo to buy tree permits and were directed to a specific cutting area. Between the numerous members of his family, we were planning to cut at least five trees, and Grams had asked me to find a small one for our house. When we arrived in the tree cutting area, Trina and a couple of the other older women set up a base camp with a fire pit and several camp stoves on which they began heating various kettles and pots. Jack shouldered a hacksaw with one hand and took Megan's hand with the other, motioning for me to follow. Sodapop loped along behind, veering off the path often to chase after unsuspecting forest creatures. He seemed to be enjoying himself immensely, judging by his goofy doggy grin as he came running back to us. We were all bundled up, including mittens and hats, for the snow. There isn't much call for heavy snow gear in Albuquerque, so I had had to search through boxes in the garage for a hat and gloves. There had been an early storm over the Thanksgiving holiday so there were actually a few inches of snow on the ground in the mountains.

"Come on, Princess. Let's show Ally how to find a really good Christmas tree."

"Come on, Ally. It's so much fun! When we get back we can drink hot chocolate with marshmallows and eat posole." Megan grabbed my hand with her free one and we were off.

Jack had to tell Megan and me that every tree looks good with snow on it, since we both tended to fall in love with every one we saw. He was surprisingly picky, bypassing trees that I thought were perfectly acceptable. It took us two hours to find a tree he approved of for his family and a smaller one for mine. He sawed through the trunks without too much trouble and Megan and I helped him haul them both back to the base camp and then stood around drinking hot chocolate and coffee, trying to warm up. Once the other family members had chosen their trees and arrived back at the camp, Trina and Jack's Aunt Gloria began serving the various kinds of soup they had brought. There is something about being outdoors in the freezing cold that makes food taste so good. Trina had thoughtfully brought a vegetarian posole for me. I found a seat beside Jack on a log and happened to glance at his spoon as he put it into his mouth.

"What kind of soup is that, Jack?" I asked suspiciously.

"My Aunt Gloria's menudo. She makes the best."

"Oh, God. Is that tripe you're chewing?"

"Yep. It is a key ingredient in menudo, querida."

"I know. I wish I didn't, but I do. Jack, I really don't know if I can kiss you after you've been chewing tripe. I think you might have crossed a line." I set my soup aside, completely grossed out by the thought of the cow stomach lining Jack was currently masticating.

"Aw, sweetheart. You wouldn't withhold those beautiful lips from me because of a little menudo, would you? It's part of my heritage, my upbringing. In fact, I think withholding kisses might qualify as racial discrimination," he teased.

"Oh, really? Racial discrimination, huh? Well, we can't have that." I leaned over and kissed him firmly on the cheek. "That's absolutely it until you find a Tic-Tac, mister."

We had an enjoyable afternoon sitting around the campfire, telling jokes and listening to stories of Jack's extended family. Little Nathan was adorable bundled up in his snowsuit, trying to help Megan build a snowman while Sodapop ran around them, excitedly biting the snow. Mat and Jack, along with several other cousins, got into an energetic snowball fight, which I watched from the safety of the sidelines. I loved seeing this light-hearted, fun side of Jack, but was alarmed when he caught my eye and began stalking me, saying, "How about we go find a nice, deep snow bank, querida?" I ran off, giggling, but he swiftly caught me, grabbed me up, and threw me over his shoulder. He carried me a short distance away from the campsite and then set me down behind a giant pine tree.

"What happened to throwing me in a snow bank?" I laughed.

"There's still time for that, but later. Right now I really need to kiss you."

"Oh, you *need* to kiss me, huh? Like you're going to die if you don't?" I teased.

"Yes, I will absolutely die if I don't kiss you right now. It's been at least four hours since our last kiss." He pressed his cold lips to mine, running his warm tongue along the seam, seeking entrance. I gladly granted it, sinking into his intoxicating kiss while I speared my fingers through his black curls, still wet from the snowball fight.

"You two wanna get a room?" Mat interrupted. "You better hope Trina doesn't catch you, Jack, or you'll get a fun-filled safe sex lecture."

Jack groaned and pulled away slightly. "Go to hell, Mat. Let me kiss my girlfriend in peace." He went back to doing that as Mat left, chuckling.

"Sorry about that." He rested his forehead against mine, breathing hard. "I don't want to embarrass you."

"Kissing you will never embarrass me," I whispered. "You can kiss me anywhere, anytime you want."

"Oh, I can, huh? God, you're good for my ego. Anywhere, huh? How about right here? You seem to like it when I kiss you here," he said as he nibbled under my ear.

It was my turn to groan. "That's not what I meant, Jack."

"Yeah, I know." He continued kissing my neck while I clung to his shoulders to keep from sinking to the ground in a puddle. After a few minutes of utter bliss, he pulled away, saying, "We better get back before they send out a search party. I've had that lecture from Trina before and it's not as fun as it sounds."

"It doesn't sound fun at all, actually."

"Exactly."

Around 5:30 the men all loaded up the trees on the flatbed trailer while the rest of us cleaned up the camp site, making sure we completely extinguished the campfire. This was all so fun and such a different experience than anything I'd ever done with my family. It was laughable to think about Grams out here searching for Christmas trees. Outdoorsy is not a term that fits her in any way. We stopped in Bernalillo on the way home for pizza, filling the entire back room of the restaurant with our loud, boisterous group. I looked around at Jack's large, loving family and felt a touch of sadness that I didn't know more of my extended family. I had no cousins; Jack had a seemingly endless supply. I had never known my grandfather; he had died when my mom was in high school. I don't even know my father's name because mom had said when he found out about her pregnancy, he denied that it was his and told her to have an abortion.

"Hey, what's wrong?" Jack noticed my contemplative mood.

I leaned against him and he put his arm around me; I loved how responsive he was to my moods and that he seemed to know when I was pondering something and needed to talk about it. "Oh, nothing. I was thinking about family and how important it is. You're really lucky, Jack. I hope you appreciate what you have."

Just at that moment, Mat dared his younger

cousin, Josue, to eat a spoonful of red pepper flakes. As poor Josue began to sweat and spit out the peppers into a napkin, Jack said wryly, "Oh, yeah. I know exactly how lucky I am." I laughed with him, putting my head on his shoulder.

"Jack, are you gonna kiss her?" Megan had appeared at his elbow.

"I don't know. Should I?" he asked the little girl. She giggled. "Yeah."

"Good idea." He leaned in and kissed me softly.

"Eww!" Megan gagged and climbed up into her brother's lap.

"Not even close, Princess," he said as he kissed her head. Within minutes she was yawning and snuggling deeper into his arms. "I think Trina and Manny will have a quiet ride home." He smiled at me.

Jack dropped me off an hour later in front of my house. Before I went inside, he pulled me close and kissed me. "Thanks for coming today," he said. "My family loves you."

"Well," I said, nuzzling his neck. "They are obviously a very smart group of people."

"Enough of that," he said, holding himself away from my seeking lips. "Behave yourself." He smiled at my pouty look. "I'll get your tree set up in a stand and bring it over tomorrow."

"Mmmm hmm," I said, trying to get back to kissing him.

He gave me a peck on the cheek and said, "Good night, Ally." He opened the door and shooed me in.

Mom and Grams were sitting in the living room, obviously waiting for me, looking rather grim-faced.

"Hey, Mom. Grams? What's wrong? Am I in trouble or something?"

"Hello, Ally," came a voice from the corner.

"Cassie!" I exclaimed. "You're back!"

CHAPTER THIRTEEN

"Truth is beautiful, without doubt; but so are lies."
–Ralph Waldo Emerson

I rushed to give her a hug. "Cassie! How was your trip? You've been gone so long. Did you find anything?"

"Slow down, Ally. Let me breathe." She held me away and scrutinized me closely.

"Sorry. I've been worried." I sat down on the couch with her, ready to get on with the news she brought. I wondered why Grams and Mom still looked unhappy. What had Cassie already told them?

"Ally," Cassie began, "the reason I've been gone so long is that I had a lot of research to do. Your situation, your apparent gift, is quite unusual. I needed to talk to a group of people about you and they needed to talk amongst themselves about how they wanted to handle what's going on with you."

"What? What group of people? Cassie, what are

218

you talking about?"

"Ally, I need you to listen for a little while. There are some things I need to tell you, things about your gift, about Seers in general, that you need to know. And then we all need to make some plans." She looked to all of us for our assent. "Now, first of all, you need to know that what you've been told, what your grandmother told you about your powers, is not the whole story."

She went on to spin a tale of ancient magic, Druid priestesses, and well-kept secrets. Grams had told me that our family had been given the power of second sight, or clairvoyance, by a grateful druid priestess about a thousand years ago, in return for saving her life. One ancient Irish booty call later, and my family, the Morans, had the gift that keeps on giving, to the females of the line, at least, in varying degrees. What Grams didn't tell me, if she even knew, was that this gift somehow made its way to other families, as well. Yeah, I don't want know how, either. After all this time, the descendants of these ancient Irish hook-ups were all over Ireland, America, even Europe. A core group of women in Ireland, called the Seer Council, felt it was their job to keep track of the descendants and what gifts they turned out to have. Some, like Cassie, were powerful in several different ways. Some, like Grams, were powerful in only one way. Some, like my mom, had a very slight power. But every once in a while, someone like me turns up, someone with some scary abilities. Cassie said that it was my vision of Megan losing her tooth, the vision that had not happened yet, that had made her realize she needed advice and knowledge beyond what she possessed.

"Ally." She took my hands between hers and looked intently into my eyes. "The Council wants to meet you. Soon."

"Why? What do they need me for?"

"Ally, they need to talk to you, to test you. They need to see what you can do. They need to see the extent of your powers so far. You are not yet 17, and already you are exhibiting powers not seen in any adult of the current generation. Powers not seen for nearly one hundred years. They're concerned."

"Sweetheart." My mom came over and sat by me. "Cassie wants to take you to Ireland over the Christmas holidays so you can meet with the Council."

"This Christmas? No, I have to stay here. I can't be gone for Christmas. Mom? Grams? I don't want to go." I could feel the pressure of tears building behind my eyes. A trip to Ireland might sound like a dream vacation to some, but it sounded miserable to me. It sounded like Christmas without my family. And what about Jack? This would be my first Christmas with him. On the way home from the mountains we had talked about our plans for the break. Plans that included shopping with Megan, taking her to visit Santa at the mall, baking cookies, watching old Christmas movies. Things that couldn't happen if I was in Ireland! Well, they could happen, and probably would happen. Just without me.

Mom came and put her arms around me. "Sweetheart, I know. I don't want you to go, either.

But Grams and I have talked, and we think this is important. You're going through some things that are very...concerning. I worry that waiting until spring break or summer could be a mistake." I started crying in earnest. Jeez, I have never cried so much in my entire life as I have these last few weeks.

"Ally, I know this is a shock, but this is an opportunity to find out what's happening to you, to find out what this means," Cassie added to her argument.

"What do you mean, 'find out what this means'? Why should it mean anything?" I wanted to know.

Cassie replied, "Well, what it means for your life, for your future. Ally, there is a path for you to follow and the Council can help you discover it. Your power is important and we need to discover its full extent. You are at a crucial point in your life. Right now you're on the path of the Seeker, but your powers are developing so rapidly. Soon you will have to make choice. Will you take your place in the realm of the Seers?" She didn't quite meet my eyes and I realized she was holding back. There were obviously still some secrets she was unwilling to share. I felt a certain sense of resentment at this. Who was she to come in here, after nearly a month of complete silence, and start messing with my life? But with both my mother and grandmother standing with her, I didn't have a chance and I knew it. I was going to be spending Christmas in Ireland. Shit.

***

221

I didn't want to talk about this wreck of a situation to Jack over the phone or by text, so I waited until Saturday night, in the middle of our date, to break the news. Not my best idea.

"So, when do you leave?" he asked as we waited for our appetizer.

"Our flight leaves early Saturday morning, right after school lets out for the break. Jack, we had so many plans for Christmas! I don't want to go," I said grumpily.

"Well, look at it this way: you get a free trip to Ireland. It's a once-in-a-lifetime opportunity. I think it's a great thing." He didn't seem nearly as upset as I had expected.

"But what about all the plans we made? Don't you care?"

"Well, sure. Of course I care. I will miss you like crazy. But it's not the end of the world, querida." He took my hand that was lying on the table. "It'll be okay."

Now, I'm not especially proud of the next few minutes and would actually prefer to skip the play-by-play, but in the interest of giving an accurate account I will go ahead and tell what happened. Could we agree that all the crazy emotions of the last couple weeks, combined with some newly active hormones, conspired to make me completely flip out?

"Well, maybe it's no big deal for me, either. Fine. I think I'd like to go home now, Jack. Can you take me home, please?"

"Now? But...we just started our dinner," he sputtered.

"I really don't freaking care about dinner!" Only I didn't say freaking. And then I stormed out. Yeah…not my best moment. I was standing outside the restaurant, freezing because of course I forgot my coat in the midst of my dramatic exit, and letting the tears run down my face. I was so angry! And yeah, I was totally feeling sorry for myself: poor little me, who has to have stupid visions about someone she doesn't even like, who has to go to Ireland over the holidays instead of spending them with my family and my seriously hot boyfriend. Boohoo. Talk about your first-world problems! Within about two minutes I went from angry and feeling sorry for myself to abject shame and embarrassment. Did I really storm out of a restaurant like some drippy diva in a bad romance novel? Was I really that big a brat? It would serve me right if Jack left me there. Jeez, I didn't even bring my cellphone. I would have to crawl back into the restaurant and retrieve my things in order to get home. So, I should probably leave the drama to professional actors and slither back in and apologize to Jack.

I was working up the chutzpah to go back inside when I felt warmth from behind as Jack draped his jacket around my shoulders, followed by his arms folding me in close.

"You're going to freeze to death out here. You stormed out without your coat," he whispered against my hair. Ouch. But I deserved it.

"I'm sorry. This whole thing has turned me into a crazy, weepy bitch. I don't know what's wrong with me. I used to be a fairly normal, even-tempered kind of girl."

He turned me around to fold me deeper into his warmth. "You are not crazy nor are you a bitch. I'm going to let you have weepy, for now." I chuckled slightly against his chest. "Hey, I've got a crazy idea. Why don't we go inside and finish eating? It's cold out here." I nodded, sniffing, and he lifted my head to kiss me quickly. "Mmmm. Salty, cold lips. Come on." He took my hand and led me back inside. The waitress was tactful, not mentioning our absence nor my wrecked face. I have mentioned before that redheads are not pretty criers—and the evidence doesn't disappear right away. I hoped Jack would leave her a good tip.

Later that night, as we sat in my driveway, cuddling in the warmth of his front seat, he looked into my eyes and said, "Listen, just because I act calm on the outside doesn't mean I'm not seriously bummed about you not being here for Christmas. It's totally going to suck without you here. I might be forced to hang out with Mat. While you're enjoying the sights and sounds of a Christmas in Ireland, I'll be working double shifts at the garage to keep from going crazy."

"There," I said, kissing him on the jaw. "That's the kind of stuff I need to hear. I need to know that you are sharing my misery."

***

Getting back to school after the short break was brutal. Thanksgiving was so late this year that we only had three weeks before we would be out again for Christmas or Winter Holidays, as the public school system calls them. I was still upset about the whole Ireland thing, but I was trying to be mature about it. I also thought more and more about trying to block the visions; maybe I could call off the whole trip if I wasn't having visions anymore. Illogical, but it made sense to me at the time.

When I saw Veronica in fourth period physics, I was shocked at the deterioration in her appearance. She had dark circles under her eyes, and her skin had a sallow, dull appearance. When she sat down at the lab table next to me, I could see that her nails were bitten to the quick. I couldn't help staring. "Holy shit," murmured Jack as he sat down and noticed where I was looking. "She looks nearly as bad as she did at the party."

"Jack, I don't know what to do. I feel so useless. I'm supposed to help her, but I don't have a clue how!" There was little time to talk during the rest of class because Mr. Chiszowski was introducing us to our final project of the semester in which we were given some skid marks from an automobile and had to be crime scene investigators, figuring out the velocity and acceleration of the car. I normally would have been into a project like that, but I had a difficult time concentrating with Veronica sitting so close by, looking so miserable. Jack was ultra-patient with me, gently taking the tape measure from my hands when I took the wrong measurement three times in a row.

"Querida, let me do it."

"Sorry," I muttered. "I'm having a hard time concentrating right now."

"I know. It's fine. We'll figure this out, I promise." He gently squeezed my hand as he took the tape measure.

I was also distracted by my hopefully subtle attempts to spy on Mr. Chiszowski. By about halfway through the period I had decided that my first instincts had been correct: there was no way that the guy who was hurting Veronica was Mr. Chiszowski. He was too old and his arms looked nothing like the arms I had seen in the vision. Those had been young, muscular, and darker than those of my physics teacher. That left Nicholas Grayson as my only suspect. I was feeling hopeless and ridiculous about this whole investigation idea.

I looked back at Veronica huddled miserably on her stool and gripped Jack's hand tightly as I suddenly felt myself being pulled into another vision.

"Ally?" I heard him say, although it sounded like it was coming from a distance instead of right next to me. Hearing his voice made me remember that I wanted to fight, to block these visions.

Veronica was walking down a hallway that somehow seemed familiar to me...

I fought to hold my concentration in the present, here in this classroom, not walking down that hallway with Veronica.

She approached a door, looking back over her shoulder...

With a slam of my palm on the lab table, I wrenched myself fully out of the vision and sat, breathing hard. Jack, still gripping my other hand, stared at me with questions in his eyes.

"Is everything all right over here, Mr. Ruiz?" It was Mr. Chiszowski coming to check on us, drawn by the noise, no doubt.

I slipped my hand out of Jack's and shook my head slightly at him.

"Um, fine, sir. I dropped something. Sorry," he said.

Mr. Chiszowski wandered away and the rest of the class turned back to their own labs.

"What was that about?" Jack whispered.

I looked around to make sure no one was paying attention, leaned close to him, and whispered back, "I just blocked a vision."

***

I soon found out why Veronica was looking so wretched. When we got to the cafeteria, she was sitting by herself at a table in the corner, while all her supposed BFFs, including her boyfriend, Danny, were at their regular table, heads together, whispering. Have I mentioned how much high school sucks?

Tara sat down, tray in hand, saying, "Well, it's all over school that Veronica cheated on Danny and has someone else's bun in her oven."

"How did everyone find out? How did he find out?" I asked.

"Apparently Veronica refused to talk about it

with her parents, so her dad went to Danny's house and confronted him. Well, Danny was shocked because apparently they've never done the deed. I heard that her dad punched him and his parents are thinking about pressing charges. And Veronica still refuses to say who the father is. This sounds like a friggin' soap opera!"

"Oh, my God. This is such a mess. Why won't she admit who got her pregnant?" I was shaking my head at how far the situation had deteriorated.

"You know," Jack spoke up, "it really seems like Veronica is terrified to say who the father is. That tells me that she has something to fear from him, whoever he is, like he has some hold over her. He may be more than simply a violent asshole who beats women and rapes them. What if he's still threatening her in some way?"

"I need to talk to her." I got up to go over to her table, but Jack held me back.

"Ally, this is getting beyond you. You could be in danger."

"Well," I said, determined, "that's too bad. Don't worry, nothing is going to happen to me at school." I leaned down to kiss him quickly. "I'll be careful." I was having very mixed feelings about having successfully blocked the vision during physics. What if it had been something important that would have helped figure things out? Was my comfort more important than Veronica's life? I didn't like the guilt I was feeling and figured I better do something, anything to help her. She was leaving the cafeteria, throwing what looked like her untouched lunch in the garbage as I caught up with her. "Veronica, wait." She ignored me and walked out of the cafeteria. She was quick on her feet, I have to give her that. I finally tracked her down in the girl's bathroom in a side hall. She was leaning against the sink, sniffling, when I came in.

"Leave me alone. I don't want to talk to you."

"You have to talk to somebody, Veronica. You look like shit. I've heard the rumors, so I know you have to be going through hell."

"I don't know why I don't get rid of it." She began crying. "Danny dumped me, called me a slut. After everything I did for him."

"What did you do for him? I mean, you said you didn't sleep with him." I winced as I said it, realizing how tactless it was.

"Forget it. If you really want to help, find out where I can get a free abortion. Do they have those? My parents refused to pay unless I tell them who knocked me up. Danny refuses to pay. Why should he? It's not his kid."

"Is that what you want, Veronica? To have an abortion? I get the feeling that you don't really want that." If she really wanted to take that option, wouldn't she have done it already?

She started crying harder. "I don't want one. I don't believe in it. I really don't. I was planning to give it up for adoption, but I don't know if I can do it. I never thought everyone would turn on me. They're all such fucking hypocrites!" she exclaimed. "Did you know that Tracy Peña, on the squad, had an abortion last year? I stood by her. I didn't judge her. Why am I being judged like this? I hate them!"

I walked over and put my arms around her and let her cry. "I'm sorry, Veronica. I don't know what to say." She seemed at a breaking point, so I didn't push for any more information.

Later that night, as I lay in bed, I thought about what she was going through. What would it be like to have that kind of stress? I mean, my life was no picnic right now, what with the visions and the upcoming trip I didn't want to take, but at least I had a supportive family. I knew, absolutely knew and would bet the farm on it, that Mom and Grams would never treat me like Veronica's parents were treating her. If I ever found myself in that kind of situation, they would be there for me. And although I haven't known him all that long, I knew in my heart that Jack would never do what Danny had done. Maybe it was because of all the crap he had gone through after losing his mother, or maybe because he felt such a responsibility to help raise Megan, but his character was so much stronger than any of the other high school age guys I knew. I was so incredibly—I don't know…lucky…blessed—to have such good people in my life. I was also still feeling plenty of guilt over having blocked what could have been an important vision. On one hand, I was proud of myself for being able to control what was happening in my mind, but at what cost had I done it? Was there any way to see the visions without completely freaking out?

I fell asleep with renewed determination to find a way to help Veronica.

CHAPTER FOURTEEN

"The more I see, the less I know for sure."
–John Lennon

I arrived at cheerleading practice the next afternoon and was greeted with the buzz that Veronica had officially been kicked off the team. I thought this was completely unfair! She really cared about cheerleading, and yet she was kicked off the team because she got pregnant. Nobody but me seemed to know she had been raped. Why didn't she tell anyone? What was she so afraid of? Was Jack right? Was she in danger somehow? Was she being threatened or blackmailed in some way? I had thought that maybe her stepdad was her rapist, but now I wasn't sure. She had spoken about her parents being so mad at her and not letting her out of their sight and I had been there at the hospital and seen her interactions with him. He might be kind of a jerk, but she didn't act like she was afraid of him or anything. I had also tried to watch Veronica and Nick Grayson, but as far as I could tell, there was absolutely no interaction between them. So, following up on the Nicks had been a dead end, apparently.

Coach informed us that rather than having tryouts yet again, they would promote one of the junior varsity cheerleaders. As we were beginning our stretching and warm ups, I overheard a couple of the girls talking about how Veronica was in the locker room right now, cleaning out her locker and turning in her uniform pieces. I really needed to talk with her, or try to talk some sense into her, so I told Coach that I was having 'feminine trouble' and needed to get some things out of my locker. Here's a hint: if you ever need to get out of class or P.E. or pretty much anything, all you have to do is mention that you are having some sort of woman problem. Nobody questions this. Guy teachers stammer and look in any direction but yours, and female teachers know better than to question the vagaries and viciousness of Mother Nature.

I found her sitting on the bench listlessly in front of her open locker. I went and sat beside her silently.

"I've spent almost every day after school here, in this locker room and in the gym or on the field. It's been such a huge part of my life. What do I do now? I was counting on a cheerleading scholarship to college. I don't have anything else. I'm just a cheerleader. I love it.

"Veronica, why don't you tell people what happened? Tell them that this isn't your fault," I implored.

She stared at me. "How...what do you know?

Who told you? Nobody else knows except—" She stood up. "You can't tell anyone! Please, Ally! Swear you won't tell anyone!" She was shaking me by the upper arms.

"Veronica! I don't know anything! All I know is that this isn't your fault! Who's hurting you? Who are you scared of? Tell me! I can help!"

She dropped my arms. "No one can help. It's too late. Please leave me alone, Ally." She turned and left without another word.

Damn it! That went very, very badly. I went back to practice, but my heart wasn't in it. Luckily, Coach thought I was having cramps.

***

"Jack, I really think I can quit cheerleading now. I mean, Veronica got kicked off, so there's no need for me to stay on the squad." We were sitting on his aunt's couch later that evening—well, he was on the floor—revising our essays from before Thanksgiving, a football game on in the background.

He held up a finger for me to wait. I watched him finish a paragraph and then click his laptop shut. He got up off the floor and sat on the opposite side of the couch, pulling my feet into his lap and stripping off my socks to rub my feet. I know, amazing, right? What a guy! I don't know how he figured out that I love to have my feet rubbed because it's not like I ever told him. So maybe the fact that I purr and melt into a puddle gave him a clue. "You could quit cheerleading now," he said, massaging the arch of my left foot. "Is that what you really want?"

"Well, yeah. Of course. Why wouldn't I want it? It's not like I'm a cheerleader-type girl, or anything. I don't even like that crowd."

"I don't know," he sounded thoughtful. "I realize that you only tried out to get close to Veronica, but I have seen you perform. I've seen your face when you're flipping through the air, scaring the ever-loving shit out of me. You look like you're enjoying yourself. And you're really good at it. Can you honestly tell me you won't miss that part of it?"

I let out a big sigh and then pulled my feet out of his hands and crawled over to straddle his lap. I took his handsome face between my hands and leaned in to kiss him. "Why do you have to be so rational? You manage to call me out on all my crap, don't you?"

He smiled that half-smile I loved so much. "Yep. You do like it, don't you? At least you like the actual cheerleading and stunts, huh?"

"Well, apparently I do. Who knew?"

"Who knew indeed? Besides, having a cheerleader for a girlfriend is hot." He flipped me over on my back on the couch and commenced tickling me. I am extremely ticklish and was soon incoherent.

"Ahh! Stop! Please stop, Jack. Uncle! Uncle!" I saw Megan come into the room wearing her footie pajamas and carrying a book, apparently ready to be tucked into bed. "Help, Megan! Save me!" She was happy to comply, tossing aside her book and jumping onto Jack's back.

"I'll save you, Ally! I'll save you from the monster!"

"Oof! Monster?" Jack roared and sat up, reaching up to grab her. "I'll show you monster! Ally, help me get this silly monkey off my back." Megan was giggling loudly. He managed to get hold of her and swung her around, placing her between us so we could both tickle her. Sodapop, who had been sleeping peacefully on the floor, got into the excitement of the moment and started barking and bouncing around. I'm not sure if you're aware of what a loud, annoying bark blue heelers have. If you want a quiet, calm dog, don't get a blue heeler.

This was the scene Trina walked into. "What on earth is going on in here?" she demanded, but with good humor. "Megan Elizabeth, you're supposed to be in bed! Jackson Iván, you go tuck your sister in! Ally…I don't know your middle name! Come with me to make some tea!"

"Yes, ma'am," we all said meekly. When adults start using middle names, it's not time to mess around. Jack carried his sister upstairs while I followed Trina into the kitchen.

Trina put the kettle on and turned to get cups out of the cupboard. I heard her sniffing and saw her try to surreptitiously wipe her eyes. "Trina," said, putting my hands on her shoulders. "What's the matter?"

"Oh, Ally," she said as she turned and hugged me close. "It's good to see him laughing and happy. He's been so sad and serious for so long. He's been through so much. Megan was too young; she doesn't remember how awful it was. Thank you for giving him a chance. So many people haven't. They just judge him for his past. He's a good boy."

"Oh, Trina. He really is. You have no idea."

"Ally," she said, looking intently and seriously at me. "Please try not to hurt him. His heart is so tender, and he's apparently given it you."

"Trina," I said every bit as seriously, "I love him. I don't ever want to hurt him."

She looked deeply into my eyes for a silent moment and then seemed to make a decision. "Yes, I can see that you do," she agreed, stepping back to wipe her eyes. "Let's get this tea."

Jack's tea was getting cold by the time he reappeared. "Sorry that took so long," he apologized as he took a swig of tea. "She begged me to finish the chapter. You know, that Harry Potter is pretty dark stuff for a first grader. I sure hope she doesn't have nightmares."

Jack and I settled into the couch with our tea, while Trina was knitting in the easy chair, the news on in the background.

"Jack, can you come to the game tomorrow night after you get off of work?" I asked. He didn't answer; instead I heard a quiet snore. Trina tssked softly. I turned and removed his mug, which was about to spill, from his hands, amused by his ability to fall asleep in seconds.

"He works too many hours," said Trina. "I'm going to talk to Manny about it."

My movement had woken him up. "Hmmm," he said, rubbing his hands over his face. "Talk to Manny about what?"

"You work too hard, Jack. Manny needs to cut your hours." Trina said as she knit.

"Leave it, Trina. Please. I'm fine. I need to save all the money I can. College is not going to come cheap."

"Jack, the lottery scholarship will pay for most of it and we will help you out. Of course we will." Trina looked hurt.

He got up and went over to kiss his aunt's cheek. "You have done enough, you and Manny. Save it for Megan. Come on, Ally. Let's get you home."

***

Ten minutes later we were in my driveway, making out and fogging up his windows. He pulled back and looked at me. "What did Trina grill you about in the kitchen? I'm sorry for whatever it was. She can be…intense."

I kissed him along his jaw, loving the feel of his whiskers. "Mmmm, you taste good. You smell good, too. She didn't grill me about anything. She told me how wonderful I am for being your girlfriend. She said how lucky you are to have me."

"Oh, yeah? Those were her exact words?" He laughed.

"Pretty much." I had moved on to his neck. I absolutely love his neck.

"You are seriously playing with fire, querida." When I increased my pace, he groaned and set me away from him, holding my wandering hands between his. "Behave yourself, you little minx." I looked up at him, I hoped innocently, through my lashes. "Not buying it, babe. Now what about your game tomorrow? Can I bring Mat? He's been moping around the garage lately since he broke up with his girlfriend. We could go out for pizza afterward. Maybe Tara can come to keep Mat company and out of our hair."

"Are you matchmaking?"

He smirked.

"I can probably make that happen. Do you mind if Travis and Dustin come too?" I moved his hands up to my mouth so I could kiss them.

His eyes were starting to glaze over a bit as I continued to nibble on his fingers. "Jesus, Ally. You can bring whoever you want, even that idiot who let you get away." He pulled his hands away from me and pulled me to him and started kissing me in earnest. When it started to get a little intense, he pulled back and rested his forehead on mine. "God, you are so beautiful. I am a lucky guy." He kissed me softly. "I need to go, querida. You tempt me too much." When he clasped my hand, I suddenly gasped, transported in my mind straight into a vivid vision. "Ally? What is it? What do you see?"

I was breathing hard, barely able to focus on his face. I thought I might be about to hyperventilate.

Blood...everywhere. Broken glass...pain. Veronica...me...I couldn't tell which was which. Everything was so fuzzy, fading in and out of focus. At the edges of the vision I could see...him. This time I could almost see his face, although it, too, was covered in blood. I knew him! But how? Where had I seen him before? Right before I faded completely out, amidst immense pain, I saw Jack's face, hovering worriedly over mine, shouting, "¡Mírame, querida! Ally, look at me!" Blackness.

I slumped against Jack, briefly losing consciousness. I woke to him shaking me.

"Come on, sweetheart. Wake up. Shit! Ally? What's wrong? Should I call…I don't know, 911 or your mom?"

"No, I'm fine. Well, sort of anyway." I wiped my hand shakily over my face.

"What did you see? Was it bad?"

"Oh, my God, Jack. Yes, it was bad…it was really bad! It was in the future, I'm sure of it."

"What did you see? Tell me," he insisted.

"No! I don't want to tell you. You'll freak out. I'm freaking out! I'm scared, Jack. I don't want to be able to see stuff like that. Nobody should be able to see that kind of thing." I sat there shaking. Why, how did I have a vision of Veronica when I was nowhere near her? That had never happened before.

"Ally, calm down. Hey, it's all right. I'm here. I'm right here." He held me close, stroking my back.

"I don't know what to do," I cried.

"Hey, shh. It's okay. You don't know what these future visions really are, do you? Maybe they're a possibility of the future or something. You've only had one other, right?"

I nodded. "But that one came true." Megan had lost her front tooth the week before, exactly as I had foreseen.

He pulled me onto his lap and smoothed my hair

back, our earlier passion forgotten. "Tell me, please."

So, reluctantly, I told him what I had seen. I told him about the blood and the pain and how I couldn't decipher whether it was me or Veronica that was hurt. His face looked like it was set in stone, the muscles in his jaw pulsing.

"Listen, this needs to stop. I told you this was getting dangerous. I don't want anything to happen to you. I want you to keep blocking these damn visions and forget about all this psychic crap."

"I didn't even have the chance to block this one; it happened so fast. I don't think I can block everything out, no matter how dangerous. I'm scared, Jack."

"Yeah. I know. Me too. I love you, and I don't want to lose you." I stilled in his arms. "Is that okay?" he asked, looking concerned.

I looked him straight in the eye. "You're not just saying that because of the vision? I don't want you to feel like you have to say it."

"I'm not just saying it, Ally. I know it's soon, but I've got to listen to what my heart is saying. I am in love with you."

I about melted into a complete puddle right there on his lap. "I love you too, Jack." And we were kissing again.

"Ally." He pulled back from me. "Can you talk to Cassie about this vision? I feel so helpless, like there's nothing I can do to help you. I don't like that feeling."

I thought back to the last time Cassie and I had spoken, when she had told me about our trip to

Ireland. I had felt like she was holding something back. I started to tell Jack, but one look at his face, still so grim and worried, and I decided to keep it to myself for now. "Yeah. I'll talk to her. It'll be all right, Jack. Like you said, we don't know what these future visions are."

But I didn't tell anyone about the vision, not Tara, not Grams, nor even Cassie. I needed some time to figure things out for myself. Probably not the best decision I have ever made.

***

Friday's game was between Oso Grande and Albuquerque High. The Bears vs. the Bulldogs. We had learned a new routine to 'Girl on Fire' by Alicia Keys. Cheesy, I know, but Jack was right; I did love flying through the air.

When I wasn't cheering, I watched the boys playing, keeping my eyes on #22, Nick Grayson. He looked pretty big and did have muscular arms and a fairly tan complexion. Hmm. Maybe. I hadn't seen any interaction between him and Veronica, but he did have the basic look of the guy in my visions. I guess I couldn't count him out yet.

We lost again, but that didn't dampen the spirits of the group that went out for pizza afterward. We were all in high spirits, three couples having a great time. Well, scratch that. Two couples having a great time and two people sitting in stony silence. Obviously, Tara and Mat had not hit it off.

"What happened?" I whispered to Jack under the guise of reaching for the Parmesan.

"Mat finally found a girl who doesn't think his every word is hilarious. I'm actually enjoying this."

"She just can't handle what a *chingón* I am." Mat had apparently heard us.

"Oh, I don't think you're a badass. I really think you're more of a *mamon*." Tara had paid attention in Spanish too, calling Mat a braggart. "Please pass the Parmesan, Ally."

"Come on, Tara," Mat wheedled. "Give me another chance. Go out with me. It'll be fun."

"No. Absolutely not."

"I see I'll have to wear you down. I can be very persuasive. And patient."

"Well, that's good. You're going to have a very long wait. Like a lifetime."

Tara didn't warm up throughout the rest of the evening. She has never been fond of loud, overly charming guys. She is a total brain and tends to like equally brainy guys. A guy like Mat, who dropped out of high school and was studying to be a paramedic at CNM, was not her kind of guy. I kind of felt sorry for him. I had gotten to know him over the last few weeks and had realized that under all his overdone charm, he was really sweet. I wished Tara would give him a chance. She always dates what she supposes are her kind of guy, but it never works out. She picks guys so similar to herself that they both get bored soon and move on. I thought someone like Mat would actually be good for her. When I tried to mention this to her later, she gave me a cold look and told me to leave it alone. Jeez. Sensitive much?

Right before he left me at my front door, Jack

pulled me close, saying, "I want to celebrate your birthday this Saturday night. Save the night for me?"

"Jack, my birthday's not until Christmas."

"I know, but you won't be here. And next weekend you're leaving. I know your mom and Grams will want some time with you. I want one evening to myself and I'll take it early if I have to."

"You can have me whenever you want," I said, completely aware of my double entendre.

He smiled and shook his head, kissing me quickly and sending me inside.

CHAPTER FIFTEEN

"The truth will set you free, but first it will piss you off."
–Gloria Steinem

I tried several times over the next week to talk with Veronica, but each time she found somewhere else to be, some other direction to turn when she saw me coming. I also hadn't been able to talk with Cassie much because she was so busy preparing for the trip, and I was still undecided as to whether or not I would tell her about my latest vision. She had completely freaked out over my first vision of the future and I really didn't relish the thought of another scene. I had plenty of those without adding any extras, thanks. I would be leaving at the end of next week for two full weeks in Ireland. Jack's equanimity about the trip had helped me to come to terms with the idea. I still didn't relish the idea of being away from my family over Christmas, but I was trying to understand the importance of learning more about my powers. This is how I felt in my more mature moments. But in my less mature, I'm-only-16-moments, it still really sucked.

When Jack picked me up from cheer practice on Thursday, I noticed his grim mood as soon as I got in the car. His kiss was…I don't know…tighter than usual. "Hey, what's wrong?" I asked, looking at his face with concern.

"I need to talk to you, Ally. Do you have time? Can we go somewhere?" He sounded worried.

"Of course. Whatever you need, Jack." Now I was worried.

He drove to a McDonald's and got us each a cup of coffee. He then pulled into a parking spot in the very back of the lot.

"Oh, boy. It must be pretty bad if you don't even want to go inside. Let me guess: you don't want another drama scene featuring me storming out?"

He chuckled slightly, taking my hand that wasn't holding the coffee. He brought it to his mouth and kissed it. "Yeah, something like that. I'm pretty sure you're not going to be huge fan of what I have to say, Ally."

"Hey, whatever it is, we can figure it out. Unless you're breaking up with me," I joked. "Oh, God, you're not breaking up with me, are you?" I looked at him, panic in my eyes.

He leaned forward and kissed me. It started out as a soft, quick kiss, but ended up pretty deep and intense when I didn't let him go. "No, I am absolutely not breaking up with you," he said hoarsely. He sat back, took a sip of coffee and cleared his throat.

"Okay, Jack. You're killing me. Tell me

already."

"Well, I went to see my guidance counselor after school today. I wanted to check on my credits."

"And?" He sure knew how to drag out a story.

He took a deep breath. "Fine. I'll say it all and then let you react however you want. I found out that I only need 2 more credits after this year to graduate: English 12 and a half credit each of economics and government. I can take them through online eCademy this next semester and graduate this spring. Wait—" He put his finger on my lips as I was about to interrupt. "I also got some information about Army ROTC at UNM. I'm really interested in applying."

"What is that? ROTC? Don't we have that at school?"

"We have junior ROTC at school. It stands for Reserve Officer Training Corps." At my continued confused look, he sighed. "Basically, it means I would join the army, they would pay for my education, give me some training, and then I would owe them a few years of active duty after college."

I sat there on my side of the car, staring at him. I wasn't really staring at him, however; I was trying to process the giant bomb he had dropped. The minutes ticked by.

"Ally? Sweetheart? Can you please say something?" Jack whispered a bit desperately.

It was my turn to put my finger against his lips. "Shh, Jack. I'm trying to process and not react. Give me a minute, okay?" He obediently sat back and gave me time. I sensed that this was an important moment for our relationship and I didn't want to screw it up. This was not the time for a big scene. "All right, Jack. I have a couple of questions. First, though," and I leaned over to kiss him. "Thank you for telling me."

He pulled me back for another, better kiss. "Always. This is the messy part of a relationship. The part where we talk and hash stuff out."

I sank back into his kiss for a few more incredible moments. Now, back to business. "All right. Let's get back to those questions." I sat back, separating myself from him so I could concentrate. I tended to lose the ability for rational thought when his lips were near mine. "First, you found out that you could graduate early, right?"

"Well, technically, it's a year late for me. I'll still be 19 when I graduate. But that's better than 20. Makes me a little bit less of a loser." He looked so vulnerable in that moment. I decided right then and there that I would be good with this, no matter how much it hurt, no matter how hard it was for me.

"You are definitely not a loser, Jack. Now," I said gently. "Tell me more about this ROTC thing."

"Well, if I get accepted, they pay either my tuition or my room and board. With the lottery scholarship, I could probably manage to live in the dorms or get an apartment. They also provide a monthly stipend. I would really like to not have to rely on Manny and Trina while I'm in college. They've done enough for me. I would take some ROTC-type classes along with my regular classes and I would have one weekend a month of training. I have to find out if my past criminal record will keep me out if it, though. I hope I can get a waiver."

"That doesn't sound so bad. I think I could deal with that. I thought your juvenile record was sealed."

He took my hands between his again. "That doesn't matter to the federal government. I would also have to go for basic training this summer. It's eight weeks."

"I'm not loving that part, to be totally honest," I said.

"Yeah, and I'll owe them a few years of active duty after college."

"That's a long way off, Jack. Let's worry about the immediate future for now. Why do you want to do this? What is it about this ROTC thing that attracts you?" I was trying so hard to be understanding and not freak out.

"Ally, you are really being so—I don't know—great about this." He leaned over and kissed me again. "Thank you. I really, really love you." He kissed me yet again. I will never, ever get tired of that. "I guess I want to do it because, I don't know…it seems like the right thing for me. It will help out with my college expenses, so I don't have to take out a bunch of student loans or take any money from Manny and Trina."

My heart melted a little more. "Jack, are you doing this because of the money? I don't think that's a good enough reason."

"No," he interrupted me. "It's not just that. It's part of it, sure. An important part, but it's also about the experience. I…I think I'd be good at it, you know? And I would have a guaranteed job right out of college. That's not a reality these days. A lot of people graduate college and then can't find a job. It's about some security in my life, I guess. I need to know if it's something you could deal with."

I was floored. What was he implying? "Jack, it's your future. I don't really have a say in it."

He took my face in his callused, work-roughened hands. "Ally, cards on the table, okay? You are my future. I know it's crazy; we've only been together for, like a month, but you are it for me. This is real, and I want you to be a part of my decisions about my future because I want you to be in my future. When I get assigned somewhere for active duty, I want you to go with me, if possible. Or if it's somewhere like Afghanistan or Iraq, I want you to be the one at home waiting for me. And I know we're way too young to be having this conversation, I mean, Jesus, you're only 16—I don't know what I'm saying. I'm sorry. You don't need to hear all this. I'll just..." He let go of me and sat back in his seat, running his hands through his hair, shaking his head.

I bit my bottom lip and looked into his handsome, worried face. He had apparently lost his nerve. Admittedly, he was throwing some pretty heavy stuff at me and people would say we were crazy, that we were too young, but that didn't bother me. The truth is, we weren't your typical teenagers with raging hormones. He had been through so much in his life already and was working a man's job, making a man's decisions. And I was dealing with some pretty freaky supernatural stuff of my own and doing a fairly decent job of it. And I felt the exact same way he did. It was time to take action because I knew he was dying a slow death in his seat. I climbed over the center console and straddled his lap. It was a tight fit, but I'm small, and when he moved his seat back all the way, we made it work. We needed to be face to face with nothing between us for the next part of this conversation.

"I'll be 17 in a couple of weeks. I'm not that young." I took his mouth with my lips, savoring the way he tasted of coffee and his own special essence.

He pulled back slightly. "And I'll be 19 a couple weeks after that. Two years is a lot right now. It wouldn't be so bad if I were like 28 and you were 26. I don't know why your mom and grandma don't want to kill me."

"Okay, old man. Calm down. They love you. Let's get back to the important stuff. You were saying some really good things a few minutes ago. Like the part where you said I was your future." I leaned in for another deep kiss. "Let's focus on that. Because I happen to completely agree with you. I'm really going to miss you at school next year, and those eight weeks this summer are going to be the longest of my life, but I want you to do this. I want you to graduate early and get into this ROTC program. And I will help you in any way I can. Now kiss me for God's sake."

"God, Ally. I don't deserve you," he said against my lips before he invaded my mouth with his tongue, stealing any further thought from me. I ran my hands through his black curls and he smoothed his hands over my back, daring to run them under my shirt. When he pulled away long minutes later, we were both panting. I rested my forehead against his and smiled at him. He reached up to rub his thumb along my cheek. "You are so beautiful, inside and out. I am such a lucky guy. I have had a thing for you since the first day you walked into our physics class, did you know that?"

I laughed a little. "What? You never even talked to me! I thought you were completely uninterested in me."

"No way. And when you decided to sit right in front of me in English, I thought I'd died and gone to heaven. But it was also hell, baby."

"Why? Was I that scary?"

"That's not it. You were so beautiful and sweet. I wasn't going to ruin that. I felt like I was nothing but trouble when I got here. I was planning to keep to myself and get through the rest of high school with as little interaction as possible. If you hadn't had that vision that day, I probably never would have talked to you."

"Well, thank goodness for that vision. Think what we would have missed out on." I moved back to his lips, and then moved on to kiss his jaw, feeling his rough, late afternoon whiskers against my lips. I kissed my way to his ear and took his earlobe between my teeth, biting gently, and then soothing it with my tongue. His hands continued caressing along my back, but then found their way to my bottom. I kissed my way back to his mouth and he gripped me tightly, pulling me against him.

"It's time to stop, sweetheart." He was breathless against my lips.

"I know." I reluctantly moved back to my seat.

"Probably past time, but I couldn't help myself. You're so damn sexy, Jack."

He laughed, as I had intended him to, lightening the heavy mood of our previous conversation. He took my hand and kissed the backs of my fingers. "Let's get you home."

**

Saturday came and I waited impatiently for Jack to pick me up for my birthday celebration. He had refused to tell me where we were going or what we were doing. When I asked him what I should wear, he looked at me blankly and said that I always looked good. Yikes. When pressed further, he relented enough to say 'wear something warm.' I chose a sweater tunic and tights combo that I felt could go in several different directions. Tara had taken the opportunity recently to help me update my wardrobe even more, sensing my vulnerability and openness to better dressing and Grams' recent loose interpretation of the purpose for my emergency credit card.

He picked me up and drove east toward the mountains. He wouldn't say where we were going, but it soon became apparent that we were heading toward the base of the tram that runs up the Sandia Mountains. 'Sandia' is Spanish for watermelon and many believe the mountains were so named because of the way the setting sun turns them a beautiful pink color, which deepened as we drove closer to them. He bought our tram tickets and we rode the 2.7 miles up to High Finance, a really nice restaurant with amazing views of the city. Before we went into the restaurant, he pulled me to a bench overlooking the city lights with the sun sinking down behind the West Mesa, turning the sky a gorgeous orange-pink, and pulled a small jeweler's box out of his pocket. "Happy birthday, Ally," he said with a soft kiss. I opened it to find a beautiful charm bracelet with one charm: a small silver compass rose.

"Jack, it's beautiful. Now we both have one."

"That's what I was thinking." He turned it over and showed me the inscription: *Never stop seeking.* "It helps me stay on the right path. Maybe it'll help you too."

"I absolutely love it, Jack. It's perfect. Thank you."

I let him fasten it on my wrist and then put my arms around his neck and gave him the deepest, best thank you kiss I could produce. At length, he groaned and reluctantly pulled away.

"We better get inside or we'll lose our reservation." He put his hands against my cheeks to warm them. "And you're freezing. It's too cold at this altitude to stand around."

We had a beautiful, romantic dinner. It felt like we were so much older than high school juniors; I felt grown up being with him like that. After dinner, I thought he would drive me home, but he surprised me by driving to the auto body shop instead.

"What are we doing here? Did you forget something?" I asked.

"No, I wanted to show you something. Come on. Close your eyes." I gamely closed them as he led me back to the garage area. He stopped several times to make sure I wasn't peeking. "All right, open them."

I opened my eyes to see a shiny, sea green classic VW bug. "Oh, Jack. How cute! Did you make it?"

He laughed. "I didn't *make* it. I painted it and did the body work. It was a wreck when it came in." He took my hand and led me closer to the car. "Merry Christmas, Ally."

I was flabbergasted. "What? You mean...? But you can't...I can't. Is this for me? Did you get me a car?"

"Yeah. I did."

"Oh my God, Jack. You can't give me a car! You already gave me a beautiful present. I can't accept. My mom and Grams would have a fit. I'll have a fit!"

"Shh, Ally. Of course you can accept. I already asked them. They actually paid for most of the parts and have helped me keep it a secret for over a month. Even Mat helped me work on it. So, it's kind of from all of us. Your mom and grandmother really managed to keep the secret."

"But you already got me a present."

"That was a *birthday* present. This is a *Christmas* present. Hey, it's not your fault you were born on Christmas. As long as I'm around there will always be separate presents." Wow. I was completely floored. The whole combo present thing had always been a pet peeve of mine.

"This year is going to be hard act to follow," I said, looking up into his dark eyes.

He laughed and kissed me hard. "I'm sure I'll manage. Come on. Let me show you your new car."

I stopped in my tracks. "Jack, you know I don't drive."

He turned back and took my hands in his. "Driving lessons included. I promise I can help you get your confidence back. I'm a really good teacher. I'm also going to have to teach you to drive stick."

"Stick? I don't even know what that means." I looked at him uncertainly. He looked right back at me, a knowing and confident smile on his face. Finally, I smiled back at him. I couldn't bear to disappoint him after all the trouble he'd gone to. "Fine. I believe you. I'll try. Thank you for my car. I love it. Now show me all the details. Then we definitely need to make out in it." I really could not believe he had done this for me. How had he done all the work in so little time? No wonder he was tired all the time! I had no idea what I had ever done to deserve such a wonderful guy. Sometimes I wondered what he could possibly be getting out of this relationship since it seemed like I was reaping all the benefits.

We got in and he started it up, sputtering and coughing. The car, not Jack. VW Bugs are noisy and smell kind of funny. Jack turned on the heater to show me how fast it heats up. "In a spirit of complete disclosure, I need to tell you the bad news." Jack looked at me with a serious look on his face.

"What? It sounds bad."

He reached past me to open the little triangular window in the passenger door. "The bad news is that *this,*" he gestured to the two vent windows, "is your flow-through air conditioning."

We both laughed, and since he was leaning past me to open the window, I decided it was time to get on with the fun part of why we were sitting in the car. Can I say that making out in a 1973 VW Beetle is not easy? That stick shift really gets in the way. Oh, calm down. Nothing much happened. Unfortunately.

Later that night, as he dropped me off—he had driven us home in the VW so I could see how it drove—I pulled him close and kissed his cold lips. "Thank you for the best early birthday/Christmas I have ever had." I kissed him again. "Oh, and the presents were really nice, too."

***

He took me driving on Sunday afternoon. We drove around this really big church parking lot so I wouldn't freak out too much and so I could begin to get the hang of a manual transmission. I lost count of how many times I stalled out, jerking to a halt. He was incredibly patient with me, never making me feel like a complete dumbass, even when I flooded the engine. This getting back into driving thing had a steep learning curve for me. I finally began to get the hang of it, but I was nowhere near ready to take to the city streets. Since I was leaving in a week, he asked if we could leave the car at the auto body shop so that he could continue to work on it while I was in Ireland.

"I have some adjustments to make, now that it's

been driven some. I think I need to put a new starter in it. You shouldn't have any trouble starting it or flooding the engine once I do that."

"You know, Jack," I said as we drove home with him now driving. "You are a pretty handy guy to have around. What are you not good at?"

"Oh, I think I should let you figure that out for yourself. No need to advertise my faults."

CHAPTER SIXTEEN

"Seeking what is true is not seeking what is desirable."
–Albert Camus

Our last week before winter break was mostly review for finals and then the final exams on Thursday and Friday. Tuesday afternoon, after cheerleading practice, I was in the main building hanging posters advertising a Christmas bake sale the cheerleaders were having during lunch on Friday. I had volunteered to hang them because I was taking the bus to meet Jack at the shop and he didn't get off work for a while. It took longer than I expected and I was actually running late for the bus I was hoping to catch, when I realized that I still had to go back to the gym and retrieve my jacket out of the locker room. I contemplated leaving it, but the temperature had dropped significantly during the afternoon; a big storm was preparing to roll in later in the week. I sighed and texted Jack to let him know I would be late.

I was closing my locker when I was hit with a violent vision that literally brought me to my knees.

Veronica, bleeding and battered, being hit repeatedly by the same hands I had seen before.

I sat down hard on the bench, head in my hands. I felt sick to my stomach with the suddenness and violence of it. I somehow knew, absolutely and without a doubt, that this was happening *now,* just like I had known at Veronica's party. I had to find her. I had to stop this. Then I did a really stupid thing for which I have no rational defense—I headed off to find her and stop her from being hurt. Why didn't I call 911 or my mom or Jack? I have no idea. It was like something took over my brain and all my good sense, and I headed off to look for her. I could tell that she was somewhere in the vicinity of the gym, because there was athletic-type stuff surrounding her. The vision kept playing on the fringes of my conscious mind. That's the only reason I can think of, now, for my irresponsible, careless behavior. *Find her, help her, find her.* It kept repeating over and over, blocking out everything else.

I ran to the gym and stood in the middle of the empty floor, listening, trying to control my heaving breaths so I could hear. The lights were off; the only visibility came from the weak, stormy winter light streaming through the skylights. The gym echoed with emptiness, with that sense that nobody else was around. I ran to the various doors that led to classrooms, offices, and closets. Most were locked;

those that weren't were empty. I was in the back hall leading from the auxiliary gym to the main gym when I finally heard it: a faint, weak cry. I followed the sound, willing it to repeat. I had to stand perfectly still and hold my breath to hear it again. *The weight room.* I had never been inside the weight room; it was the realm of football players and wrestlers. It was completely dark in the room and I had to grope my way toward a sliver of light coming from under a door on the far wall. I banged my shins hard on some piece of equipment and struggled to keep in a curse. Something was niggling at the fringes of my consciousness, some sense of familiarity, but I pushed it away impatiently. I could hear garbled voices coming through the heavy fire door. As I crept closer I could make out a female crying and screaming with a deeper voice yelling some of the foulest words I have ever heard in my life. I stood listening for a heartbeat before I heaved it open, hoping to gain an element of surprise.

The sight that met my eyes was horrifying and is now forever, unfortunately, burned into my memory: Veronica half-lying on a desk in the weight room office, nearly unconscious, one eye completely swollen shut, blood dripping from her nose and mouth. Her jeans and underwear were pulled down around her ankles. Standing over her, hands on his open belt buckle, was Coach Trevino, the young, muscular boys wrestling coach and weight trainer. I've only ever seen him a few times before; he apparently spends the vast majority of his time in the gym and its environs—a place I had never had much reason to visit until recently. I had heard girls giggling about how good-looking he was, but I had always thought he seemed rough and crude somehow. Not my type at all. He certainly wasn't good-looking right now. The look that was frozen on his face as I threw open the door was one of complete and abject *rage*. He was obviously out of control, having severely beat Veronica and was now about to inflict even more suffering and humiliation by raping her. Her head rolled toward me, her one good eye widening with surprise.

"Help me." It was no more than a whisper.

"Get the fuck out of here!" Coach Trevino screamed.

I should have been terrified; I was, I know I must have been. But a cold, steely calm crept over my entire being and I slowly advanced toward the desk. "Get away from her." I didn't even raise my voice.

I have never seen anyone in a killer rage before; I devoutly hope never to again. He roared—I can't think of any other way to describe it—and launched himself at me, his belt dangling and the top of his pants undone. I turned to run, hoping at least to get him away from Veronica. He slammed me up against the door before I could even get it open, knocking the breath completely out of me. He grabbed me by the back of the neck and the hair and lifted me up to his eye level. My 5'1", 100 lb. body was not much of an obstacle for him.

"You're dead!" he screamed. I believed him. He slammed me into the glass trophy case beside the door. I heard and felt the shatter of glass, much of it imbedding itself into the back of my head. I slid down the broken front of the case into a pile of glass shards, now mixed liberally with my blood. I know I must have screamed, but I can't remember. He stood over me, breathing heavily. When he saw I was still conscious, not quite dead, he reared his foot back, preparing to deliver what probably would have been a fatal kick to my head. At the last second, Veronica, who had managed to pull herself up from the desk, hit him in the back with a folding chair. That would bring most people down, but he was in such a rage—hyped up on something?—that it merely distracted him. She saved my life, but at great cost to her own. He was distracted, but became even more violent. He turned on her with a scream and smashed his fist into her head. She fell, unconscious, as he began viciously kicking her in the stomach and ribs. She would be dead in seconds, if she weren't already. With my last vestiges of strength and consciousness, I crawled over to a large trophy that was now lying close to me, picked it up, and with enormous effort, smashed the heavy marble base into the back of his head. I don't think I will ever forget the sound of that moment: the *thunk* of the solid trophy base connecting with the hard flesh at the back of his skull. I wasn't even able to tell if it knocked him out, or if he was still standing. I fell into a heap of blood and glass, consciousness finally, mercifully slipping away.

***

When I awoke, it was to a dark room, antiseptic

smells, and a beeping sound. There was none of that 'where am I?' stuff that you always see in movies. I knew exactly where I was and I was so glad to be there that I felt tears start to build. I sort of thought I might be waking up *somewhere else,* if you know what I mean. Or, rather, not waking up at all. I slowly turned my head, sucking in my breath at the pain, and saw Jack's beloved face; he was slumped in an armchair next to my bed. I realized he was holding my hand, loosely, through the bed rails. He had fallen asleep. He looked rough; dark stubble covered the lower half of his jaw, his hair looked as if he had run his hands through it repeatedly. He looked like he was wearing scrubs, which I couldn't figure out. I stared at him, loving that I still could, for a moment before I squeezed his hand gently.

"Jack," I whispered, scratchily.

He woke up immediately. "Ally. Oh, God." He leaned over me, looking intently at my face, trying to determine if I was really with him or not. "Jesus, Ally. I was so scared." A tear threatened to escape his eye and my heart split in two.

"Jack," I whispered again. He leaned in and kissed me so, so softly, on my lips. "Tell me," I insisted as he pulled back. "Veronica." I feared what he would say.

His eyes clouded. "She's alive. Barely. She's in ICU. That bastard nearly killed her. She's in really bad shape."

"The baby?" I whispered. He shook his head. I didn't even know how to feel about it or how to process this. "What about...him? Did I...?" I couldn't find the words.

He again shook his head. "No. You fractured his skull, but he'll live, unfortunately," he said bitterly.

I couldn't help the sob that escaped. Jack held me carefully. "Shh. It's all right, Ally. It's okay now. It's over." He sat back. "I need to text your mom. I sent them downstairs for coffee, but I had to swear to text immediately if you woke up. Tara's here too."

It turned out that I had a pretty bad concussion and 17 stitches in the back of my head, along with a lovely shaved spot. Hats were going to be part of my daily wardrobe for the foreseeable future, and it would be a while before I could shampoo. Gross. The doctors kept me overnight for observation, but I was allowed to go home the next day, as long as I spent it resting.

Veronica was not nearly as fortunate. She was in a coma, mostly drug-induced, to help her heal. She had to have surgery to repair internal damage done by the vicious kicks, including a torn uterus. They also had to remove her spleen. It was unclear whether or not she would ever be able to bear children because the damage was so severe. She had also suffered a severe concussion from Coach Trevino's fist.

Coach Trevino, the rat bastard who did this, was fine. Isn't it always the way? He had to have a few stitches and had a minor skull fracture. He was currently being held without bail in the Bernalillo County Metropolitan Detention Center awaiting trial for multiple counts of rape and attempted murder. I should have hit him harder. I don't mean I wish I had killed him or anything. I would never want to actually take a life if I could avoid it; I think it's unfair that out of the three of us, he suffered the least damage. He also wasn't talking; he had lawyered-up immediately. I've always wanted to say that. We would have to wait until Veronica was awake to find out what had happened, why she had ever gotten involved with him, and why she had not told anyone he had raped her.

Grams and my mom were amazing when I got home, waiting on me hand and foot, bringing me tea, juice, and putting DVDs in for me. My head hurt too much to read. It actually hurt too much to even enjoy watching movies for long. The doctor had given me some hefty Tylenol that didn't do much for the pain. All I wanted to do was sleep; I could barely stay awake long enough eat. I hoped I would start to feel better soon so I could enjoy milking this for all its worth. Both Mom and Grams had tried to get me to talk about what had happened in the office with Veronica and the coach, but I couldn't bring myself to talk about it to anyone. I was trying hard not to even think about it. I know they were both worried sick about my emotional health as much as my physical health.

Jack came by after school; he looked worse than I felt. I had finally been able to persuade him to leave the hospital around 5 a.m. so he could at least shower and change before going to school. He couldn't afford to stay home because of the physics review and we were planning to go over his notes this evening. I was hoping to be allowed to return to school the next day to take my finals, but was starting to worry that my head would still be hurting too badly. He hadn't shaved and looked ruggedly handsome, yet completely exhausted. I tried to convince him to go home and get some sleep, but he wouldn't listen.

"Let me sit with you for a little while. I need to hold you. Then I'll go." He sank into a corner of the couch. I nestled into his arms and pulled the blanket over both of us. We were asleep in seconds. We awoke hours later to the delicious smell of lasagna wafting out of the kitchen. Grams served dinner on trays in the living room while I finally got a chance to ask Jack about the details of what happened the previous afternoon. How did I get to the hospital? Who found us? I had no memory of those events, only the horror leading up to them.

"When I got your text message, I was finishing up at the shop and decided to surprise you by picking you up at school. I couldn't find you anywhere and you weren't answering your phone. I was literally running all over that damn school, looking for you, when a janitor mentioned he had seen a redheaded girl by the gym. Ally, sweetheart, why didn't you call me? Or the police?"

"I don't know, Jack. I'm so sorry. I'm so sorry, Grams. I had a vision and it kept playing over and over in my head. I couldn't think of anything else except finding Veronica and helping her. It was stupid." I buried my face against his chest.

"No, Ally," Grams said. "It was brave. Perhaps not wise, but you saved that girl's life. I'm very proud of you."

"Your Grams showed up about the same time I did. She knew you were in trouble. We both started frantically searching for you. When I opened that door, and saw you lying on the floor in all that blood and glass…I don't know. I think I went a little crazy. I thought you were dead. I thought I'd lost you." He closed his eyes, leaned his head back on the couch and sighed deeply.

I tried to remember any part of what he was telling me, but I couldn't. What I did remember was another vision, the vision I had of Veronica with all the blood and pain, the one in which I couldn't tell if it was Veronica or myself that was being hurt. The vision that I had decided to keep from Cassie.

"Jack!" I clutched his hand, gasping. "The vision! It was the vision!"

So, of course I had to tell Grams about it. She was concerned and disturbed that I hadn't told anyone, especially Cassie. "Why, Ally? What were you afraid of?"

"I don't know, Grams. I feel like Cassie is hiding something, keeping something important from me. I'm sorry, I just—"

"Look, Mrs. Moran, I don't think now is the time to go into all of this," Jack interrupted, pulling me back into his arms, kissing the top of my head. "Ally's not up to it. Why don't you finish telling Ally what happened yesterday so she can get back to resting?"

Wow. I have never seen anyone stand up to her like that. She looked at him intently for a moment before nodding and then continuing. "Once we had ascertained that you were alive, I called the police and found something to tie up that horrible man's hands with in case he woke up. I couldn't get Jack to leave your side. He sat there, holding you, getting absolutely covered in your blood, until the paramedics came. I don't think I'll ever forget that sight as long as I live." She suddenly let out an involuntary sob.

Poor Grams! This had been really hard on her and Mom. I got up and went over and put my arms around her, hugging her from behind. "I love you, Grams."

She sniffed and cleared her throat. "Well, anyway. Your mother met us at the hospital and we sat with poor Jack while they stitched your head. We were all very concerned when you didn't wake for so long. I couldn't budge Jack out of your room. Your mother, Tara, and I had just gone down to get some coffee when you woke up." She paused to blow her nose.

"So that's why you were wearing scrubs when I woke up, huh? You got my blood all over your clothes. God, Jack, I am so sorry." And I kissed him right there in front of Grams. "I love you, you know," I whispered.

"I know," he whispered back and kissed me.

"I don't understand why this all happened," I said as I disengaged from Jack. "Why would Veronica be involved with Coach Trevino? And why did she call him 'Nick' in my visions? His name is Jonathan. I don't understand." I noticed a look, some sort of unspoken communication passing between Grams and Jack. "What? What are you guys not telling me?"

"Tell her, Jack," said Grams.

"I don't think she needs to hear it all right now.

She needs to rest."

I sat up and turned to look in his face. "I'm fine, Jack. Please tell me what you know."

He sighed. "All right. It's not that much, actually, since Trevino's not talking. While the cops were searching his office, they found a large stash of steroids. It looks like he was selling them to some of the students. At least that's what I'm guessing from the questions I was asked by the cops. There were cops all over school today. They even had drug dogs, so I think they might be looking for more than steroids. Ally, you may have busted a drug ring at school."

There were really no more details he could share with me, so after a few more questions I curled up next to Jack while he got his notes out for the review and started going over them with me. I couldn't keep my eyes open and fell asleep within a few minutes. I woke up as Jack was carrying me to bed, which would have been much more exciting in another context.

"Jack, I can walk. You don't have to carry me."

"Shh. Let me. It's the first time I've felt useful in days." He laid me on my bed, tucked the comforter up around my chin, kissed me, and turned to go. I caught his hand.

"Stay with me, please? Just until I fall asleep."

He lay down next to me, on top of the comforter, and pulled me into his arms. "Go to sleep, querida. I love you." His warmth and nearness helped me fall into a mercifully dreamless sleep.

It turned out that I didn't go to school the next day. My head was still killing me, and the school called to say my teachers had all decided to give me a special exclusion from my finals. I would get the current grade I had in the class. Since they were all A's and B's, I graciously accepted their offer and went back to sleep. All I wanted to do was sleep. When I was asleep I could forget.

***

Cassie came over later that afternoon to check on me. I'm sure she was wondering if I would be able to travel on Saturday.

"Ally, honey, we need to talk. I know you're hurting and I know you're not trusting me much right now."

"I can't believe Grams told you."

"I'm glad she did." Cassie reached over and took my hand. "I'm so sorry I've been so secretive, sweetheart. I'm not really trying to keep secrets." At my disbelieving look, she held up her hand. "Hear me out. Fine, so maybe I have been keeping secrets, but for a good reason, and never to hurt you. Ally, I didn't want to tell you too much too soon, especially before we really know anything."

I looked at her for several moments before sighing in resignation. It was too exhausting to stay angry; I simply didn't have the energy for it. "Okay, Cassie, but no more secrets, huh? I need you to be honest from now on. I can handle it."

"Deal, as far as it's up to me. This trip to Galway will make so many things clear. Things I can't explain right now."

I simply nodded, too tired to do anything else. I

lay my head back down on the arm of the sofa and closed my eyes.

"Ally, what you went through was truly horrifying, but you can't shut yourself away like this. You need to talk about it, to process it, so you can begin to deal with it, to begin to heal."

"Cassie, I don't even know how to feel about it. Maybe we should leave the counseling to Grams. When I start to think about it, to remember, I can't handle it."

"Honey, I know. You saw some things that no one should have to see, much less a 17-year-old girl. I can help, Ally. You can share what you saw with me through our gifts. I can help you bear this burden, just a little bit, until you have had some time to come to terms with it." She held out her hands to me.

"Cassie, why should you have to see it, or experience it? It was so awful—"

"Because that's what Seers do to help each other, if we can. Please, Ally. Let me help."

So I sat up and put my hands in hers and remembered; I remembered the horrible, foul words Coach Trevino was shouting at Veronica. I remembered her, lying half-nude across his desk, begging me to help her. I remembered him undoing his pants, preparing to violate her once again. I couldn't catch my breath; it felt like I was hyperventilating as the scenes ran through my brain over and over. I felt Cassie squeeze my hands; I knew she was seeing what I saw. My breathing started to calm down. It wasn't that I was no longer seeing the memories; they were no less vivid. I can't really explain—it sounds selfish to say that knowing Cassie saw it too, made it easier for me to bear. I didn't like that about myself. Who would wish these memories on anyone?

"No, Ally. It's not selfish. It's human. We are made to bear each other's burdens. Especially for those we love." She set my hands in my lap and broke the connection. Tears were running down her face. "It is a horrible memory and I don't relish having it in my mind, but I'm so glad I could help you. It's my gift and I must use it. Just like you must use your gift. You can't run away from it."

"I don't think I deserve this gift, Cassie," I said in a small voice.

"What are you talking about? It's not a matter of deserving."

"But why couldn't I help Veronica before she got hurt so badly? I tried so many times." Now the tears were running down my face as I silently wept—wept for myself for failing to help Veronica before she was attacked so violently, wept for Veronica who would never be the same after all of this, and wept for that tiny life that was over before it had a chance to begin.

"I don't know, Ally. You were handed a very difficult situation before you were equipped to handle it. I don't know why. You also need to realize that people have free will. We can try to help, but if they won't accept, there's only so much we can do." She held me and let me cry for a while. It was the first time I had really allowed myself to think about everything since the attack. "There," she said when I had control of myself once more.

"Now I'm going to ask you to do something that will be very difficult for you."

I looked at her hesitantly.

"I want you to share the details of what happened with your grandmother, your mother, and with Jack. Probably even Tara, too, since you share everything else with her."

"No." I started shaking my head. "They do not need to hear all the gory details. Why should I tell them? I've told them the basics. That's all they need."

"You are not in charge of protecting them, Ally. That's not what love is all about. You're holding back from the people that love you the most in this world, and it will damage your relationships. Trust me on that."

I didn't want to hurt my relationships with any of them, so I said, "All right, I will, if you think it's that important." I had something else I needed to ask her, but I was hesitant. "Cassie, did you see the vision that I...blocked?" I finished in a whisper.

She looked very serious. "I did. Ally, I had no idea you could do that. I feel so bad that I wasn't here for you."

"Cassie, what if I hadn't blocked it? What if I could have—"

"No, Ally. Stop right there. You can't know what would have happened. I don't really understand about your future visions, Ally. That's one of the main reasons I feel you need to see the Council. Seers who can see the future are extremely rare. I don't know if you see possibilities or concrete events. We need to get you to the Council as soon as possible."

CHAPTER SEVENTEEN

"Proclaim the truth and do not be silent through fear."
–St. Catherine of Siena

Veronica had been allowed to wake up on Thursday afternoon as her doctors weaned her off the medications that had been keeping her asleep. By Friday, she was moved to a regular room and I was feeling well enough to pay her a short visit. I knocked softly on her door and wasn't surprised when it was her mother who opened it for me.

"Oh, Ally, come in. She's been asking for you. She's awake, but I doubt it will last for long. I'll give you a few minutes alone to talk with her." As I moved past her, she grabbed me in a tight hug. "Thank you," she cried against my hair. "I can't ever say that enough. You saved her, Ally."

I hugged her back, this woman I hadn't spoken to since elementary school. "It's okay. Veronica actually saved my life, too." She let me go, sniffing and muttering about needing a tissue.

I approached the hospital bed with a feeling of dread at what she would look like. She turned to look at me, and, wow. She looked really bad. One eye was swelled almost completely shut and the rest of her face was a mass of purple bruises. "Hey, Veronica," I began lamely. "How are you?"

She shook her head very slightly. "Not too good. How are you doing?"

"Oh, I'm fine. I only needed a few stitches." I took off the slouch hat I was wearing and turned to show her the gash on the back of my head.

"Oooh." She winced. "That's going to make for some interesting hairstyles. Hey, sit down, please? I want to talk to you about what happened."

"You don't have to talk about it if you don't want to, Veronica. I know you probably want people to leave you alone."

"No, I want to tell you what happened. You deserve to know, Ally. You tried so hard to help me for weeks, and I pushed you away. I remember we used to be really good friends. I wish we could be again."

"Sure. Of course we can. You need to take care of yourself and get better."

She smiled at me, sadly, it seemed. "I never thought I would be the kind of person to be involved in something like this, Ally. It all got so messed up so fast."

"Something like what? I haven't been back to school and Jack hasn't said much, except that the coach had a bunch of steroids in his office. What's going on?"

"You haven't been watching TV? You haven't

seen the news?" she asked incredulously.

"No, nothing. I've mostly been sleeping."

"Oh my God, Ally. You exposed a steroid scandal at Oso Grande High School. Coach Trevino was selling steroids to a bunch of the guys on the football team and the wrestling team, even some basketball players."

"Wow, Jack said something like that, but I had no idea it was so big. I didn't do anything. I only tried to keep that asshole from raping you." This was shocking news to me. Jack had certainly downplayed the whole thing.

"I don't know how you haven't heard anything about it. I've heard there were drug dogs and searches at school and that they've arrested another coach. All the boys have been kicked off the teams. My dad's talking to our lawyer because I might be in trouble too."

"Wow. I had no idea." I stood there, unable to believe what had been going on. I had done a superbly bad job of figuring *anything* out. Jack had been closer to figuring it out; at least he had called it on the steroids thing. "Veronica, how did you get involved with Coach Trevino? He was seriously terrifying. I've never seen anyone that angry before."

"That's what steroids can do to you, I guess. It's so embarrassing to tell you about him. I really thought I loved him, but he changed so much over the last few months as he started using more and more steroids."

"Wait, you *loved* him? I thought you were being raped!"

"I was, Ally. But there was a time when he loved me. At least I thought he did." She started to cry quietly. "I know now he was just using me. I was an easy lay for him. God, I'm pathetic."

"How did this happen, Veronica?" I couldn't see how all the pieces fit together.

She sighed and wiped her eyes, being very tender around her injured eye. "I had heard about the steroids from some of the girls on the squad. Their boyfriends had really bulked up over the summer and were suddenly playing so much better. Danny wanted me to find out how they were doing it. Long story short: I found myself in Coach Trevino's office trying to get him to let my boyfriend into his special inner circle. He did, but not without coming on to me. I bought it all, thinking I was special, that what we had was special. I really thought we were in love. I let him convince me to have sex with him. You'll probably be shocked to know that I was a virgin until him. Then I got pregnant and he got angry. I was scared and tried to call it off, but he went crazy. That's the first time he raped me. I didn't understand that it was rape, because I had said yes in the past. I was so stupid. I let him hit me and use me. I thought I deserved it. To be honest, I'm still having some issues with that last one. I start therapy as soon as I get out of here." She paused and reached for her styrofoam water cup, but was having trouble reaching it. I got it for her and helped her take a sip from the straw.

"I'm so sorry, Veronica. Nobody should have to go through this."

She continued, "But I couldn't bring myself to

get rid of the baby. And every time he texted me, I would go to him. And every time, he got angrier and angrier."

"What was he so angry about?" I still didn't totally understand; this was so far beyond my experience.

"Everything. Nothing. Sometimes he was mad because I was pregnant; sometimes he was ecstatic, talking about how we would get married and raise the baby together. I never knew which Nick I would be getting: the nice Nick or the crazy one. Lately it was mostly the crazy one."

"His name was Nick? I thought his first name was Jonathan?" When Tara and I had checked out all the teacher's first names, the only Nicholas that had shown up was Nicholas Chiszowski.

"It's his middle name. That's what he wanted me to call him so it would be more secret." I had never even considered that Nick might be a middle name. Suddenly, the impossibility of what I had been trying to do was apparent.

Veronica dissolved into tears at this point. I looked around and found some tissue for her and then sat beside her, patting her hand uselessly until she fell asleep.

I had the answers I had been wanting, but I was more confused than ever.

***

I didn't go back to school before I left; I rested and packed on Friday afternoon. Tara came over after school and Jack came when he got off work.

Mom brought home a Chinese take-out extravaganza for dinner and we celebrated my last night before my trip. After dinner, I sat them down in the living room and told them exactly what had happened, leaving nothing out, including what I had heard from Veronica that afternoon. Mom and Grams had tears running down their faces by the time I was finished. Tara looked pissed. Jack's jaw kept getting tighter and tighter; at the end of my accounting, he muttered a very bad word, kissed me hard, and wrapped his arms around me, holding me tightly.

"This whole Seer-thing is complete bullshit! Can you tell that Council they can have their damned gift back?"

Tara, Mom, and Grams were trying not to smile. I pulled back to look at him and said, "I don't think that's how it works, but I'll try. Jack, Veronica told me more about the whole steroid scandal at school. I had no idea it was so big! They kicked all those players off the teams? You kind of downplayed that part, you know?"

"Ally, querida, I only wanted you to get a little stronger before you had more to deal with. I really wasn't trying to keep anything from you."

"We all thought it would be better for you, Ally-Bear," Mom apologized. "I'm sorry if we were wrong."

I moved out of Jack's arms and into hers. "No, you weren't wrong, Mom. It was probably for the best. I'm so confused right now. What's going to happen to Veronica? "

"I don't know, baby. I don't know."

In the long run Cassie was right; telling my mom, grandmother, Tara, and Jack the whole truth about what had happened actually made me feel better—not a lot, but at least I could deal. And stay awake for more than an hour at a time.

***

They all came to see me off at the airport on Saturday, even Megan. She hugged me as she handed me a small, beautifully wrapped Christmas present.

"It's from me and Jack. We wanted you to have a present to open on Christmas." I was touched and, predictably, started to get teary-eyed. You would think I wouldn't have any tears left by now, but I managed to find a few somewhere.

"Hey," said Jack as he took his turn to hug me. "None of that. You'll be back in no time. But I will miss you like crazy. I love you, you know." He gave me the best kiss yet, soft and soulful.

"I know." I gave them all a last hug and followed Cassie through to security.

***

As I opened the present on Christmas morning, also my 17th birthday, in my hotel room in downtown Galway, I thought about how much I missed all of them. I opened the box to find a silver cheerleading charm to add to my bracelet. I turned it over and read the inscription: *Do what you love.* It was beautiful and perfect. I could hardly wait to talk to him on Skype later.

Tomorrow I would meet with the Seer Council and perhaps discover what this gift was about. I went to sleep that night both scared and excited to begin this next chapter in my life.

The End

ACKNOWLEDGMENTS

There are so many people who have supported me and believed in me as I embarked on this new adventure. First and foremost, I want to thank my family: my wonderful husband, Lyle, who patiently put up with many fend-for-yourself dinners; my beautiful daughters, Cat, Bri, and Lacey, who all told me I could do it; my mom, who has read every word I have written. Thanks also to Sheila, niece-in-law extraordinaire, who believes in book boyfriends. Ginormous thanks to Carol, my BFF since high school and writing buddy/beta reader. Thanks to my students, especially Shella, Nicole, Sam, and Chana, who gave me so much encouragement. You are extraordinary.

Special thanks to the amazing team at Limitless Publishing. Thanks for believing in me. Thanks, Toni, for your awesome editing skills! You guys ROCK!

ABOUT THE AUTHOR

Amy Reece lives in New Mexico with her incredible husband and two ridiculous mutts, Greta and Sodapop. When she's not writing, she's teaching high school English and social studies or maybe wandering through a thrift store in search of the next lucky teapot for her vast collection. She is an unrepentant bookaholic and has overflowing bookshelves in nearly every room of her house. Her favorite authors include J.R.R. Tolkien, J.K. Rowling, and C.S. Lewis–must have something to do with initials! She loves to travel and is hoping to need many research trips for future writing projects.

Facebook:
https://www.facebook.com/areeceauthor

Twitter:
https://twitter.com/AReeceAuthor

Website:
https://amyreece.wordpress.com/